DARRYL'S REUNION

BY

JOHN B. WREN

DEDICATION
To my daughter, sisters and sons.

INTRODUCTION
The Patient...

The waiting room in the doctor's office was quiet at 4:30 on this cool March afternoon. The walls were freshly painted a pale institutional green and all the art work hung about were soothing landscapes with trees and flowers, but no people. The patient sat in one of the brightly upholstered waiting room chairs, nervously thumbing a well-worn periodical, watching the clock on the receptionist's wall for the appointed time and not really looking at the magazine in hand. When a door opened next to the receptionist's window, Doctor Schrader peered into the waiting room and said to his only remaining patient, "Please come in."

As the patient stood and approached the door, the doctor said, "My office is at the end of the hall." The patient walked ahead of him, entered the office and as the doctor closed the door, he said, "Please sit down, there are a number of things to discuss." The patient complied, taking a seat in one of the two stuffed leather chairs facing the doctor's desk. Dr. Albert Schrader was a silver haired man, looking taller than his actual 5'-11" height and very commanding in appearance. He sat at his desk, shuffled a few papers, took his glasses off, allowed them to half drop on the papers and continued, "There's no easy way to say this, but you have to know the truth. Your condition is rare and we are still learning how it affects the body."

The patient, squirming in the leather chair said, "Please, don't try to soften it, just tell me how long I have and when will I be, you know, hurting, unable to do things."

"This is a strange new condition to me as well as to you and I am dependent on the analysis of others at the hospital," returned the doctor.

"Doctor, please..."

"Okay, indications are that initially everything will appear normal; you should have complete mobility and feel little discomfort. Soon, you will begin to experience slight dizzy spells and feel periodic aches and pains in your arms and legs. These may continue intermittently for a week or a month, possibly more. We just don't know."

The patient looked at the floor, then back up at the doctor, "Please..."

Dr. Schrader leaned forward in his chair, "The little aches and pains will become more frequent and not dissipate. Most of these may be addressed with medications, allowing you almost normal activity." He paused, looked at his patient and said, "Shall I continue?"

The patient had turned, looking out a window at the trees swaying gently in the breeze and imagining a deep breath of cool, fresh air. "Yes, please do."

"As these discomforts increase in frequency and duration, you will find yourself tiring easily. You will require more sleep than usual and you will lose your appetite." He leaned back in his chair and continued, "You will be able to walk short distances comfortably for a while, and then you will need to rest more often and find going up a flight of stairs will become more difficult."

The patient turned toward Dr. Schrader, "What about driving a car?"

"Driving requires that you are in control and can respond quickly to various situations. I would recommend that you give up driving at the first sign of any problem in moving your legs or arms."

Head bowed, the patient asked, "When should I expect that to happen?"

"I would guess definitely within the next two months, possibly sooner," responded Dr. Schrader.

The patient forced a smile, more from discomfort than pleasure, looked at the doctor and said, "What about working, will I be able to continue working?"

"You are in no way contagious, so, if you wish to work, you may, at least for a short while," responded Dr. Schrader. "I can write a letter to your employer, explaining the situation and possibly get you a reduced schedule."

The patient turned again towards the window and said, "Yes, that would be good. But I don't want it known around the office, no pity parties."

"Okay," said Dr. Schrader, "I'll write it up and you can hand it to whoever is appropriate."

The patient thought for a second or two and said, "Thank you, I appreciate that. Now, can you tell me more about what I can expect to happen?"

Dr. Schrader paused, looking at this young person and wondering if he would have remained as composed as his patient under similar circumstances, and continued, "As I was saying, you will begin to notice little aches and pains in your arms and legs, these will increase as you lose energy, you will want to be more sedentary. I'll prescribe some medications that will be able to address the discomfort but not the tiredness."

Again, the patient gazed out the window, then turned toward the doctor, "What about my mind, will I lose anything in that respect?"

"Not that I am aware of, but again, we are still learning about this syndrome and you are the first case I have ever directly encountered."

The two sat in silence for a minute and the patient finally said, "What will happen next?"

Dr. Schrader took a deep breath, "It could go different ways. You may be completely mobile for weeks and suddenly require a wheelchair. Your pain will be manageable for an undetermined period, and then suddenly escalate, requiring adjustments in your medications on a continual basis. There are no hard and fast rules for this, we assume that it will be over in two or three months, but even that is not certain." Dr. Schrader lowered his voice, leaned forward and continued, "Nobody knows for sure what will happen, but know that I will be there for you whenever you need me. I am going to suggest that you move into a Palliative Care Center soon and we can better utilize the entire team in your treatment."

The patient looked at the doctor, "Do you mean like hospice?"

"Sort of, yes, but this approach is just as dedicated to finding a cure as in giving you comfort through the end."

"When should I expect to make this move?"

"We will be ready to move you as your symptoms become more pronounced, and the discomfort increases or your mobility decreases. It may be weeks or even months before this step is necessary, but I will start the paperwork part of the process now while there is no rush, so we will walk slowly through this phase, with you in control."

The patient stared at the floor for a minute, then looked out the window again and said, "What should I do now?"

The doctor leaned back in his chair, "I think that you should stop working, if you can. Rest as you need, your body will let you know when. Before you lose mobility, do something that you've wanted to do, but never took the time - visit with your family, climb a mountain, make the most of the time you have left."

"I don't have any immediate family, my father passed while I was in college, I lost my mother a few years ago and I was an only child. I guess I'm out here alone..." The patient paused, looked down at the floor for a moment, then looked up with a forced smile, "There is a class reunion coming up this spring for my high school. That's only two months away, so I guess I'll give it a try. I missed the fifth and tenth year reunions, so maybe I'll make the fifteenth."

Doctor Schrader smiled, "There you go, keep your head up, believe that tomorrow will bring something new and good, maybe you can prove all our predictions wrong."

"Thank you, Doctor. When should I come in again?"

"Let's make an appointment in a week, unless you feel the need to come in earlier. We close at 4:30 every day, but I'm here until 6:00 or 7:00 pm, wrestling with e-mails and other paperwork. You call anytime and know that I will see you any day at this time."

"Thanks again."

As the door closed behind the patient, Dr. Schrader sat in his chair, the bright smile fading as he thought about this unfortunate young person and the all too few days left to live. He straightened, put on his glasses and began shuffling papers again, "Reunion, hmm, maybe a good thing to do. Fifteen years..."

* * *

CHAPTER ONE
The Town...

Vaneksburg, Virginia is west of the Nations' Capitol, straight out Route 66 about thirty miles, then a short drive south on a state route. The town has a population of approximately 9,800 plus or minus a nickel or two and Vaneksburg's main attraction is a small, peaceful community where nothing ever happens. The local high school is Vaneksburg High where most of the area's teenagers gain their secondary education. Located a half mile south of the center of town proper, the high school is a reasonable walk in the morning and afternoon for most of the southern portion of the district and an early morning bus ride for the northern half and the outlying areas. The high school is fed by two elementary schools, Thomas Jefferson Elementary on the west side and George Mason Elementary on the east. The two elementary schools are spaced such that most of the younger children can easily walk and only a few require bus service from the outlying areas.

The high school class of 1997 was having its fifteenth year reunion in May of 2012. The school graduated 78 students that year and anticipated 50 to 60 attendees, including spouses and assorted mates. Last years' reunion planning committee had booked the banquet hall at the Vaneksburg Hotel, the most convenient venue that could easily serve 100 people. The buffet style sit down dinner would be preceded by a cocktail hour beginning at 4:30, dinner at 6:00, followed by a few speeches at 7:30, with a cash bar at 8:00. A DJ playing music from the mid-nineties would host the dancing. Closing time was set at midnight.

"Sounds civilized," said detective Ian McLarry, "I don't think we should have a problem. Let's figure two men stationed near the hotel, maybe rotate in and out, to let them know we're there. Maybe we won't even have to issue any tickets."

"Nice thought, McLarry," said Chief Bowen, "Nice, but not real. Those folks will drink too much, just like any other group. We're gonna' have a few visitors in our jail that night."

"That's pretty negative, Chief."

"Yeah, yeah," said the chief, grinning, as he walked back into his office.

Ian went back to his desk and studied a calendar on the wall thinking, "May 26th, that's about, one, two, three... six weeks away. It'll be here before you know it; maybe I should go over to the hotel and get a feel for the place." He turned, picked up his coat, poked his head into the chief's office, "I'm going to check out this hotel, never been there."

"Good idea," returned Chief Bowen and added sarcastically, "You need a map?"

"You're a funny guy, Chief."

*   *   *

The Vaneksburg Hotel is located at the northern end of the incorporated township and visible from Route 66. Ian parked his unmarked car in the front lot and entered the lobby, looking for the front desk. The clerk was signing someone in as Ian approached and finished his conversation with, "The elevators are down that corridor a few steps and on your left." He turned his attention to Ian with a smile, "May I help you, sir?"

"Just a few questions," said Ian, "My name is Detective Ian McLarry, I'm with the Vaneksburg Police Department. I understand there will be a high school reunion held here on May 26th and I wanted to coordinate with your management, just in case there is an incident. Is there someone here I can talk to?"

"Sure, give me a minute and I'll get our manager," said the young man. He disappeared into a room behind the counter and returned almost immediately with an older gentleman wearing a pinstriped suit.

"May I be of assistance?" said the man.

"Detective Ian McLarry, Vaneksburg Police department," Ian said as he extended his hand.

"My pleasure, sir," returned the gentleman, "I am Harold McGowan, manager of this hotel. How can I help you?"

"As I told the clerk, I know there will be a reunion held here in May and I wanted to introduce myself in case there is an incident. It's always good to know who to talk to when I make a formal visit."

"Understood, detective. I can assure you that in the past these events have posed no real problems and I have no reason to suspect any this time either."

"Good to hear," said Ian, "Please consider this a courtesy call and my introduction. I have only been with the Vaneksburg Police department since the beginning of this month."

"Well, I appreciate your calling on us. The occasional incident does occur with guests, but rarely. As long as you are here, allow me to give you a brief tour of our facility, and please, call me Hal."

*   *   *

Ian McLarry had come to Vaneksburg three weeks prior and started his new job early that week. After an eight-year stint in the Marine Corps and two years at a community college in Pennsylvania, Ian joined the Pittsburgh Police force in 2001. Ten years as a street cop with a constant eye toward a gold shield, Ian had anxiously looked forward to sitting for the detective exams. He applied as soon as the examination date was set. He and approximately two hundred others were told to be at a local community college at 7:30 on a cold December morning to sit for the detective's examination. He did well on the test and was given credit for his military experience, but the six available openings were not sufficient to accommodate all the qualified candidates. Ian was number eight in line and he decided to look around the country for other opportunities.

Early in February, the small town of Vaneksburg in middle Virginia presented an opportunity that could result in a pleasant change from the busy streets of Pittsburgh. An opening was coming up in April, when one of the town's detectives reached his sixty fifth year and planned to retire. Ian applied for the position and less than two weeks after sending his resume to Vaneksburg, he was pleased to find a letter in his mail box, inviting him to meet the Chief of Police in a formal interview. Ian accepted, and a few hours' drive south had him sharing lunch and conversation with Chief Ned Bowen and Frank Barnes, the mayor of Vaneksburg.

"We don't require a large police presence or the need for solving complex crimes," stated the Mayor, "But we do get enough to maintain the interest of a few full time detectives."

"I should add there have been a few cases that challenged our uniforms a little more," added the Chief.

The conversation ranged from crime statistics in Vaneksburg to the purchase of new cars for the uniformed force, to the computer system in the department and gradually dipped into a favored fishing spot in a nearby river. The proximity to a minor league baseball team, the short drive on Route 66 to the Nation's Capital and the beautiful Virginia countryside rounded out the conversation. The pay was less than Ian had hoped for, but he was pleasantly surprised at the appeal of the entire package and expressed his positive interest in the opening.

"Well, you take your time, give us some thought and we will discuss what we learned today. We'll contact you by Friday with our decision," said the Chief.

"Fair enough," replied Ian, "I look forward to your call." He left the center of town and drove around the perimeter past the two elementary schools, a few shopping centers and meandered around the countryside before heading north and home. That Friday, Ian received a call from Chief Bowen asking about his availability to start in four weeks' time. "Four weeks is no problem," he returned.

"Great, Monday, April 9th, 8:00 am, my office. See you then, Detective."

*   *   *

CHAPTER TWO
The Committee...

"Reunions need organization. Every reunion has to be coordinated with the school, the graduates, the venue, the caterer, the entertainment, other places for things like golf outings, tennis courts, and barbeque grilles. The list could go on and on," said Barb.

"Agreed," said Brent, "Are you volunteering to drive this bus?"

"Well, I could. I mean, I am here in town, I teach at TJ Elementary and I know most of the local grads," replied Barb.

Sandy volunteered to help next, "Great, Barb count me in. My schedule at the hospital is fixed for the next few weeks, so I have time to help in the afternoons and early evenings."

Lisa and Audrey both sat quietly and nodded acceptance. They would pitch in wherever they could. It was set. Barb would coordinate everything and assign tasks to whoever was available. The date of May 26 was already set by the previous year's committee and, as was the norm, the event would take place at the Vaneksburg Hotel.

Barb Nessman had attended and now taught the fifth grade at Thomas Jefferson Elementary School on Vaneksburg's west side. She was also a member of the graduating class of 1997 from Vaneksburg High School. Barbara Saunders Nessman had been very popular in high school, able to get along with just about everybody and was a natural to chair the committee to coordinate the reunion. Widowed after a very brief marriage to Kevin Nessman, a Navy pilot who went to Iraq and was brought home in a flag draped coffin, Barb was happy to busy herself with the reunion. Every late afternoon and evening she was on the phone calling old friends, trying to cajole the attendance of her classmates to this reunion.

Barb had met Kevin at UVA and as soon as she graduated, they married. He was two years her senior, a graduate of the engineering program and looking forward to finishing his tour in the Middle East and pursuing a career as a civil engineer, designing and building bridges. It took several years to get past that tragedy and planning this reunion was about the best therapy she could manage.

A call from Barb to Mark Lindstrom, always one to help her out, added a volunteer to help with the music selection and choice of a Disc Jockey. Mark was 40 years old and still single. He would have said yes to anything that Barb asked of him. A mechanic at the local Ford dealership, he often talked about opening his own garage, "A dream, I don't have the money yet, but I have been saving and I'm getting close." He had purchased a small two-bedroom house with 53 acres which he leased out to a neighbor who grew corn.

Barb also contacted Lisa Harkins, who agreed to volunteer. Lisa's duties would consist of composing and printing the official invitations, menus and programs. Lisa had been a cheerleader at Vaneksburg High along with Barb and Sandy Lansing. She was a quiet girl in her first year of high school, but a girl with a dark side. As she met and made new and different friends, she began to play on the edge of danger. In her third year at Vaneksburg High, her on-and-off boyfriend, Sam, took her out on his motorcycle. They rode with a tough gang, smoked and drank more than most and Sam was arrested several times for minor offenses. By the time she was in her last year, Sam had ridden off into the sunset, bound for California with a new babe on his bike. Lisa took the high road, applied to several colleges and was accepted into Christopher Newport, where she seemed to outgrow Sam and his wild streak. Her degree in business administration served her well in the retail field, finally achieving a position as a manager of a high-end women's clothing boutique.

Sandy, a surgical nurse at Vaneksburg Hospital, was never too busy to get involved with anything that might just be fun. In high school, she was often sent to detention for outbursts in the classroom and still had the occasional verbal confrontation with other drivers on the highway. Sandy was very bright and initially planned on medical school, but settled for nursing as money became tight and she tired of classrooms and examinations. She would help with the phone calling and fill in where needed, if available.

The four of them arranged to meet at the Vaneksburg Tavern that Wednesday for dinner, where they hoped to meet with the owner, Jim Schuster, another classmate. Jim had taken over the family business only two years ago and was doing double duty as the manager and the head chef, so he would be very helpful in coordinating the menu with the Hotel.

Audrey Redding sold real estate in Fairfax, an hour's drive east of Vaneksburg. She visited less and less since her mother passed away two years ago. Her father had died nine years ago while she was in Charlottesville at college. Now an orphan with no brothers or sisters, she was alone in the world. Neither of her parents had any siblings, so she had no close relatives. She was not a social butterfly and her limited group of friends led her to consider the Vaneksburg population as her 'next of kin'. Her elementary and high school years saw this quiet, shy little girl grow into a bright and attractive young woman. She considered modeling at one point, but found the attention too intense. Her forte was more in the line of negotiating with people, an asset that served her well in the real estate business. Audrey would coordinate the specifics with the venue, The Vaneksburg Hotel.

Brent Coyle was a moderately successful architect, living in Leesburg, Virginia about an hour's drive north of Vaneksburg. As his design practice became busier, his visits home became fewer. Brent specialized in high-end homes and the occasional shopping center when he could team up with a developer.

The committee was rounded out with Phil Kline, a veterinarian with a thriving practice in Vaneksburg. Phil had two daughters attending Thomas Jefferson Elementary and had been married to Eileen for nine years. She had graduated two years behind him, also from Vaneksburg High. He would split the phone duties with Sandy and fill in where and when time allowed.

The committee decided Wednesday evenings would be the most convenient meeting time for the majority of the members. The business end of these meeting would probably be short and the group knew they would likely spend more time reminiscing, and that meant sooner or later the subject of Darryl Zamanski was bound to come up.

*   *   *

The patient drove home after the meeting feeling good about having become involved with the reunion. "Things to do, people to see and now I have a great reason to look up old friends. This is good." The patient arrived home with thoughts of paying off all debts, perhaps selling some furniture and the car. Maybe donating some things to charity and finding her closest relatives. "Maybe that cousin in Colorado, George... I think he has three kids, two in high school with college tuition right around the corner for him," muttered the patient as the car was turned off and the patient walked toward the door. "I have two insurance policies, the one Mom and Dad started for me in high school and the one from work." The patient opened the door, placed the car keys on the kitchen table and stared at them. "The car, it's almost paid off, but I will never get the full value from selling it, maybe George could use it." The patient wandered from room to room, wondering what should be done about the furniture, heirlooms that should be kept in the family.

Sleep came early that night and in the morning the sun rose, flooding the bedroom with light and warmth. The patient went back into the kitchen and looked at the car keys again.

*   *   *

CHAPTER THREE
Darryl...

In 1993 Darryl Zamanski was a slight boy given to math and science rather than football and baseball. He was shorter than most boys his age, quiet and friendly if approached. Like so many young boys in their pre-teen years, Darryl was sought out by those trying to make their way up the social ladder by toughness. Darryl was the first stage in their climb; beat up Darryl and maybe you are ready for the next step up the ladder. The prospect of going to high school both terrified and excited Darryl. The opportunity to learn more and maybe find a group of like-minded boys who did not care about being "Tarzan" or the "Hulk" made him want to get there faster as the actual time approached. As a result, a whole new world of toughs with a new ladder to climb was giving him a whole new world of nightmares.

The first day of his high school career in 1993 was a beautiful September day, the sun was shining, the air was clear and crisp and Darryl had met several new kids from George Mason Elementary. Three old friends from Thomas Jefferson Elementary joined him in the cafeteria at lunch and they were in turn joined by new acquaintances. Soon, Darryl was surrounded by both old and new friends. He hoped that this would be a whole new world, hopefully without the constant battles with toughs he had experienced before. The conversation was lively, fun and informative. He learned he was not the only one used as the first rung on some tough guy's ladder. He also hoped there would be less of that sort of thing now they were in high school. "The jocks can play football or join the wrestling team if they want to be tough," said one of his new friends. "Yeah," said another, "Put on a helmet and play chicken. Now that takes a load of smart." The ensuing laughter drew the attention of a group of girls who joined the crowd and his circle of new acquaintances increased even more. He saw a girl he had known at TJ, but rarely spoken to. She was even shorter than he was, with long dark hair and big blue eyes. This was a girl he wanted to know better and he now felt bold enough to wink at her and say, "Audrey and I were at TJ together, I'm glad to see you." Audrey blushed, smiled and sat next to him.

After the first week passed and life in high school was starting to become routine, Darryl found another circle of friends in the school's Science Club. Meetings were on Thursday afternoons and the first session was everything he had hoped for. He casually let slip to his mother that he was going to help on a project with two seniors. He felt a rush of pride similar to that of the Tarzans scoring a touchdown in a varsity game as a freshman.

The next Monday, Darryl was in the cafeteria with a group of his new friends and as the lunch period ended, a nemesis from the past spotted him. David Branch decided to flex his muscles and reinstate his physical dominance over Darryl. "Hey, Zammy," he called from two tables away, "You shouldn't be sitting with the girls, it's hard to pick you out."

Audrey looked angry but hesitated and Barb Saunders noticed her reaction. She stood, smiled at Audrey, turned toward the loud voice and said, "Darryl, isn't that Dave Branch, he's in his fifth year here, you know. He can't seem to pass his phys-ed course."

Everybody within earshot snickered. Then Barb leaned over and kissed Darryl on the cheek and said, "You're much better looking than him, too."

More laughter. Darryl blushed, Audrey giggled, and Dave turned on his heel and hurried out of the cafeteria, muttering to himself. The laughter continued. Darryl had scored a victory and he hadn't even thrown a punch. As Darryl and Audrey walked together toward the door, several others joined them. They continued the lunchtime conversation with no mention of Dave or his dismal phys-ed record. The friends met each day at noon in the cafeteria, discussing the various activities they had all joined. Darryl mentioned his project with the Science Club. "The next meeting is Thursday afternoon and they want me to do some of the artwork."

Thursday arrived; the Science Club meeting began at 3:00 and went until 6:30. Heavily into a discussion about the rotational velocity required to maintain normal gravity on a space station, the time flew by. At 6:30, several group members had to rush home, and they all dispersed in different directions. The evening air was significantly cooler and Darryl was still thinking about space stations and his drawings as he walked up Vaneksburg Road toward Garland Avenue. His mind was on the discussion with the Science Club for moving mass around the space station by pumping water to various tanks, thereby maintaining balance. He imagined the pipes, pumps and tanks while walking through a small industrial park. It was still light and he had gone this way before, but this time he was dreaming, not paying attention. His mind drifted, the walk home was a pleasant time to think, to dream, to imagine. His mind was still toying with the club's project, but he also thought about Audrey, Barb, the friends he was making. Life had never been better. He was walking past a deserted building, "Some kind of storage facility, a warehouse," he thought to himself, as he continued walking.

As luck would have it, a group of older boys, Dave Branch and three of his buddies, were drinking beer and smoking in that building when Darryl passed by. They had left the door cracked open enough to see out. It was Bob's turn to sit by the door and keep an eye open for anyone that might interrupt their activity. He spotted Darryl and waved Dave over to look. "Dave, ain't that Darryl whatshisname?"

Dave was sitting on an empty crate with a cigarette in one hand and a can of beer in the other. "Where?"

Bob stood next to the door, looking out, "There, he just walked past the door," he said quietly, pointing at Darryl's back, "Half way down the block."

"I want that little son of a bitch," Dave said to his friends as he pushed on the door and started to jog after Darryl. The others followed, and catching up, they surrounded Darryl. "Well, ya little punk, what do ya have to say now that you don't have your girl friends to protect you?"

Darryl was pushed from one bully to the next, back toward the door, and forced inside the building, where the beating continued. He was punched by each of the boys, and when he fell to the ground, he was kicked and hit with a slat from a broken pallet. The kicker was Bob Dorsey, a senior and a devoted follower of Dave. If Dave jumped off a cliff, Bob just might follow him. Dave was a hitter. He enjoyed punching people and he exhausted himself hitting Darryl.

The other two boys were also seniors at Vaneksburg High and just as drunk. They had been playing with a cattle prod they had stolen a week earlier and now they took turns poking Darryl as he lay on the ground.

After twenty minutes of abuse, the four boys were about to leave when Carl said, "Hey, Dave, he ain't movin' — You think he's dead?"

Dave went pale, "What! Dead! You think we killed him?"

"No, I think you killed him," replied Carl as he and the others stood staring at the limp body on the floor.

Dave rolled Darryl over and looked at his eyes. They were open but saw nothing. He checked for sounds of breathing, nothing. Dave gagged and said weakly, "Yeah, he's dead."

Carl looked to be the most-sober of the group. "Dave, get his wallet and his watch. Bob, get his backpack, don't touch nothing where you could make a fingerprint. We'll make this look like a robbery. Did anybody touch anything in this place that could leave a fingerprint?"

The other three were all on stun. Dave slowly took the wallet and watch and walked toward the door. Bob walked back in with the backpack held up with a stick.

"Wait a minute," said Carl as he took the backpack and emptied it on the floor, "Where are the other guys tonight?"

Ron looked at Carl and said, "I think they went down by Bradley's Wharf, they were gonna' try to catch some catfish."

"Perfect," said Carl, "That's where we've been all night. You guys understand we have been at the Wharf, catfishin'. Now let's pick up our cigarette butts and empty beer cans. We'll take 'em with us to the Wharf and spread 'em around." He kicked the contents of the backpack around as if it was rifled and found some loose change which he pocketed. The group stood next to the door and looked over the scene. Bob found a stray cigarette butt and pocketed it. They left the building with everything they thought could be evidence and piled into Carl's car.

Carl paused, turned and looked at the others, "When we get there, don't say anything about the warehouse. Don't make any noise about getting there or what time it is. We get there, we spread out and get comfortable. Everybody take a few cigarette butts and a couple of beer cans. Quietly spread them around when nobody's looking. We should stay as late as we can and when it comes time to leave, we have been there since about 6:30. You all understand, no mention of the warehouse, no mention of Darryl."

Fifteen minutes later Carl drove into the Wharf parking lot. The four boys exited the car and looked through the trees and bushes toward the dock where the others had gathered. Carl turned and looked at his three friends, "Remember, we been here since 6:30. Now, one at a time, just wander in and join the group."

A few minutes later the four had filtered in. Carl sat off to the side and lit a cigarette. Dave wandered over toward the water's edge and sat down. Nobody seemed to notice the new arrivals and as the evening passed, each of the boys distributed his cache of beer cans and cigarette butts around where he was sitting.

Carl noticed that it was almost 9:30 when two more boys showed up. He casually mentioned to one of them that they were late, "We've been here since 6:30," he said quietly. "Beginning to think you weren't coming."

Dave sat on a log and took out Darryl's wallet. Carl saw him and quickly moved to sit next to him. "Dave, give that to me. That and the watch," he whispered, "I'll take care of them. I'll lose them on my way home tonight."

It was approaching 11:00 and there were now ten boys sitting around, talking, casting lines into the water, drinking beer and smoking as if they all had been there all evening.

*　　*　　*

Darryl's mother worked at a department store in the mall and got home at 10:00 pm. Darryl was not there and she wondered if he was still at his Science Club meeting. At 11:00 pm she began to worry and at 11:30, she began the phone calls. It was almost midnight when she called the police and reported him missing. The police checked the school and found nobody there. They traced the several routes that he may have taken to walk home and found nothing. A patrol car drove through the industrial park and noticed nothing. The door to the vacant building was closed and he didn't look inside.

The next day, Darryl was noted as missing at school. The police showed up asking questions, but nobody knew anything. The boys that went cat-fishing were sure he had not been at the Wharf. Several other groups were equally sure they had not seen him. The Science Club members said he had left at about 6:30 pm when the meeting ended and they all went home. Nobody knew which way he had gone. The search reached out to the freeway on the north and circled around the same distance to the south. Nothing was found. Then, on Saturday morning, a security guard checking the buildings in the industrial park noticed the unsecured door on a deserted storage building, entered and found Darryl.

The news broke his mother. She was no longer able to cope with the real world and was taken in by her older sister. She lived for another three years, deteriorating, and finally passed away in 1996. It was said she never smiled after Darryl disappeared. Never.

Darryl had very few friends, but the funeral was well attended. Dave Branch was there along with Bob Dorsey and Carl Wilkins. They all acted humble and had no idea what happened to Darryl.

Detective Andy Ferguson caught the case and questioned a number of students at the school, including Dave Branch and Bob Dorsey and could not find enough evidence to focus in on any one individual. The ten boys fishing at the Wharf stuck to their story, never wavering. The final police file entry noted that Darryl had been beaten to death, his watch and wallet had been stolen and the perpetrator or perpetrators of this crime were never identified.

Darryl was murdered, mourned, buried and all but forgotten before the end of what would have been his first year of high school. The assumption by the police department was that it was a robbery by someone passing through town, because "Nobody from Vaneksburg would be a part of that sort of thing." After seven months with no new information or clues, the investigation had gone cold. Detective Ferguson kept the file on his desk and periodically would browse through it and seemingly drift off into the dream world. When Andy Ferguson retired and moved away, the file was relegated to the basement with all the other 'cold cases', gathering dust.

* * *

CHAPTER FOUR
Cold Cases...

The patient visited the doctor after two weeks and was still relatively pain free. Some minor discomfort in the back and shoulders, but no real pain helped Dr. Schrader to determine which medications they might try and he prescribed one that would present the fewest side effects.

The patient had attended two reunion Committee meetings and a third was scheduled for the coming Wednesday. Participation in planning and coordinating the reunion had proven to be a pleasant and welcome distraction for the patient. Conversations with people the patient had not seen in years definitely diverted attention from the inevitable. The prospect of an entertaining social gathering kept the patient interested and occupied.

The patient's current position, held for the last several years, had given the patient the financial means to take a leave of absence that allowed time to take care of some personal matters. A very frank conversation with the Personnel Director about the condition which "May not end favorably," allowed the patient to take a day or two here and there to assure that all personal matters were in order and to be prepared for the outcome of the various tests and treatments that were coming.

* * *

Det. Ian McLarry was accustomed to a busy work schedule and Vaneksburg was even quieter than he had expected. In order to make himself more useful, Ian asked the chief if he could review cold cases and maybe, "Fresh eyes will see something."

"Okay, Pittsburgh," responded Ned Bowen. "The file cabinet in the basement has a few that you could chew on, have at it, but if something new happens, you come outta' the basement and back on the front line."

"Thanks, Chief. I'll dig into it today."

The file cabinet had a number of minor unsolved crimes, including eight robberies, two hit-and-runs near the north side Mall and one murder. Ian opened the file and read aloud "Darryl Zamanski, fourteen years old, 1993, beaten by person or persons unknown, died of internal bleeding. Initially reported missing by his mother Thursday, September 9, 1993 at 11:55 pm, body found by security company during a regular weekly check of the facility on Saturday, September 11, 1993 at 10:22 am." He carried this file back to his desk and read on.

Chief Bowen noted Ian sitting at his desk, apparently absorbed in a single file. He thought for a moment then walked out to Ian's desk and sat down. "Darryl Zamanski?"

Ian raised his head, "Yeah, sad. This reads like he was a nice kid. Took a walk one night and got killed."

"Yeah, back then I was sitting at a desk like this one. I didn't catch the case, but we talked about it in the department for months. Nothing ever happened. No evidence, no suspects, no arrests, no damn justice." Bowen suddenly looked exhausted. "I'll collect my thoughts and we should sit and talk about this one. Andy Ferguson was the lead on that case. He retired about two years after, in '95 and moved to Florida or somewhere in the Carolinas. I haven't talked to him in over ten years. Anyway, come see me when you have finished reading the file. I'm gonna' give Andy a call."

Ian continued reading. Some of his classmates and several others from Vaneksburg High were interviewed. His friends relayed the story of Dave Branch and the embarrassment he suffered in the cafeteria several days before Darryl was killed. He and seven of his friends were questioned. Dave had an alibi, he and his friends were at a pizza parlor, Franco's Pizza, on the east side, celebrating someone's birthday early in the day and wound up at Bradley's Wharf trying to catch catfish until ten or eleven that night. All seven of his friends swore that Dave was with them all evening and others remembered the group including Dave as being there until 11:00 pm.

Ian continued, a fingerprint on a library book in Darryl's backpack was a match to a Ronald Nestor, one of the group celebrating at the Pizza Parlor and the Wharf. The explanation followed that Ronald worked part time in the school library and his prints were probably on a number of books in that library.

Ian closed the file, looked at the ceiling and walked into the chief's office. "That was depressing."

Chief Bowen took off his glasses, put them on his desk, leaned back and said, "Just talked to Monica Ferguson. They are in North Carolina, near Greenville. Andy doesn't remember where he was last week, last month, last year. He even forgets his own kids' names. She told him I was on the phone and he asked who I was."

"So chief, no other fingerprints, no DNA, no witnesses, no little pieces of clothing, nothing," said Ian.

"Right, nothing. We looked for anything that could be considered evidence, nothing was discovered, no prints that were worth anything and back then we couldn't even spell DNA. Do you still want to do this?"

"Yeah, even more now. This just ain't right," said Ian as he walked back to his desk. He stopped just outside the chief's office, turned and went back in. "That reunion coming up at the Hotel, that would have been his graduating class." He grinned, turned and began to walk away again. He stopped and said loud enough for the chief to hear, "Chief, it's been nineteen years, and they'll be gathering at a Hotel right down the road. I'm going to talk to every one of them before this is over." He turned again and walked back into the chief's office, "The years spent in high school can be looked back on by someone in his or her thirties or forties and the events of the day can then be viewed from a completely different perspective. It's no longer important to be viewed as being cool or being on the right side of a bully. Now the slight geek who wore thick glasses and couldn't throw or catch may be an attorney or a doctor. The game may be the same but the ground rules have matured and an answer from 1993 may differ in 2012."

"You may be on to something, Pittsburgh, good luck," said the Chief. As Ian walked back to his desk, the chief grinned, looked down at his desk and muttered, "Got me a bulldog. Go get 'em, kid."

* * *

Two more weeks passed and again, the patient returned to the doctor's office for another visit and a checkup on vital signs. A brief examination and Dr. Schrader looked out into the corridor, then closed the door. "Have there been any changes you have noticed?"

"I don't think so," replied the patient. "I feel tired continually and those little aches in my back and neck seem about the same as before."

"Okay, but no pain that the medications can't handle?"

"No, and I try not to use the meds if I don't really need them."

Dr. Schrader smiled and thought for a second. "Okay, let's make it two weeks again, same time."

"Thank you doctor," said the patient, standing to leave.

"By the way, how is that reunion thing coming along?"

The patient smiled, "Oh, there is going to be another meeting this week, on Wednesday. We have already divided up the main tasks and we'll see what kind of progress has been made and maybe make some adjustments."

"Just remember, no lifting and carrying," said Dr. Schrader as he put his stethoscope away.

"No worries, I will only volunteer for light duty work," laughed the patient.

Dr. Schrader thought for a second, his patient was going to die and life is far too short as it is. This person had barely begun to live, thought Dr. Schrader. He thought about all the bad, unhealthy things he had done in his younger days and blurted out, "You should do something you have always wanted to do. Hell, have a cigarette, drink too much whiskey or beer, eat the wrong food and have seconds for dessert."

The patient smiled, "I'm going to spend a little more time with friends, doctor, and I have a cousin living near Denver, I've already written to him." The patient thought for a second and continued, with a grin, "My mom was my beneficiary on my insurance policies, but she's gone, so I am leaving almost everything to my cousin George. Maybe his family will remember me after I am gone." The grin faded and the patient looked at the floor.

Dr. Schrader put his hand on the patient's shoulder, "I still hope we will find something."

"No false hope Doctor, I'm slowly getting used to the idea and I'm going to make these last few months, or weeks, mean something."

Schrader was impressed at the patient's perspective, or apparent perspective. "You have a cousin in Denver? Perhaps a trip west may be in order."

The patient looked thoughtful, "He is the only one that I could find right off, but maybe he knows other family members. I was happy to find him. We have not seen each other since I was in college, so maybe a little ride to Denver and as you said, a second helping of apple pie and ice cream, it sounds almost evil, but what the..."

"That's the spirit," said Dr. Schrader, "Now get out there and go do something bad."

The patient found humor in that and grinned, "Maybe I will, Doctor, maybe I will."

*   *   *

CHAPTER FIVE
The Committee Meets...

Ian contacted the high school and found out the Reunion Committee was being chaired by Barbara Nessman. A call to Barbara after regular school hours got him an invite to join them for dinner that Wednesday evening at 6:00 at the Vaneksburg Tavern. Ian arrived about fifteen minutes early and told the hostess Barbara Nessman was expecting him. The hostess immediately led him to a small private dining room and told him the group usually met in that room.

A minute later a man wearing a green knit shirt with the restaurant's name and logo entered the room carrying an armful of menus, "Detective McLarry, I presume."

"Yes," replied Ian, "And you are?"

"Jim Schuster, this is my restaurant and I'm on the reunion committee. They usually get here right on time, so any minute now. Can I get you something to drink while we wait?"

"A little coffee would be great," replied Ian.

"You got it," said Jim and he turned to a waitress standing in the doorway, handed her the menus and said, "Carol, how about a fresh pot and several mugs?"

The waitress smiled, said, "Right away," and hustled off.

Jim turned back toward Ian and said, "Detective McLarry, what is your interest in our reunion?"

"Please call me Ian, and I'm interested in finding out more about a crime that was committed about nineteen years ago."

Jim thought for a second, then looked Ian in the eye and said with a very heavy voice, "You're looking into the Darryl Zamanski killing?"

Ian was surprised at the gravity in Jim's voice, "Yes, do you remember it?"

Jim pointed to a table and pulled out a chair. The two men sat at the table as Jim continued, "Remember it, hell, yes, I remember it. I can't forget it. Darryl was a nice kid. We were not tight, I mean we didn't hang out together, but that whole thing was brushed aside altogether too quickly. I'm not sure the police back then really looked into it. So what is your interest?"

"I joined the Vaneksburg force in April. So far I have met the office staff, all of the patrol officers, the mayor, several councilmen, the hotel manager and a couple of business owners. This is a nice, quiet community, not a lot of crime for me to investigate, so I'm looking into cold cases. New eyes, a fresh approach and who knows, we might come up with some answers."

Jim leaned back in his chair, "Very interesting, do you like this cold case work?"

"Jim, I'm a cop, I come from a family of cops. If there's a bad guy out there, I want to find him. If I can keep this kind of thing from happening again, then that's what I want to do. When I looked into the file on this case, well, I couldn't just put it back in the basement. I want a shot at it. I want to solve it and arrest the bad guy."

Jim nodded with understanding, "I hear you Ian, and I appreciate that. If there is anything I can say or do to help you, just ask. The others we are meeting with tonight will all probably say the same thing."

Right on cue, the door opened and an attractive, blond, athletic looking woman entered the room. "Hi Jim, and I assume this is Detective McLarry," she said as she extended her hand, "I'm Barb Nessman."

Ian stood and shook her hand, "My pleasure, Barb, I don't want to get in your way, but meeting this group is a perfect opportunity to learn some things about Darryl."

Two others, a tall, thin man and a slight woman with long dark hair, entered the room and approached the three. "Good evening everybody," said Phil Kline, "I'm a little late, I had to zip the windows into my Jeep, it might rain tonight."

Jim said, "Phil, you are right on time." He looked at the woman and said, "Audrey, glad you could make it. Is everybody good with burgers again?"

This was met with four yeses and a blank stare from Ian. "I'll make it six and the good detective can join us for dinner and ask us all the questions he wants," said Jim. He walked out of the room and spotted Carol. "Let's have six burger platters, three medium and three well done and come in and take some drink orders when you have a minute."

"Okay Jim," she replied and turned toward the kitchen. Jim surveyed the dining room crowd, grinned and turned back to the small dining room mumbling, "Nice crowd tonight."

Barb led the conversation by introducing Ian as the new detective from Pittsburgh. "He's new to our community and is looking into the Darryl Zamanski killing. He will probably have a lot of general questions that will be old news to us, but new to him, so we should be ready to get into detail whenever we can." She turned to Ian, "Detective, this is Phil Kline and Audrey Redding and now you have the floor."

Ian stood, faced the group and began, "First, my name is Ian and I do not want to knock your reunion business off track, so I'll keep it brief."

"Not to worry," said Phil. "You got questions, maybe we have answers, maybe not, but we can try."

Ian extended his hand to Phil, "Thanks, Phil, but you guys have business to take care of here."

"Well, more time is spent talking about other things, including Darryl, so you will fit right in, Detective," said Jim as he came back into the room with two waiters.

"That's very kind of you," said Ian.

They arranged the tables so that everybody could eat and write in their note pads. The six chairs were spread around a table that could accommodate twelve people.

Jim surveyed the arrangement, satisfied and said, "Pull up a chair, Ian, the coffee is coming in a second and the food will be here right after that." He leaned closer to Ian and confided, "The service in this place is fantastic."

As Ian began to speak, a waitress came in with a coffee pot and a basket of sugar and creamers. Another waitress brought in a tray of mugs and spread them around the table. "I'm looking into the incident that occurred in September of 1993, nineteen years ago. I realize your memories may have dimmed over that length of time. But, the process here is to talk to each of you individually and try to rebuild the puzzle. I have the previous detective's notes and have had a conversation or two with people who are still with the police force today. I am going to ask you not to talk to each other about this until I have had a discussion with each of you. Then we will get together and do a round table type thing. This will allow me to get different points of view and hopefully, I will find something that may have been overlooked."

Barb was the first to respond, "We have talked about this several times in the last few weeks, and haven't identified anything new, detective."

"Well, let me try this approach, it's sometimes beneficial when new eyes and ears join the parade," said Ian, "So, if I may suggest, let me take each of you separately off to the side and see what shakes out."

Jim said, "Food will be here in a minute. Let's eat, then we can do our business while Ian takes us aside one at a time."

*　　*　　*

Jim set up a second table in the corner for Ian to use while talking to each person individually. Ian finished his dinner and seemed anxious to get started. Barb noted his restlessness and said, "Why don't you and I get this started while the others finish eating?"

"Okay," replied Ian, "Come on over here and bring your coffee."

Barb smiled and said, "Finished my coffee, but I will bring my wine. Is that okay?"

"Sure," said Ian. He pulled out a chair for Barb and they sat down to talk. "Tell me Barb, how long have you lived in Vaneksburg?"

"Oh, all my life, except when I went to UVA, and when I was married for a couple of years to a Navy pilot. We moved to Virginia Beach for a few months. We had a house and a van and were planning to start a family." She paused, looked down at her wine, took a deep breath and continued, "Then I came back here and started teaching, but I still have the van." She forced a smile and Ian sensed that all was not well.

"Your husband?"

"He was killed in Iraq."

"Sorry, I didn't know."

"That's one thing about this town. Everybody knew me and after the funeral, I came here for a little break and the people were just so nice to me, well, I never left."

"Was your husband from here too?"

"No, we met at UVA, he was from the Virginia Beach area and was two years ahead of me. When I graduated he visited me on leave and we got married. We had two good years when he was home." Barb looked down at her wine glass and was quiet for a few seconds.

Ian paused while she reflected and he began, "You graduated in '97 from Vaneksburg High?"

Barb raised her head, smiled again and said, "Yeah, I did."

Ian opened his notebook, "And Darryl would have been in that class?"

"Yeah, he was such a nice kid," she said.

"Did you know him well?"

"No, not very well, he was just a nice little guy, smart and very quiet."

Ian leaned back in his chair, "So why would anyone want to hurt him?"

"Well, I always thought it was that group of tough guys. They pushed everybody around, big and small. You know what I mean?"

Ian looked a little amused and said, "Yeah, I've met the type before."

Barb twisted her face, "You, you're one of the big ones. You wouldn't have gotten pushed around."

"Oh yeah, I had my little run-in with the toughs long before I grew into this larger size," said Ian.

"How did you handle it?"

Ian smiled, "I have a cousin. His name is Lucas. He just retired after 32 years in the Marine Corps. For the last twenty years, he has been an instructor in hand-to-hand combat schools. Toughest son of a bitch I have ever known. The first time I came home with a bloody nose, Cousin Lucas taught me how to convince others not to bother me."

"He taught you how to fight?"

"No, he taught me how to win. There's a difference. I could get into a fight every day and maybe even come out on top once in a while. Lucas showed me how to have one fight and make it obvious that I was not to be messed with, ever. It's not about getting a punch in here or there, more like get that single finishing punch in as soon as possible."

Barb looked stunned, "And that worked?"

"Oh yeah," said Ian, "There was a family, four guys, brothers or cousins or both, that jumped me one day and one of them kept saying something about breaking my arm. He wanted one of the others to hold my arm out where he could jump on it."

"That's terrible," said Barb.

"Yeah," said Ian, "Well, I remembered what Lucas taught me and all of a sudden I turned and grabbed one guy by the throat and tried to rip him open. He screamed and started to cry. I let him go and punched another guy as hard as I could in his throat. He didn't talk right for a week. Anyway, that was all it took. Those guys never bothered me again. Half of the school never came near me again, the other half seemed to stay closer than ever before. One fight where I got crazy and it was over."

Barb cleared her throat, "Well, Darryl was not that sort of kid. He was not a fighter, he just wanted to be himself. He enjoyed the difficult stuff like math and science and might have been a scientist, or an engineer or a teacher today. We'll never know."

Ian opened his notebook again, "This group of toughs, who would they be?"

"Well, the one that sticks out is Dave Branch. We had a little run-in one day in the cafeteria just a few days before Darryl was killed."

"Tell me about that," said Ian.

"We were sitting around a table in the cafeteria having a good time. Darryl was sort of in the middle of everything. I remember him laughing. Then Dave said something to Darryl about him looking like a girl. I had to open my big mouth and say something about Dave being in his fifth year of high school."

Ian made a quick note and asked, "What did Darryl do?"

"Nothing, he let Dave have his say and he let it go," said Barb.

As he was making notes, Ian said, "Sounds like Darryl was a smart kid. It's kinda' hard for someone else to finish a fight if you're not willing to let it start. So he just sat there and you threw the next rock."

Barb looked troubled, "Yeah, I've thought about it over these last nineteen years. Did I get Darryl killed?"

Ian had heard this sort of reasoning before, "No way, you can't absorb any heat on this. Dave may have been the bad guy here, but not on account of you. If he was involved, it's all on him."

Barb seemed to relax again, took a sip of wine and said, "That's what the police told me in the interviews. Then, when they decided Dave couldn't have done it, well, that kind of took the pressure off."

Ian could tell that Barb still harbored some feeling of guilt. "So you didn't know him very well, but you stood up for him."

"I guess," said Barb. "It was more that Dave made me angry. It could have been anybody he jumped on, I would have done the same thing. Dave was a jerk and the whole school knew it. Something just had to be said."

"Okay, so after you said something to Dave, then what happened?"

"Then I kissed Darryl on the cheek and said he was better looking than Dave too."

"And?"

"And Dave left, kinda' stormed out. I thought that was the end of it. A few days later Darryl was found dead."

Barb looked drained and Ian said, "Let's leave it there for now. I'll talk to the others and probably have a few more questions for each of you as we go down this road." He walked back to the large table with Barb and said, "Who wants to be next?"

As he asked, Ian looked around the table and noticed a new face. The young lady stood and said, "Hi, I'm Sandy Lansing. Running a little late tonight and I will probably be called back, so can I go next?"

Ian didn't hear any objections and said, "Sure, let's go over here," he said pointing toward the smaller table. "Please sit. First, my name's Ian McLarry, I'm..."

"I know, we were talking about you while you were talking to Barb. So what can I tell you?"

"First, let me get my notes squared away, your name is Sandy, is that short for something?"

"Oh, yeah, Alexandra Maria Lansing. L–a–n–s–i–n–g."

Ian wrote her name down, "Thanks. So how long have you lived here?"

Sandy looked up at the ceiling, then at Ian, "My dad was with an airline for years. We used to live in Texas and he was transferred here in '82. So I hardly remember Texas, this is my home, I really like it here."

"Okay," said Ian, "So when did you first meet Darryl?"

"We were in the first grade together, but we didn't talk. He was shy and kinda' stayed to himself," Sandy responded.

"Did he have any friends?"

Sandy thought for a second, "Yeah, Phil Kline and he got along. I remember the two of them having lunch together a lot and I think that their houses were close."

Ian continued making notes, "Did Darryl have any of the opposite, guys he didn't get along with?"

Sandy wiggled in her chair as if she was ready to start dancing, "Well, Darryl was one of those kids who never seemed to catch a break. He was not a big kid. He was small and other kids picked on him a lot. I remember him getting beat up pretty badly by an older boy when we were in the fourth grade. I remember because Mr. Barnes, our teacher, took him to the school nurse to get patched up."

"Do you remember who the older boy was?"

Sandy's face showed disgust, "Yeah, I'll never forget, it was Dave Branch."

Ian checked his notes from Barb's conversation, "Dave Branch, was he a bully?"

"He was a jerk, a complete ass. I never could stand him. I even asked a different nurse to take care of him when he came into the ER about two or three years ago."

Ian looked up at Sandy, "So, you are a nurse?"

"Yeah, at the hospital on Gradison. I work in the ER," she replied.

As he noted the hospital in his book, Ian continued, "And this Dave came into the ER with what?"

Sandy rolled her eyes in a thoughtful way, "I think it was a cut on his arm, a nasty cut as I recall," she said with an evil grin. "I think he caught it in some farm machine, not really sure. But the other nurse that took care of him, she did too good a job."

Ian looked confused, "Waddya" mean, too good?"

"The son of a bitch lived," she said with a touch of fire in her voice.

"You don't like him, I'm getting that drift," said Ian.

"I think the only ones who did like him then or now are the other creeps he ran with."

Ian readied his pen, "You have any names for me?"

"Sure," she answered, "Let's see, there was Bob Dorsey, Ron Nestor, Ken Murray and Paul Burger. Let me see, oh yeah, Joe and Ben something."

"Were these guys always together?"

"Pretty much, as I recall. If you saw one of them usually there were two or three of the others."

Ian was writing in his notebook, "Still today?"

"Yeah, except for Ken Murray, he was killed in a car accident about nine or ten years ago. I was in the ER when they brought him in. As much as I didn't like him, I hoped it was quick. He was a mess. Oh and one of the others moved away, I forget his name."

Ian looked up from his notes, "Did any of the others confront Darryl?"

"I have no idea, but I'd guess no. Darryl was small and those guys were older and bigger than he was."

"Meaning?"

"Meaning that beating up Darryl was something only the new kids would do. It would be like you punching Audrey over there."

Ian turned his head and looked at the slight woman at the table. "The little one with the long dark hair?"

"Yep, Audrey Redding. I think she liked Darryl and he liked her. She was shorter than him and pretty smart. They seemed to get along pretty well."

"So you have known them since the third grade?"

"Yeah, oops, that's me," she said as a pager sounded, "Gotta' go, but any time you want to talk, I'm not hard to find." Sandy stood and hurried out the door.

Ian walked back to the table, looked at the crowd and said, "Phil, let's talk."

Phil pushed himself up from the chair with a slight groan; when he noticed Ian looking, he said, "I wish I could say it's an old football injury, but it's not. I think I slept twisted in a knot last night."

Ian grinned, "I know what that's like." They sat at the small table and Ian said, "Okay, what can you tell me about Darryl?"

"Well, first, we were friends. We went to TJ Elementary together and we both seemed to like the same stuff. Darryl was always looking at books about stars and space. He was excited about taking physics when we got to high school. I think he knew all the dinosaurs' names and most of the constellations. To Darryl, working out a math problem was fun, he started doing geometry on his own before we got to high school. He never got to take physics, that was something he talked about, he was really looking forward to physics. I leaned more toward the biology stuff and wound up a Vet. Darryl, well, he might have been the next Stephen Hawking, or Albert Einstein. We'll never know."

Ian looked up again, "Was he really that smart?"

"Probably not, but it's nice to think of him that way. I liked him, a good friend."

"So what do you think happened to him?"

"Well, that day in the cafeteria when Barb planted a big one on Darryl's cheek and said something to Dave Branch that made him look dumber that dumb, well, that made me think that Dave and his buddies probably jumped Darryl and got carried away beating on him."

"Was this Branch fella arrested?"

Phil leaned back in his chair, "No, not that I recall. I remember he had an alibi, something about him and about ten other guys fishing down at the Wharf when it happened. Then we heard it was some drifter passing through town that beat him and stole his money and his watch. I guess it's possible."

"But you really like this Branch guy for the beating?"

"It would have to be more than just Dave. He could take Darryl in a fight, but I think he must have had help to do this much damage. Branch is too wussy to have done that on his own."

"Who were Dave's friends?"

"Dave, let's see, there was Carl Wilkins, Ron Nestor and Paul Burger. They were kinda' tight. Oh, Ken Murray and Bob Dorsey. They all seemed to end up in the same place. There were others too, but I'll have to think about it. Murray is dead. He was always doing drugs or drinking or both and when he drove his car into a bridge support a few years ago, we all figured that drugs were in play. The guy was a mess, he had a closed casket. He lived with his folks and couldn't seem to hold a job for long."

"Do the rest of these guys still live around here?"

"Not sure, I know that Marve moved to California years ago. He has a little brother that was in our class and they moved before we graduated."

Ian paused his writing, "Marve?"

"Oh yeah, Marve Korbut," said Phil.

Ian asked, "Did these guys ever hassle you?"

Phil sat up straight, "Oh yeah. It was a regular thing for a while, but after a bit they found others to pick on. Darryl was smaller than me so he was a target for a longer period. We used to talk about getting to high school where there would be a lot more kids and we could fit into a crowd. Kind of like getting lost in a friendly forest."

Ian sat up straight, "Just be one of many, hide in plain sight."

"Yeah. And after Darryl was killed, the toughs kinda' blended into the woodwork. It seems like none of us were bothered again. I guess it still goes on, but for me and other guys I knew in high school, the bully trash seemed to stop that year."

Ian finished another note and said, "Okay, I'm going to talk to the others and then we can all sit at the big table and compare notes."

Phil went back to the big table, "Okay, who's next?"

"I'll take a turn," said Audrey.

Ian led her to the small table and opened the conversation, "Are you originally from here?"

Audrey sat up straight, a little like a school girl, very proper. "I was born here, stayed through high school and went away to college."

"Do you live here now?"

"No, I moved to Fairfax a few years ago, to be closer to my work. I have a lot of weekend appointments and close is better."

"What do you do?"

"Oh, I'm in real estate. Mostly private homes, but I've gotten in on a few commercial deals."

"You were in school with Darryl before high school?"

"Yes, we were at TJ together."

"Was he a nice guy?"

"I thought so, we got along very nicely and he never pushed me."

"Pushed?"

"Yeah, some people don't like it if you walk slowly. Darryl walked as slow as I did. Some people eat fast, Darryl waited and didn't push me. He walked slow for me and ate slow for me. I always felt comfortable with him. When we talked, he let me say what I was thinking and he didn't laugh at my silly ideas. If we played a game he let me take all the time I wanted for my turn. He didn't push and he smiled a lot, a happy smile."

"You liked him and he liked you?"

"I think so. I guess if we had gotten through high school we might have made a couple." She lowered her head and stopped talking for a moment. "Maybe I loved him. I think today that I did."

"What do you think happened to him?"

"I think that Dave Branch and at least two of his friends killed him. I don't think they set out to kill him, I think they just beat him so much that he died."

"Dave Branch, that name keeps popping up. The police cleared him though. He and about ten others were fishing when it happened."

"Yeah, that's what they say. But I still think he did it."

"Because of the incident in the cafeteria?"

"That and all the other times Dave pushed Darryl around. Dave couldn't push many people but Darryl was small and not a fighter. He was an easy target and Dave couldn't handle kids his own size."

"So he used Darryl as a punching bag."

"Yeah, but only when he was with someone else. Dave is a coward. He wouldn't have attacked Darryl if he didn't have help."

They returned to the larger table. Ian looked at Jim, "Jim, you want to add anything to what we already covered."

"I've told you most of what I know," said Jim.

Ian pulled up a chair and sat down, "Then it's time for the group to talk."

"What about you," asked Barb, "You must be forming some opinions by now?"

"I am," replied Ian, "But it's a little too soon to put them on the table. First, the reports indicate Darryl was on his way home from some school meeting."

"Science Club," said Phil.

"Yeah, so he had a backpack with books, a wallet, a watch and some loose money. His mom said he had about twelve dollars when he set out in the morning. He apparently was taking Garland Avenue to get home. That is question number one. Somehow he went into that empty building. He could have walked in, been asked to go in, was forced in, we don't know. That is question number two. The markings on his clothes and on the floor indicate he was beaten there. Question number three is: Who was in that building?"

The group was listening intently when Barb said, "We knew that, and we are pretty sure we know the answers."

Jim leaned forward and added, "Darryl was a good kid, detective. I don't think he would have gone into that building to do anything like have a cigarette, or drink beer."

Phil offered, "If he was passing that building and a stranger asked him to step inside, I think he would have run, or at least put up a fight outside."

"What if someone inside called out for help. He would have tried to help if someone was in trouble," said Audrey.

"The possibilities are countless and often we find that the least likely is the answer," said Ian. "Years ago, in 1991, I was in my last year of high school. My father and uncle went to Cleveland for about a week. My cousin had gone missing and the family gathered to look for her. As it turns out, she had been kidnapped and murdered. It took a number of years and some dogged determination on the part of another cousin, a detective with the Cleveland Heights Police Department, to identify a suspect, but the guy was finally found in 2000 and he paid for what he did."

"Is he in jail now?" asked Barb.

"That's a story for another day," said Ian.

"Sounds ominous," said Audrey.

"Let's get back to our case here," said Ian.

Barb sat up straight and said, "I've always thought Dave Branch and his pals did this. Can we talk about that?"

"Yes," said Ian, "We should. Let's start with the unpopular theory that it was somebody passing through town."

"Okay," said Jim, "First: Why would anybody passing through town hole up in that building? It's not on the main drag, not near the highway and probably not obviously empty. No, it makes more sense some locals knew it was empty and knew where an open door might be. They would hang-out in there and do what they can't do at home. Smoke, drink, snort, be tough, and beat up Darryl."

"We have had this conversation a few times, Ian, and we all agree the 'stranger passing through theory' doesn't work," said Barb.

"Well, if that doesn't work, what does?"

"Dave and his band of goons," said Jim. The others nodded in agreement.

"Once again, they all have an alibi."

"They are each other's alibi, doesn't that smell just a little bit funny?" asked Audrey.

"Listen, I am going to take all of this and run the files again. I'll check out each of the guys you have listed for me and see what pops out," said Ian.

The group stayed for another hour talking about everything from the reunion to Darryl to baseball. They broke up at about ten and went their separate ways.

*　　*　　*

CHAPTER SIX
Review...

The next day Ian dug through the file again. He was looking for anything that may have been written down about Dave Branch or his friends. Dave's name was there, he had been questioned about the cafeteria incident and his whereabouts on the night of the murder. The report made Dave look like an innocent bystander. No side notes about suspicious behavior and no indication he may have orchestrated an alibi at the wharf. The names of three other boys were also listed. Each had been questioned, each claimed to have been at the wharf and each listed the others as a part of their alibi. All four boys also listed six other boys at the wharf as part of their alibis.

"Chief, is there anything else on this case?' asked Ian. "What I have found is next to nothing. The interviews with potential suspects were bland, handled as if the detective was questioning his girlfriend."

"You mean the interviews with the boys?" asked Ned.

"Yeah, there is nothing there. Each one of them was asked where they were and they all said they were at the wharf, fishing and BOOM, case closed."

"Waddya' want me to tell you, Ian?"

"Tell me this Darryl was more than a punching bag for a small minded hood. Tell me someone actually cared about him."

Ned leaned back in his chair and spread his hands, "Ian, back then I was just another cop working a desk. Andy Ferguson handled that case and when he said the boys were cleared, well, what could I say? He was the lead, he conducted the interviews and he determined it was someone passing through town, not one of those boys that had killed Darryl. I had no reason to question his conclusions."

"What about forensics, did they find anything, and is anything left that might be rechecked?"

Chief Bowen leaned back in his chair, grinned at Ian and said, "Ian, you have to remember we are a small community in the middle of Virginia. We don't have a fancy forensic lab like on the cop shows, and this happened nineteen years ago. Back then if someone said DNA, we might scratch our heads and not know what to say."

"So what sort of physical evidence do we have?"

"Outside of the cattle prod and a piece of wood with a little blood on it, zip. Those two items and the files that you have in front of you are the extent of our evidence. We wrote things down, we took pictures, we interviewed people, and all that is in the files. You have everything that was collected and saved."

"That's not a lot to go on, chief," said Ian. "Is anyone else still here that I might talk to?"

"Well, you know about Andy. He can't remember his kids' names anymore, much less the details of a case like this. That's it, I was here, Bill was here, and you can ask the receptionist, Monica, she was on the front desk."

"Okay," said Ian. "I'm going to try everything I can. You never know, a little piece here and a piece there and we start to build a chain."

"By the way, there was a minor bumper wumper last night out near the interstate, in the entry to the hotel parking lot. Nobody hurt badly, just some vehicle damage and some bruises and the SOB took off. You check that one out this morning. Cindy will get you the file as soon as she collects all the forms."

"Okay, Chief, I'll jump on that right away." Ian dropped the files on his desk and walked over to Cindy. "Good morning, Cindy, Chief says you are building the 'hit-and-run' file. As soon as you have it built, I'll check it out."

"Timing is everything Detective, I just finished," she said as she handed Ian a fresh file complete with case number, colored filing tabs and a handful of forms inside. "That's all we have thus far. As you collect more stuff, I'll type it up and keep it as current as I can."

Ian opened the file as he walked back to his desk. He noted the incident happened in an intersection between a shopping center and the hotel. It was a simple enough case, a little paint transfer, check the local repair shops, interview the witnesses, catch the bad guy. "Simple, should be left to the uniforms," he mumbled to himself. Ian walked out to the front desk and asked Monica what she remembered about the Darryl Zamanski case.

"I was just starting on the front desk then and didn't see much of what was happening in the back rooms."

Ian pulled up a chair next to Monica and said, "Tell me what it was like here back then. Like was the front desk very busy?"

"There were some days when we had people waiting to see someone, but that was not very often. People came in and out a lot but it was more like a constant flow of people, not a crowd in the morning and another in the afternoon."

Ian leaned a little closer and asked, "Do you remember people coming in to talk about Darryl Zamanski?"

"Oh yes. There was a lot of people in for that one. I remember Andy – Detective Ferguson, had four or five people waiting to talk to him for a full week."

"Do you remember who they were?"

"I don't remember their names, well, some I do, but not all of them."

Ian sat up straight, "So who do you remember?"

"Well, there was Bob Dorsey, and his mother. I remember them because she and Detective Ferguson had an argument one day and she was not a happy person when she left here."

Ian was making notes, "What was the argument about?"

"Oh, I have no idea, they were in an interview room with the door closed and I couldn't hear what was said, but it got loud and like I said, she was angry when she left."

"How did Bob look, was he angry also?"

Monica thought, then said, "I don't think Bob was with her. I think she was alone that time."

"Did she come back again?"

"Not that day, but over the next few weeks she came in a few times. I remember because I wondered if there was going to be another argument."

"Was there, another argument?"

"Nope, she came and left a few times, never stayed very long and left without any fuss."

"What else do you remember?"

"There were a couple of other boys brought in for interviews. I do remember the Murray boy. He was killed in an accident sometime after that and it stuck in my mind. He was high on something and hit a bridge abutment."

"Anything else?"

"Oh, that Branch boy, David, was brought in several times for 'disorderly' and even spent a night or two in the back."

"Anybody else come to mind?"

"There was another one, I don't remember his name, but he was a cocky son of a bitch. I didn't like him. I remember he walked in the first time with his father and a lawyer. His father said it was just to keep everything legal, or something like that."

"He said that to you?"

"No, he was talking to Detective Ferguson. I don't know if I was supposed to hear it or not."

"Anything else you remember?"

"No, I think the whole thing was dropped soon after that and we went on to other things. The whole thing lasted about a month and it was over. I think the killer or killers turned out to be some drifters passing through town and they were never identified or caught."

"Thanks Monica, you've been a big help." Ian started to stand.

"Oh, wait a minute, Carl, I think his name was Carl, the snotty one," she said as she reached for a ringing phone.

Ian got up and walked back to his desk thinking about what he had learned. He was pouring over the file and his notes when he decided to shift gears and get a little fresh air. He picked up the Hit and Run file and walked over to the chief's office. "Chief, I'm going to run out to the hotel and check on this new one. See you later."

"Okay, hey, by the way, I called Bill and told him to find you when he checks in today."

"Thanks Chief, this won't take long," he said as he went out the door. "Bill Aikens, right?"

"Yep, Aikens," smiled the chief. He was pleased with his new detective.

* * *

CHAPTER SEVEN
Investigation...

Ian drove out to the hotel, checked at the front desk and located Hal in the main dining room. "Hal, I understand there was an incident in or near your parking area this morning."

"Good morning, Detective. They have you checking out these little problems? I expected to see a uniformed officer, not a detective," chided Hal.

"Well, we are not as busy as we could be, a very quiet spring. Let's hope it stays this way for a long while," replied Ian with a grin.

Forcing back a smile, Hal addressed Ian's concern, "The 'incident' you are referring to is a bit of damage to one of our guest's cars. He was backing out of a parking space when another car turned a corner and struck Mr. Westin's vehicle. Both he and his wife were shaken up and have gone to the hospital to be checked out. I can show you their vehicle."

Ian made another note in his book, "The other car and driver, did they leave before giving any information?"

"Yes, I'm afraid so. We do not have much of a description for you. A dark blue SUV, no make, no model and no license plate, but Mr. Westin did note that it was a Virginia plate," replied Hal.

Ian entered the information in his notebook, "Well, that's a start, I'll take anything I can get."

Hal returned to the question about Ian working a traffic incident, "Is this what you expected to be doing when you joined our local constabulary, traffic accidents?"

"All part of the program," replied Ian, "Catch a thief, track down a serial killer, ferret out an embezzler and find a hit and run bad guy. I hope there won't be too many of these, but I did do a number of them in Pittsburgh while in uniform and like I said, it's all part of the program."

Hal laughed and opened the door to the parking area.

"Actually, I'm just starting to get into a cold case that is looking interesting," said Ian in an almost defensive manner.

"Hmm," said Hal, "Cold case, aren't those old ones that nobody can solve?" He led Ian across the parking area to a vehicle with a broken tail light and some body damage.

Ian made a few notes, photographed the damage with his phone camera and started to scrape some paint chips from the damaged area. "Cases that were not solved when they occurred and the detectives have hit a wall. The case is going nowhere and it gets shelved but not closed."

Hal was watching as Ian took several paint transfer samples from the dented fender, "Interesting, anything that will come this way?"

Ian finished scraping paint samples into two separate small envelopes, labeling them as he said, "You know, that's interesting in itself. Were you in this area twenty years ago?"

Hal replied, "Twenty and then some. I grew up in Fairfax, did a little tour with the army in the early eighties and joined this hotel in '85 after I was discharged. Been here ever since."

As they turned to go back into the hotel, Ian asked, "Do you remember the Darryl Zamanski incident in 1993?"

"Yes, that occasionally comes up in conversation. I was not very interested in it initially. Over time, and a number of conversations later, my interest increased. I still don't know as much as others around here."

"What do you remember about it?"

"Well, as I understand, it was a robbery gone bad. Apparently, the robber or robbers got carried away with beating the kid. Why couldn't they have just taken his money and run, I mean, why kill him?"

"That's a good question. What do you think?"

"Well, either they just overdid the beating and never intended to kill him, or they were going to be in town for a while and didn't want to be identified."

"What else do you remember?"

"That's it. Not much help, is it?"

"Maybe something else will come to mind."

As they walked across the parking lot toward the hotel, Bill Aikens drove in. He lowered his window as he pulled up next to Ian and Hal, and called out "Hey, Ian, the chief said you wanted to talk to me about the Zamanski case."

"I do, Bill. Do you know Hal McGowan?"

Bill opened his door and stood with one foot still in the car, extended his hand toward Hal, and said, "Sure, how you doin', Hal?"

"Pretty good, Bill."

Bill leaned on the open door, "So, Ian, what can I tell you?"

Ian stepped closer to Bill, "The Darryl Zamanski thing, do you remember anything at all about it?"

"Yeah, we never caught the bad guys. That one bugged Andy till the day he left the department. It probably still keeps him up at night," said Bill.

Ian had opened his notebook again, "It really bothered him?"

Bill stood up straight and stepped away from the car, closing the door, "Yeah, he spent hours of his own time talking to people. It sometimes kept him at the station all night."

Hal looked down at the ground and cleared his throat in an uneasy way. Ian noted the discomfort and asked, "Hal, are we keeping you from something?"

Hal looked troubled, "No detective, I think there may be something else you should know."

Ian stepped toward Hal, "What's that, Hal?"

"Are you referring to Andy Ferguson?"

"Yeah, Andy Ferguson. He retired a few years ago, moved to North Carolina," replied Ian.

Hal shuffled his feet, cleared his throat again, "Yes, I knew he was no longer here, but I didn't know where he had gone."

"Chief Bowen gave him a call this morning, to ask about this case. Seems as though Andy won't be of much help, he can't remember his kids' names much less any details of this investigation."

"Well, he did spend a lot of time at night away from home, but it was not all at the station or work related."

Ian looked at Bill, then turned toward Hal, "What are you saying Hal?"

Hal lowered his voice as if he were divulging secrets, "Look, Andy is a great guy. I think everybody was his friend. He always seemed to have a smile on his face and a kind word. I really don't want to drag him down."

Bill stepped a little closer and said, "Yeah, but?"

Hal hesitated, then said, "Well, there were several boys who were questioned, but they were all cleared. The Dorsey boy, Dave Branch, Carl, I forget his last name and Nestor, Ron Nestor. You probably have the records of all of their conversations."

Ian noted each of the names, "All of their conversations?"

Again, Hal hesitated, "Well, yes, I mean the ones at the station and those that occurred here."

Ian continued to make notes, "You never know, a little piece here and another there, and all of a sudden we have a puzzle coming together. How many conversations were held here?"

"Several," replied Hal. "I couldn't tell you how many, maybe two, maybe more. It just seemed like business as usual for a detective. Interviewing people at home or at work. I wish I could tell you more."

Bill was about to ask another question when Ian said, "What was the attraction to talking to the boys here?"

Bill grinned, backed up a step and patted Ian on the shoulder.

Hal responded, "As I said, he spent a lot of time away from home. Some of that time was here on the fourth floor."

"Come on Hal, give me more," said Ian.

Hal glanced around, "He was never alone."

"I'm still looking for a connection," said Ian.

"There were a number of young ladies that he —, entertained," said Hal.

Ian stopped writing, looking up from his notes at Hal, "And this is significant because?"

Hal paused again, then said, "Janet Dorsey for one."

Both Bill and Ian looked at Hal, then at each other. Bill shrugged his shoulders, Ian turned toward Hal and said, "As in Bob Dorsey's mother?"

"Yeah."

* * *

CHAPTER EIGHT
The interviews...

Ian walked into the station and went directly to Ned Bowen's office. "Chief, we have to talk."

Bowen took off his glasses, leaned back in his chair and said, "Come on in, Ian."

Ian entered, turned around and closed the office door.

"That's never a good sign," said Chief Bowen. "Do we have a problem, Ian?"

"Maybe," said Ian as he pulled a chair a little closer to the chief's desk. "Andy Ferguson, he was your friend?"

Chief Bowen sat up straight, leaned forward, "And he still is a friend, Ian. Where are you going with this?"

Ian cleared his throat, "I never met the man, but everybody seems to agree that he was, or is a nice person."

"Yeah, I'm listening," said Chief Bowen.

"Apparently Andy was playing motel bingo with a number of young ladies."

Chief Bowen leaned back, grinned and said, "We all knew he fooled around some. So what, a lot of people do."

"Yeah, well he was doing some of his extra-curricular activity with Janet Dorsey," said Ian.

"As in Bob Dorsey's mother?"

Ian grinned, "That's what I said."

Bowen picked up his glasses, "Can you prove it?"

"Don't have to chief. It's not about Janet Dorsey or Andy Ferguson. This is about Darryl Zamanski. I don't care about either of them. I checked and Janet Dorsey is almost as far out in space as Andy. She is about ten years younger than Andy and is in an assisted living home down near Richmond. She apparently watches the same DVD movie over and over on her television and she doesn't remember seeing it an hour before."

"So what do you have?"

Ian sat up straight, "What I have is an idea of what happened. If Andy was bouncing around with Janet Dorsey, he wouldn't want to jeopardize the kid, Bob, or his relationship with Janet. He interviewed several of the boys and either intentionally or stupidly did not file meeting notes from all of their conversations, and allowed the boys to be ruled out of the equation. So, an alternative scenario had to be developed. The strangers passing through town was it."

"Ian, all notes from interviews are filed immediately and reviewed by someone watching the video while they read the notes. If Andy had a conversation, it would be recorded," said Bowen.

Ian held up a finger, "Not if it were held somewhere else. Not if it was a casual conversation, friend to friend."

Bowen put his glasses back on, "Or between the sheets?"

"Yeah, that too."

Chief Bowen thought for a minute, then looked at Ian and said, "Okay, so where do you go from here?"

"Square one. I'll take it from the top and work through it," replied Ian.

Bowen paused again, then said, "Okay, you can pass the traffic thing off to Bill and put some time on the Zamanski case."

Ian stood and turned toward the door, "Thanks, chief."

"Leave it open," said Ned Bowen. As he scanned his desk trying to remember what he was doing before Ian came in, he smiled and mumbled quietly, "Got me a bull dog."

*   *   *

Ian went back to his desk, opened the file and his notes. He started to make a list.

Dorsey, Robert DOB 1975 Real Estate Local

Murray, Kenneth DOB 975 Deceased Car, DUI

Korbut, Marvin DOB 975 Teacher California

Grayton, Ben DOB 975 ? ?

Branch, David DOB 1974 Farmer Local

Wilkins, Carl DOB 1975 Sec. Co. Sales Local

Burger, Paul DOB 975 ? ?

Nestor, Ronald DOB 75 Auto Sales Local

Spallen, William DOB 975 Deceased Texas

Baines, Joseph DOB 975 Pharmacist Leesburg

"First order of business—who are these characters?" Ian mumbled to himself, "Next, where are they today? What is their story?" He pulled his chair up close to the computer screen and punched in 'Branch, David.'

All ten names were checked against warrants, both current and past. None were open. He checked all past warrants and found some of the boys had been questioned about various minor offenses, but none had been arrested, except Will Spallen. He was a long haul trucker and had been arrested, tried and convicted of rape in Texas in 2005. His sentence was cut short when several of his fellow inmates explained the disadvantages of harming the cousin of another inmate. Spallen's body was buried in Texas when no one from his family in Virginia claimed it.

*   *   *

Ian began to plan the interview sessions with the eight men who were still alive. He allowed about an hour for each interview in the office and planned on talking to all of them as soon as possible. His search located the first four, Branch, Dorsey, Wilkins and Nestor locally. Baines lived in Leesburg and Korbut lived in California. Murray and Spallen were dead and he still had to find Burger and Grayton. He called Bob Dorsey first and asked if he could come into the station at 2:30 on Friday to help clarify a few confusing points from the interviews held back in 1993.

*   *   *

The next day, once Dorsey was in the building, he called Dave Branch and asked if he could come in at 4:30 that afternoon. Branch agreed and Ian went to the interview room where Monica had placed Bob Dorsey.

"Bob, I'm Detective Ian McLarry. Thanks for coming in on such short notice."

"No problem, detective. You say that there are a few loose ends from the Zamanski thing?"

"Yeah, it appears there were several conversations with Detective Ferguson back in '93 when Darryl was killed. They apparently took place at the Vaneksburg Hotel. The problem is, we have not found his notes from those meetings, yet."

Bob Dorsey was composed, relaxed and very calm. "I do recall going to the hotel and having dinner with my mom and running into the detective back then, but honestly, I can't remember what was said. Have you spoken to the detective about this?"

"Well, no. He retired and moved south to the Carolinas a number of years ago. He is on my list of people to talk to. I thought I would talk to you and several others before driving down there to meet him."

Bob looked relieved and said, "Detective, I really wish I could be of more help, but, as I said, I can't remember the conversations at all, other than that they happened."

"Bob, I really appreciate you coming in to talk to me. As long as you are here, could you give me a rundown of the events of that day? As best as you can remember."

Bob wanted to get out of the station, but he thought it would do no harm to relay the Wharf story. "Sure, Detective. It was a nice night, somebody got some beer and we each had cigarettes. A few of us met up early that evening and went out to have pizza, then at about 6:30 we went to Bradley's Wharf to meet some other guys. We had a little beer, some cigarettes and some fishing gear. So we hung around there smoking, drinking and talking. Didn't do much fishing. We left there around eleven and went home."

Ian made some notes in his notebook and casually asked, "What do you think happened to Darryl?"

Bob was slightly flustered by the question. "I don't know. I heard it was somebody passing through town. That's all I know."

Ian finished making notes and closed his note book. "Bob, I have to check on something, I'll be right back." He stood, walked out of the room, closed the door and went into the adjacent room. The two way mirror allowed Ned Bowen to observe and record the interview. Bob sat in his chair looking very nervous. He sat there for five minutes biting his fingernails and slouching in his chair.

Ian looked at Chief Bowen, "How do you read that behavior?"

"Once upon a time, I was guilty of something," said Bowen.

Ian grinned, "Yeah, once upon nineteen years ago."

"You know we don't have enough to arrest or charge him with anything."

Ian picked up his notebook and started for the door, "I know, but now I also know that we are moving in the right direction." He went back into the interview room and sat down across from Bob. "Bob, thanks for waiting, there are so many loose ends to clear up on this case before I close it and put it in storage. One last thing, who was with you that night at the wharf?"

Bob fidgeted and cleared his throat, "Ah, Dave Branch, Carl Wilkins, Ron Nestor," he paused, "And Will, Joe, Paul, Marve, and Ken Murray."

"Do you remember a last name for Will?"

Bob tensed a little and said, "Yeah, it was Spallen, Will Spallen."

Ian slowly noted the last name in his notebook, "Thanks Bob, what about Joe, what is his last name?"

Again Bob was wary, wondering if the detective was trying to trap him into saying something that would cast a bad light on him. "Joe's last name was Baines, yeah, Joe Baines."

Ian again slowly wrote down Joe's last name in his notebook. He looked up at Bob, smiled and said, "I have to write everything down. Every word. Procedure, you've heard about procedure, haven't you Bob?"

Bob was beginning to perspire as he shifted in his chair, "Yeah, I've heard about that."

"That's good Bob, now what about," Ian paused as he looked at his notes for a moment, "What about Paul, what is his last name?"

"Paul Burger," Bob blurted out, "His name was Paul Burger."

Ian flipped a few pages in his note book, "You know what Bob, I think I already had that information. But just to be sure we are all on the same page," Ian smiled, holding a single page in his notebook, "I'll write it down again," he went back to the page where he was making notes, "Hmmm, let me see, Paul Burger. Well, I think that's all of them." He leafed through his notes and said, "Ah, one more, what about Benjamin Grayton, I have his name in here for something. Was he also with you and the others?"

"Ben, yeah he was there with all of us."

"Great, that's great, you all got there about 6:00 in the evening together and stayed until 9:00 or 10:00?"

Bob looked confused and cautiously said, "No, no we got there about 6:30 and met the other guys there. Then some more came a little later, like 7:30. And we were there till 11:00."

Ian flipped through his notes again, feigned a frown and said, "Ah, here it is, yep, 6:30 when you arrived." He looked up with a smile and said, "Who was with you when you arrived at 6:30?"

Bob twisted in his chair again, thought for a second and replied, "Dave Branch, Carl Wilkins and Ron Nestor."

Ian made some more notes, "And the others were already there?"

"Yeah, I mean some of them were and some more came later."

Ian made some more notes, looked at his watch and said, "Bob, give me another minute, I have to check something."

Bob was breathing as if he had just run a race, "Sure, okay, I'll wait."

Ian walked out of the room with his notebook and went directly into the adjacent space. Chief Bowen had been watching the interview on the monitor. "Any thoughts, Chief?"

"Yeah, this guy is ready to burst. What about the meetings at the hotel?"

"One step at a time, Chief. We don't have a record of any of the meetings at the hotel, so there is nowhere to go. I am going to put it on the table again and see how he reacts. If he says there was no discussion about the Zamanski thing, I have to let it go. Maybe in another conversation I can bring it up again and see if he 'remembers' anything. I don't want to push yet, and I don't want him to 'lawyer up' as they say on TV." Ian went back into the interview room.

"Okay Bob, just a few more items to cover. The several meetings with Detective Ferguson at the hotel, we are reading through his notes from back then to see what transpired. Do you recall any of those conversations?"

Bob knew the meetings with his mother and Andy Ferguson were supposed to be kept quiet, a secret. He knew Carl Wilkins and his father were there at one or two of them, but he and the other boys were not involved in the conversations. The meetings were not discussed even when the boys were alone, without their parents. Everyone was supposed to remain quiet about them and that was what happened, they were not discussed. He looked at Ian, "I don't remember anything from those meetings at the hotel."

Ian took his time completing another note and looked up at Bob. "So Bob, have you ever been in that warehouse on Garland?"

"Where the kid was found? Not that I can remember. I mean, maybe, I could have been, but I don't remember."

"It was empty for a long time, like four or five years, great place for guys to hang out."

"Yeah, I guess. But I don't remember."

Ian closed his notebook, looked at Bob and said, "Bob, thanks for coming in. I know it doesn't seem like much, but every little piece fits somewhere into this puzzle. It may take time, but I will get to the bottom of this mess." He walked Bob out to the front door and thanked him again for coming in.

Ian went back to the observation room and sat down. Chief Bowen looked at him, "Okay, detective, what's next?"

"Dave Branch at 4:30. I'm looking forward to this one. Then we will invite Ron Nestor in for a little chat tomorrow and finally the Wilkins character."

"What about Grayton, Burger, and the others?"

"They will follow this group of four later, but did you notice who Bob mentioned first and who seemed to be secondary. Tells me he's trying to cover Branch, Wilkins and Nestor as well as himself. My money is on them. They were involved and the others are just backing up their alibis. Not to worry, Chief, I'll get to them all before we are done."

*   *   *

Dave Branch was late. He arrived at 4:52 pm and made no excuses. Monica rang Ian's phone and said, "Your 4:30 appointment is here. Shall I put him in the interview room?"

"Yes, please, and thanks, Monica."

"Not a problem, detective. I just made a fresh pot of coffee, would you like a cup before you go into the room?"

"I would like it very much. I'll be out there in a minute." Ian gathered his notebook, pen, the case file, his coffee mug and walked out to the reception area. As he poured himself a cup of coffee, Monica returned from the interview room and Ian asked, "Did you give our guest some of this coffee?"

"Hell, no. That man is nasty, smelly and late. He gets nothing."

Ian grinned and walked into the interview room. "Good afternoon Dave, I'm Detective Ian McLarry." He gestured toward a chair and said, "Thanks for coming in on such short notice. Please have a seat. This shouldn't take long, it's Friday and you probably have things to do this weekend."

Ian set his coffee down on the table, sat down and said, "I'm trying to clean up several old cases and your name comes up in one of them. I assume you remember the Darryl Zamanski murder about 19 years ago."

"Yeah, I remember it. Very unfortunate, a young kid gets robbed and killed like that."

Ian smiled, "Yes, well, it happened long before I got here, so right now I am trying to understand what happened, organize the file so we can close it out and put it down in the basement." He paused, "We have to get on with today's business."

Dave forced a smile, not sure where this was going. "What can I tell you that hasn't already been stated?"

"As I said, I'm reviewing the file. I want to put it to bed. There are other things that need our attention. You understand, don't you?"

Dave started to feel less tense, "Yeah, sure, but I don't know what I can tell you."

"Let's begin with the meetings held at the Vaneksburg Hotel with Detective Ferguson back in '93 when Darryl was killed."

Dave looked a little puzzled but remained calm. "Yeah, I remember talking to Detective Ferguson out there once. I was with my dad, we went out to have dinner there 'cause my mom was sick or something, but I can't remember what was said. Have you talked to Detective Ferguson about this?"

"Well, no. He retired to North Carolina a number of years ago and he is on my list of people to talk to. I thought I would talk to you and several others before driving to North Carolina to meet Detective Ferguson."

Dave relaxed, leaned back in his chair and looked at Ian. He had nothing else to say.

Ian looked at his notes from the conversation with Bob earlier that day, "Dave, I really appreciate you coming in to talk to me. As long as you are here, could you give me a rundown of the events of that day. As you remember it."

Dave twisted and sat up straight, "Sure, let me see, we were down at the Wharf, fishing. We had gotten some beer and we each had cigarettes. We met up at about 6:30 down at Bradley's Wharf. We were gonna' catch some catfish. I was busier drinking and smoking than fishing. We left there around eleven and went home."

"Where were you before going to the Wharf?"

"We were at Franco's havin' pizza."

Ian made some notes in his notebook, looked back at Bob's responses and casually asked, "What do you think happened to Darryl?"

Dave was relaxed and answered the question, "I don't know. I heard it was someone passing through town. That's all I know."

Ian made a few notes and again checked Bob's responses to the same question. He closed his note book, "Dave, I have to check on something, I'll be right back." He stood, walked out of the room, closed the door and went into the adjacent room with Chief Bowen. Together they watched Dave on the video for a few minutes. Dave appeared confident as he sat back in his chair and smiled.

Ian looked at Chief Bowen, "How do you read this one's behavior?"

"His answers are remarkably similar to Dorsey's," said Bowen.

Ian grinned, "Yeah, interesting ain't it?"

"We still don't have enough for any arrest warrants."

Ian flipped open his notebook, "Franco's?"

Ned smiled, "Pretty good pizza, but long gone, about ten years ago."

Ian picked up his notebook again and moved to the door, "I know we need more, Chief, but I'm getting more comfortable with the direction we're heading." He went back into the interview room and sat down across from Dave. He looked in his note book, "Dave, thanks for waiting, there are so many loose ends to clear up on this case before I close it and put it in storage. One last thing, who was with you that night at the wharf?"

Dave was ready for that question, and he sat up straight, "Carl Wilkins, Bob Dorsey and Ron Nestor."

Ian was a little surprised that Dave only named those three people. He looked at Dave and said, "That's all?"

Dave was suddenly defensive, "Ah, no, there was Marve Korbut, Ben Grayton, and Joe Baines. Then there was and Ken Murray and Will Spallen. Oh, yeah, and Paul Burger."

Ian made notes in his notebook, compared the answers to Bob Dorsey's and said, "Thanks Dave, you're sure about those names?"

Dave was looking a little uncomfortable, "Yeah, I'm sure."

Ian flipped through a few pages in his notebook, looked up at Dave, smiled and said, "I have to write everything down. Every word. Procedure, you've heard about procedure, haven't you Dave?"

"Yeah, sure."

"That's good Dave, now what about those meetings at the hotel? I have to tell you, we are still going through Detective Ferguson's files and eventually those notes about the meetings will turn up. What do you remember about them?"

"Like I said, I remember talking to Detective Ferguson out there once with my dad, but I can't remember what was said. You should talk to Detective Ferguson about this."

Ian made more notes and said, "Okay, Dave, let's go back to the Wharf, you arrived about 6:00 in the evening together and stayed until 9:00 or 10:00?"

Dave immediately replied, "We got there about 6:30 and met the other guys that were already there. Then some more guys came a little later, like 7:30 and we were there till 11:00."

Ian flipped through his notes again, feigned a frown and said, "Ah, here it is, yep, 6:30 when you arrived." He looked up with a smile and said, "Who was with you when you arrived at 6:30?"

Dave moved in his chair again, thought for a second and said, "Carl Wilkins, Bob Dorsey and Ron Nestor."

Ian made some more notes, "And the others were already there?"

"Some of them were and more came later."

Ian made some more notes, looked at his watch and said, "Dave, give me another minute, I have to check on that fax again."

Dave said, "Yeah, okay."

Ian walked out of the room with his notebook and went into the adjacent space. Chief Bowen had again been watching the interview on the monitor. "Whatta ya think, Chief?"

"I think this guy is much better prepared to answer questions, but I still sense that he's hiding something."

"Yeah, we're on the right track, now we need evidence. Like maybe a conflicting statement from one of the boys."

"So it looks as though the four that you have targeted are the ones that did the deed. The others are part of the same 'gang' and don't want to give them up."

"If one of them cracks, and we give him immunity, it could tear the whole lie apart."

"Could, but the story could change to the four were out roaming around, and when Darryl was discovered, they knew they would be suspect, so they got the others to give them an alibi."

"Not enough to convict."

"Nope, not enough." Chief Bowen started toward his office, "You gonna' call the Nestor guy in next?"

"Yep, after I finish with this turnip. Nestor is probably still at work. I was going to wait until tomorrow, but maybe I can get him in here tonight, and then get Wilkins to come in first thing in the morning." He went to his desk, opened the file to called Ron Nestor at the car dealership and set up an appointment for that evening, then went back into the interview room.

"Dave, we are almost done here. I understand the warehouse where Darryl was found was vacant for quite a while. A great place for guys to hang out, have a cigarette, drink a little beer. How often did you go there?"

"The warehouse? I don't remember ever going there," blurted Dave. He paused, thought and continued, "I guess I coulda' been there once or twice, but I don't remember."

"So maybe some guys hung out there, maybe a vagrant or two slept in the building once in a while, whatta ya think?"

"Sure, I guess that adds."

"Well Dave, that will do for now. You have been a big help." Ian stood and walked out of the room.

Dave waited a minute and left.

* * *

Ron arrived at 8:45 that evening. He was still in sales mode when he extended his hand, smiling from lobe to lobe and said, "Hi, I'm Ron Nestor."

Ian returned the smile with a slightly smaller grin and guided him into the interview room. "Hi, Ron, I'm reviewing old case files, trying to clean up several loose ends."

Ron, still smiling, replied "Yes, the Darryl Zamanski incident from '93. I remember it well. He was severely beaten during a robbery by a group of people passing through town. We spoke to a Detective Ferguson back then, is he still part of this little investigation?"

Ian was surprised by his enthusiastic response, "No Ron, Detective Ferguson has retired, moved somewhere south to the Carolinas. He will not be joining us today, but I believe he is available."

Ron's smile faded slightly. "What can I tell you that has not already been said?"

Ian leafed through his notebook to a previous page, looked up at him and said, "Loose ends Ron, I want to clear up the loose ends. We have more important things going on here and these open cases are a nuisance. I want to close them out, put them in permanent storage. Hell, Ron, it's been twenty years since this kid was murdered." He looked at Ron for a reaction, grinned and said, "Now there were several meetings held at the Vaneksburg Hotel back then and I have not yet reviewed Detective Ferguson's notes from those meetings. I was hoping you could shed some light on the conversation from back then."

Ron looked a little less comfortable, "I remember going to the hotel with my mother and Detective Ferguson was there. I don't remember what he told us though."

"Do you remember how many meetings there were, Ron?"

Ron fidgeted, "Like three or four maybe, I don't remember exactly."

Ian made some notes and leaned forward, "Did your dad ever go to one of the meetings?"

"No, my mom went, my father was always traveling, so he was never there," replied Ron.

Ian continued, "Do you remember anything about those meetings?"

Ron again twisted his face and responded, "No, mostly we were not part of the conversation."

Ian looked quizzically at Ron, "We?"

"Yeah, me and Carl and Dave, we just sat out in the lobby until they were done."

Ian sat up straight, "Really, why were you not part of the conversation?"

"I don't know," said Ron. "They asked us a few questions and we were told to go wait in the lobby."

"How long did these meetings last?"

Ron thought for a second, "Not long, fifteen, maybe twenty minutes I guess."

Ian checked his notes, "Did they ask you any questions?"

"Yeah, like did we know anything about the Zamanski thing."

Ian looked at Ron, "And you all told them the same story, right?"

"Sure," said Ron. "We were fishing when it happened."

Ian slowly turned a page in his notebook, "Where were you fishing?"

Ron was breathing more heavily, "At the Wharf, Bradley's Wharf."

Again, Ian made a quick note and slowly turned a page, "Do you remember what time you arrived at the Wharf?"

"Yeah, it was 6:30," replied Ron.

Ian nodded as he looked at his notes, "And when did you leave?"

"At 11:00," said Ron.

Ian leafed through a few pages, pausing briefly then looked at Ron, "Who was asking the questions back then?"

Ron thought for a moment and answered, "The cop, Ferguson."

"Did he ask all the questions?"

"Yeah, when he was there."

Ian did not react, but he could sense Chief Bowen in the next room was not sitting quietly, listening. "Ron, will you excuse me for a minute or two, I have to check on a fax I'm expecting."

"Sure, no problem."

Ron relaxed and Ian went into the observation room. Chief Bowen had been watching and listening. "Ian, this is turning into a mess. It looks as if our detective coached these kids on how to respond to any questions that may come up. Or he coached the parents and they coached the kids. I don't know if he really thought they were not guilty or if he was just covering his own ass with his lady friends."

"Chief, you said that Andy played around and everybody knew it. Do you think he might have been sharing time with Ron Nestor's mother too?"

"I have no idea who or how many women he entertained. This is a small town and the pool of available and willing women ain't all that big, I think. Hell, Ian, I didn't get into that stuff, and it's not illegal. I just don't know."

"Do you think his wife might know?"

64

Chief Bowen rolled his eyes, "As I said, this is a small town. Playing bedroom bingo with one may stay quiet, two and the talk begins, three and you're lucky if it's not on the nightly news."

Ian scratched his chin, "I think I may have to talk to Janet Dorsey. She may just have a little piece that will help pull the puzzle together."

Bowen opened a file in front of him, "What about Ron's mother, I have it here, her name is Myra."

"We make a great team Chief," Ian noted the name in his notebook.

Ian went back into the interrogation room with Ron. "So, Ron, did you and your mom talk about these sessions after you went home? Like about the cigarettes or the beer?"

"She was a little mad about that but mostly about having to go to the hotel to meet with that cop, Ferguson."

"She didn't like him?" quizzed Ian.

Ron shrugged, "I don't know. She acted like she didn't know him, but I think she did. Like maybe he went to our church and she was embarrassed about the whole thing."

"Is that why you met at the hotel instead of the police station?" asked Ian.

"Oh, yeah," said Ron. "So not as many people would see us and talk."

"Small town probably has a huge gossip mill," Ian mused.

Ron half grinned, "Yeah."

Ian started to close his notebook, then, "One other thing, Ron. You and your friends would hang out in the warehouse on Garland on occasion. Did you ever note anyone else in that same building?"

Ron tensed, "That place where they found the kid? No, no I didn't hang out there. I mean some guys did, and I was probably there a few times, but I didn't hang out there."

Ian scratched a note and added, "Do you recall ever seeing anyone else there, like someone you didn't know, like a stranger?"

Ron was visibly shaken, "A stranger, sure. I guess. I mean there coulda' been strangers there. I don't remember."

Ian made a brief note and closed his notebook, "Ron, that takes care of my questions for now. You enjoy the weekend. If we have any more questions, we'll call you, and thanks for coming in."

Ron left in more of a hurry than when he arrived and Ian went back into the observation room. "Next will be Carl Wilkins, but that won't be until Monday."

Ned closed the file in front of him and said, "You could ask him to come in tonight."

"Yeah, but I want the others to talk to him first, let him think he has an edge."

"Crafty, and sly. You just might grow up and become a detective someday."

"I'll call him now and set it up for first thing Monday morning."

Ned Bowen grinned, "Enjoy the weekend."

"I will, chief, I will."

*   *   *

Ron pulled out of the police station parking lot, drove three blocks, turned into a strip center and nervously opened his cell phone. "Dave, it's Ron. We have to talk."

Dave Branch cursed under his breath and said, "Hey, Ron, why don't you stop over here in the morning and have a beer. We should catch up."

Ron doubted that the phones were bugged but responded as if they might be, "Sure, I was going to see if Bob wanted to drive down to the river and try a little fishing. Maybe you want to join us?"

"Yeah, maybe. See you there about ten."

"Okay," said Ron, "Ten sounds good." He checked his speed dial and pushed another number, "Bob, it's Ron. Just talked to Dave and I'm going over there tomorrow morning about ten. I told him you and I were going down to the river to do a little fishing. He may want to join us."

Bob thought for a moment and said, "Yeah, fishing, that's good. I'll be ready between 9:30 and 9:45. See you then." Bob put his phone back in his pocket and walked out to his garage. "Fishing, I hate fishing," he muttered.

Dave checked his phone book and dialed another number. "Hey Carl, I may be going down to the river in the morning, do a little fishing. Bob and Ron are going to be there. How would you like to join us?"

Carl replied, "Did they call you into the cop shop for a discussion?"

"Yeah, and Ron and Bob too. Did they call you?"

"Just got off the phone with the new cop, McLarry. I have an appointment with him on Monday morning, like 9:00 am." Carl thought for a second and continued, "Fishing may be good. What time are you going to get there?"

"We're leaving my place at ten."

"Okay, I'll see you guys there."

*   *   *

CHAPTER NINE
Meeting ...

Saturday morning was chilly, with temperatures in the 40's, and promising to reach into the 50's. The four men met at the Wharf parking area and walked down to the river's edge. They stared at the water for a few seconds and turned toward a nearby picnic table.

Carl shivered as he said, "Fishing, who's idea was it to go fishing today?"

Dave pulled his coat closed and said, "First thing that popped into my head, fishing, and you all know where it is."

Carl leaned into the middle of the table and said, "Look guys, just like we did back then, we stick to the story. We were here, drinking, smoking and fishing. We got here at 6:30 and stayed until 11:00. If they ask what we think may have happened, we got no idea. As far as we know, the kid was killed by some bum passing through town. That's what the news reports say and we don't know anything different. Now what was the big deal about these sessions yesterday?"

Dave said, "The cop says he's trying to close this case, put it in the basement file room for good, but he wants to tie up a few loose ends."

Carl leaned back, "Yeah, like what loose ends?"

Bob responded, "He asked if I had ever been in that warehouse."

"Oh yeah," said Carl. "And what did you tell him?"

"I told him that I didn't remember ever being in there."

Ron nervously said, "He asked me about those meetings at the hotel, with our parents and that cop."

"Why should that bug you, your mom was meeting that cop for a couple of years," said Carl.

Dave smiled, "Your mother was banging a cop, and you didn't know it?"

The three men laughed at Ron and Carl looked at Bob, "Why are you grinnin', your old lady was jumpin' in bed with the same guy for years."

Bob was angered at the accusation, stood, looked at Carl and said, "Yeah, what about your mother?"

Dave stood and looked at the group, "Look, maybe the cop was jumpin' from bed to bed, that's not our problem here. We have to keep our stories straight and keep our butts outa jail. Now, that cop had a reputation for playin' around, and maybe he scored with my mom, too, way back when, I really don't know and I don't care. You guys need to settle down and let's take care of today."

Carl added, "Dave's right. Today counts, yesterday don't."

The four men sat at the table for a few minutes in silence and Ron finally said, "It's too damn cold to fish, I'm goin' home, and I don't need any coaching. I know what to say and not say." He stood, looked at the group, picked up his fishing gear and turned toward the parking lot.

Bob stood, picked up his gear and walked away without a word. Carl and Dave were left at the table and Dave said, "You shouldn't have said that to Ron. He didn't know about his mom."

Carl grinned, "Everybody else did. I remember my old man talking to a group of guys at a party and they were laughing about it. I think half of them had been in her shorts."

"Nice, Carl, real nice. Let's hope both Ron and Bob keep quiet about this."

"It's cold out here, and those damn fish can stay in the river. I'm going home," said Carl.

Dave stood first, "Fishin' was a bad idea." He turned and went back to his car.

*　*　*

The patient was about to get in the car and drive to the supermarket for some basic supplies. Standing to begin this little trek, the patient felt weak and light headed. "I don't think I will be going anywhere tonight." Sitting down and regaining control of both legs, the patient decided to call Dr. Schrader's office and schedule an appointment for Monday or Tuesday afternoon.

The phone rang three times and was answered by an automated system. When the chime sounded the patient left a message asking for an appointment early in the coming week.

The patient hung up and walked to a window overlooking a children's play park. A tear formed in the patient's eye and slowly trickled down a cheek.

*   *   *

Monday morning came with thick clouds and sprinkles of cold rain. Not enough to merit an umbrella, but enough to be annoying. Carl arrived at the police station at five minutes after 9:00 and was shown into a conference room. He sat at the conference table playing with a nail clipper and muttering to himself. He did not look happy as Ian walked into the room.

"Good morning Carl, I'm Detective McLarry," said Ian as he took the chair opposite Carl and placed his tape recorder on the table. "We are trying to close out old cases that have been gathering dust in the basement. There are bigger fish to fry today and these things are just in the way. So, I have asked you here to clarify a few points for me and hopefully close one or two of these avenues."

Carl sat up straight, trying to figure out what McLarry's game actually was. Did he really want to close the file as conveniently as he could? Had something new come to light, or was he playing a game with the four men? Carl replied, "I'm not sure what I can tell you that has not already been said, Detective."

"Sometimes it's as simple as finding out everything was written down, but sometimes a new detail is remembered and a new avenue opens up. Maybe you will recall something that was said or happened back then that seemed insignificant at the time and now, well, who knows," said Ian.

Carl sat motionless and was about to speak when Ian continued, "For instance, you know the area where Darryl was found, in that abandoned building, a warehouse, right?"

Carl nodded and was about to say something when Ian cut him off again, "Maybe you and your friends saw someone in or near that building and it could prove very beneficial."

Carl paused, almost twenty years had passed, he could easily say he had seen someone hanging around that building back then. Someone average looking, ordinary, someone that would not stick out. Maybe that would send this cop off in another direction, maybe and maybe not. He looked at Ian, "No detective, I don't recall seeing anyone that stands out. There may have been someone, but I don't remember."

"But you had been in that neighborhood, you had driven through, or walked through, maybe even stopped somewhere to have a cigarette, or talk to your friends. So it would be natural to see other people there, other boys who were looking for a place to hang out away from others. A place where they could smoke and have a drink without being bothered."

Carl thought for a moment and decided to deny everything. "No, I don't recall hanging out in that building. I mean, yeah, I drove through the area several times, but I'm not sure I ever stopped and got out of my car."

"It was just a thought, Carl. Let's move on to a few other things," said Ian as he opened his file and clicked his pen, ready to write. "The Wharf, when did you arrive at the Wharf that night?"

"We got there at 6:30."

"And when did you leave?"

Carl was still thinking about getting to the Wharf and wondered if any of the others had said they had been on Garland Avenue, ever. "We were there till 11:00 that night and..."

"Where did you go at 11:00 that night?"

"Ah, we went home."

Ian made a note in his book and looked at his quarry, "Carl, when is the last time you were in that building?"

Carl was not expecting that question, "I don't think I was ever in there, at least I don't remember ever being in that building."

"Who else was at the Wharf that night?"

Carl looked a little flustered, "Dave Branch, Ron Nestor and Bob Dorsey. Oh, and Marve Korbut, Ken Murray, Paul Burger, Will Spallen and Joe Baines."

"Well, Carl, I have already spoken to Dave, Bob, Ron and now you. I have to find the others and talk to them."

"Yeah, well, Marve moved to California and Ken was killed in a car accident. Will, well, Will got arrested in Texas and was knifed in prison and he's dead."

"Yeah, I know about that. That leaves Paul Burger and Joe Baines. I want to contact them next. Carl, if you remember anything at all about that night or about the building on Garland, give me a call. I would appreciate that."

"Sure, Detective, I'll call you."

Ian stood, smiled and said, "Carl, thanks for coming in. You have been very helpful," then he turned and walked out of the room.

Carl sat motionless for a moment, then slowly got up and left.

*   *   *

Ian located a Joe Baines in Leesburg, working as a pharmacist. A phone call later Joe agreed to come in and talk to Ian after he got off work. "I finish up at 4:00 and the ride will take about 20 minutes, so let's say 4:30 this afternoon."

"I appreciate that," replied Ian and he began a hunt for Paul Burger. After an hour of dead end phone calls, Ian contacted the FBI and finally got a little help. Paul worked as a heavy equipment operator and had moved several times. He was currently living and working in Minnesota on a highway project, operating a heavy crane, setting steel for new bridges. Ian caught him on a break, Paul had a three hour wait before his next lift.

"Sure, I remember that night," said Paul. "We went down to the Wharf to catch catfish. I spent more time drinking and yammering than I did fishing."

Ian asked, "Do you recall what time Dave and Carl arrived?"

"Oh hell, I got no idea, they were there when I showed up," replied Paul.

"What about the building on Garland Avenue, did you ever hang out there?"

"Garland, you mean where that kid got killed? No way, man. After that happened, I steered clear of that place."

"Before the incident, did you ever notice anyone that looked out of place hanging around the building?"

"I never really thought about it. I can't remember what it was used for years ago, but when we were in high school, it was empty. There were a few doors left open at different times. Some of the padlocks were busted and you could pretty much just walk right in whenever you wanted. There was nothing there to steal or break, so we never thought much of it. A place to get out of the rain or have a cigarette, I guess. There were some people that walked by once in a while, but I can't remember anyone looking out of place."

"But you and your friends did hang out in that building when it was empty?"

"Yeah, a few times, like five, maybe ten."

"Were there other guys with you on these occasions?"

"I guess, sure, couldn't tell you who though. Probably Dave, Marve, Will, I guess all of us at one point or another."

"Dave, Marve and Will, what about Bob or Ron?"

"Yeah, sure, they were there a few times."

"Carl?"

"Yeah, Carl too."

"Okay, thanks for your help. I may call back again if more questions come up."

"Sure, anytime."

*   *   *

The day dragged on until 4:30 when a man entered the police station and approached the receptionist. "Good afternoon, my name is Joe Baines and I have an appointment with a Detective McLarry."

Monica smiled and said "One moment please," as she pressed Ian's line. "Detective, there is a Mr. Baines here to see you." She unplugged her headset and led Joe Baines to a conference room, "Detective McLarry will be right with you."

Ian came into the reception area as Monica was returning to her desk. He was carrying a folder, notebook and his coffee cup. Monica stepped in his direction, took the coffee cup and said, "Mr. Baines is in room 2 and I will bring you a fresh cup of coffee in one minute."

Ian started to ask, "Did you offer Mr. Baines anything?"

"Hell, no," she replied and turned toward the break room.

Ian entered the conference room and Joe stood to meet him. Baines was a slight man, well dressed, with thinning dark hair, thick glasses, manicured hands and a tan that was either the result of a tanning bed or a spray bottle. They shook hands and Ian said, "Please sit down. This will only take a few minutes."

Baines grinned and looked a little uneasy. "The last time I was questioned by the police was twenty years ago," he said, "That was about the Zamanski kid. Somebody killed him and I guess the cops thought I was involved."

"Nothing to worry about, Joe. Just want to ask you a few questions about that night."

"Like I said, that was a long time ago, I don't remember much today. I mean, we were at the Wharf, fishing and drinking. More drinking than fishing. I guess some things stick in your mind, like where you were when some big event happened. Like 9/11, you know where you were that day. You might even remember some of the things you did or said."

Monica came in and put Ian's cup on the table, smiled and went back to her desk.

Ian opened his notebook, flipped through a few pages and looked at Joe. "Do you remember what time you arrived at the Wharf?"

"Time, no. I remember that Marve called me and said that one of the guys had scored a few six packs and they were heading for the Wharf. It was after dinner and we usually ate around 5:30, my dad got off work around 4:00 and he was ready to fall asleep by 7:00. Anyway, I remember after dinner I told him I was going out for a little while. Like I said, he was usually asleep by 7:00. I could have stayed out half the night and he would never know."

"What is your best guess about what time you got to the Wharf?"

"I would guess a little after 6:00 and I remember I stayed until about 10:30 or 11:00," said Joe.

Ian paged through his notes, "Do you recall what time others arrived at the Wharf?"

Joe paused and thought for a moment, "No, not really, I mean different guys came in at different times."

"Joe, does anything stand out, did anyone do or say anything that you can remember?"

Joe looked around the room and up at the ceiling, then back at Ian, "Yeah. Ron was spreading his beer cans around and I asked him why he didn't just throw them away."

Ian turned his notes back to his conversation with Ron. "Do you remember what he said?"

Joe puzzled for a moment, "Something like he was gonna' pick 'em up later. Then he took a handful of cigarette butts outa his pocket and dumped 'em on the ground."

Ian stopped writing in his notebook and asked, "Why did he do that?"

"No idea, he was acting a little weird but I just let it go."

Ian looked up, "Was Ron there at the Wharf when you arrived?"

Again Joe thought for a second or two, "No, I don't think so. Marve was there and Will. We sat around and talked for a while before anybody else showed up."

Ian paused, made another note and continued, "Do you remember how long before anybody else got there?"

Joe responded, "Not really, maybe half an hour. Then Ken came in, said something about drinking before 7:00, downed a beer in about one gulp, and then belched as loud as he could. The others came after that."

"You're sure of that?"

Joe laughed, "Yeah, I remember one of us telling Dave about Ken when he walked in, and he said he could do it too."

"So Dave got there after Ken?"

"Yeah."

"How long?"

"I don't know, maybe twenty minutes, maybe half an hour."

"And Ken got there after you?"

"Yeah."

"How long?"

"Like I said, about half an hour."

"And you got there a little after 6:00?"

"Yeah."

"So that means Dave got there about an hour after you, maybe more."

"Yeah, that sounds about right."

"Just one more question. How late could it have been when you got to the Wharf?"

"Like I said, a little after 6:00."

"Okay, so you finished dinner and went right over there?"

"When we finished dinner and put the dishes in the dishwasher, my dad usually turned on the television to watch the news. I would sit there with him until he fell asleep."

"Is that what you did on that night?"

"Yeah, sort of. Then Marve called and I left."

"Did you drive to the wharf?"

Joe grinned, "In what? I didn't have a car. No, I walked over there."

"How long did that take?"

"About twenty minutes. Not long."

"Joe, did you ever hang out in the empty warehouse on Garland? "

"You mean the one where the kid was killed?"

"Yes, that one."

"After the kid got killed, I never went in there. Not like it was haunted or anything, more like, like if it happened to that kid, it could happen to me."

"But you did hang out there before Darryl was killed?"

"Oh yeah, it was a good place to be out of sight and the cops never bugged us there. I guess they knew we were there sometimes but we weren't doin' anything 'cept smokin', and maybe havin' a beer. We always cleaned up after, didn't leave a mess. So nobody cared."

"Did your friends hang out there also, like Dave Branch, or Bob Dorsey?"

"Yeah, we were kind of a gang, or a club. There was about ten or twelve of us that were kinda' tight."

"Like who else?"

"Let's see, Dave and Bob, like you said. Then there was Marve Korbut, he moved to California. Carl Wilkins and Ron Nestor, I think they are still in Vaneksburg. Will Spallen, he got killed in prison a few years ago and Ken Murray, he drove his car into a wall or somethin', anyway, he's dead. I don't know where Paul Burger is or Ben Grayton."

"Anyone else?"

"Probably a couple of others, but I can't remember any names."

"You all hung out in that warehouse?"

"Different guys at different times. Yeah, I guess."

"Maybe sometimes all of you at once?"

"Oh, I don't know about that, more like two, three or four of us at one time."

"Like you and Dave or you and Bob?"

"Yeah, sure."

"How about Carl, was he ever there?"

"Yeah, he usually could score some beer and a few of us would meet him there."

"Joe, thanks for coming in."

Baines left the station and Ian went back to his desk. He sketched a time line for Joe's activities that evening.

Dinner: 5:30 to 6:00; clean up dishes: 6:00 to 6:05; television with dad 6:05 to 6:10; phone call with Marve: 6:10 to 6:11; walk to the Wharf: 6:11 to 6:31; sit around with Marve and Will: 6:31 to 6:51; Ken Arrives: 6:51; sit around with Ken, Marve and Will: 6:51 to 7:21; Dave arrives: 7:21.

The Chief approached Ian's desk, "What have you learned, Ian?"

Ian turned the time line around so the Chief could see it, "It appears as though our foursome didn't get there until around 7:30. That is assuming the times Joe listed are accurate."

"If he's working off his memory, how can you check them out?"

"First, he said they usually had dinner at 5:30 and his dad watched the news after dinner. He said he was watching the news with his dad when Marve called. That puts him at home at 6:00. The call from Marve and the walk to the Wharf, he allowed about 20 minutes for that. I want to check the distance from his old address to the Wharf. Anyway, the other times are all guesses and there is no good way to check them out."

They walked over to a large map on the roll call room wall. The distance from Joe's house to the Wharf worked out to 2.25 miles. "That would take about half an hour, maybe more," said Ned.

Ian looked at Ned and said, "Add another 10 minutes to that time line and Branch and company didn't get to the Wharf until after 7:30. Yet they are all on the same page with their 6:30 arrival. Hmm…"

*   *   *

CHAPTER TEN
Planting the seed...

The reunion committee was meeting on Wednesday night at the Tavern. Ian decided to join them again and arrived at 6:30. Jim was greeting people near the door and when Ian approached, he asked if he was there for their meeting.

Ian responded with a guilty look. "I thought I might be able to ask a few more questions, if that's alright."

"Only if you stay for dinner," Jim laughed. "The others will be here soon. You know where the room is, so go on in and I'll join you in a minute or two."

Ian continued into the dining room and was looking out the window when a small voice behind him said, "Good evening, Detective. I'm glad to see you will be joining us this evening."

Ian turned and looked at a small, slight woman with big blue eyes and long dark hair, "Audrey Redding, right?"

Audrey smiled, "Right."

Jim came in with a steaming pot in one hand and two mugs in the other. "Ian, how about some coffee?"

Ian lit up and responded, "Absolutely."

Jim looked at Audrey, "I didn't see you come in, Audrey, how about some coffee?"

"Thanks Jim, that would be nice," she replied quietly.

Jim went to the doorway and called out to Carol, "Carol, could you please bring in a few more mugs and the basket?" As he was talking to Carol, Phil and Barb approached. "We have a guest tonight," said Jim.

Barb and Phil joined Audrey and Ian at the table and Carol brought in a tray of mugs and the basket with sweeteners and creamers. Barb settled in next to Audrey and said, "I talked to Sandy and Brent, they will be here."

Audrey smiled and said, "I think we can count on Mark as well."

Barb blushed and said, "Great, we have a full house." She looked at Ian, "Detective, what brings you here tonight?"

"I have been looking into several possible sources of information and turned over a few rocks."

Barb smiled and said, "Yes, you were talking to the bad boys club. What have you learned?"

"How do you know just who I have been talking to?"

"Ian, this is a small town. I know everybody and everybody knows me. Of course I know who you question and even some of what was said."

Ian twisted in his chair so that he was facing Barb, "You care to tell me who in my police department has been talking out of school?"

Barb paled, realizing she could get her friend in the detectives' area in some hot water and replied, "Maybe I guessed what was going on and you just confirmed it. So, detective, you are my source."

Mark walked in and took a chair next to Barb. "Evening, all. Have we already ordered?"

Jim counted noses and said, "That makes us eight for tonight, so four medium and four medium well," he said as Carol approached.

Carol came in the room, set a pitcher of iced tea on a service table, turned and walked toward the kitchen. She returned within a minute with pitchers of regular and diet sodas. "Dinner will be ready in about ten minutes. Jim, will you be ready?"

"Sure," he turned toward the others, "Ten minutes, guys. Let's get some of the business out of the way."

Barb took the cue and reported on the status of invites and acceptances, then continued to the topics of music and food. It took the entire ten minutes to run down the agenda and then dinner arrived.

After dinner, Ian was given the floor. He began, "Tell me why all of you feel it was just these four guys."

Phil replied, "They were tighter, those four, than the others. Yeah, they were all in the same group, but those four were more likely to get physical. Like it was their job. They had to be the toughest guys in the school. The others were filler, just backup, so nobody would challenge them."

"That's right," said Brent, "If someone else had done this, those four would rat them out in a heartbeat."

Ian asked, "Even their own friends?"

Jim stepped in, "Yeah, even their own friends. But between the four of them, no way they would talk. Of course that was then and today is an open question. Isn't that right, detective?"

"I am talking to each of them individually, maybe the bonds have loosened over the years. But understand, if one or all of them was involved, it was murder, maybe second degree, but murder none the less, and there is no statute of limitations on murder. So if one goes down for this, they all could."

Barb chimed in, "No sympathy from this group. If they did it, they should all be hung, or shot or whatever the punishment is for murder."

Ian replied, "In the Commonwealth of Virginia, the condemned can choose between electrocution and lethal injection." He paused, looked at the group and continued, "The other element is that three of them were minors at the time of Darryl's murder. I don't know how the courts would deal with that today in terms of charges and possible sentences."

Audrey raised her hand as if she were still in high school and quietly asked, "Could they get off without any punishment?"

Ian looked at her big blue eyes and said, "Well, I suppose if the evidence was not strong enough, and a jury could not be convinced beyond a reasonable doubt. And remember, Dave Branch was 18 at the time, so, he would certainly be tried as an adult, but the others might be tried as minors. That's a question for the lawyers and the courts. As minors, they might be given a nominal sentence and some kind of credit for being good since then."

"Or not," said Mark.

*   *   *

The patient was tired and noticed a definite weakness in the right leg again during the ride home. The additional medication prescribed by Dr. Schrader on Tuesday addressed most the numbness and feeling had returned, but walking was soon going to be difficult. The negatives were outweighing the positives and the thought of having only a few months left to live was painful. "I don't want to die. What have I done in this life that will be remembered?" Then the patient thought about Darryl. "He really got cheated, only 14 when he was killed and here I am at 33 feeling sorry for myself."

The patient drove on in silence for a few minutes. Thoughts of fairness, privilege, truth and honor raced through the patient's head. "If I could only do something that would be remembered, something good, something like finding Darryl's killers. Hell, we all know who did it, I don't think there is any question about that. Even the new cop has zeroed in on those four, but he can't find enough to arrest or charge them." The patient continued on in silence again, thinking.

"If I could only do something that might convince them to talk, to confess."

The silver sedan stopped for a traffic light and the patient had a thought. A smile broke out on the patient's face. "Dr. Schrader said I should do something bad, what if I took them with me to see Darryl. We could have our own little reunion."

*   *   *

CHAPTER ELEVEN
Reconnaissance...

A number of questions arose as a plot began to form in the patient's mind. Driving past the high school and the industrial site where Darryl was found, the patient wondered how all four men could be brought to one place at the same time. It would have to be some sort of lie that would appeal to all four, or four different lies that would draw them individually.

The warehouse would have been the ideal location, but as the patient drove past the building, it was obviously occupied and busy. There had to be another place that could be used. A place where they could be drawn in and, and what? Just what would be an appropriate action, maybe get them to confess, and then call the police? Perhaps torture them all as Darryl had been tortured, then call the police, or leave them to die as they left Darryl to die? Perhaps shoot them, or hang them. Questions, so many questions and now to figure out the answers.

The patient began by defining who these four characters were today. Where did they live? Did they have families? What are their interests? What might draw them to a common place at the same time? The phone book answered one of the questions. The patient made a list of the four men:

Branch, David E.   16732 Lomond Road

Dorsey, Robert A.   4231 Crestview Lane

Nestor, Ronald F.   2354 Hemming Drive

Wilkins, Carl J.   5347 Slater Avenue

Lomond Road ran north and south about a mile east of town center. The Branch farm was about six miles south of town center on Lomond and as the sedan approached from the north, the patient slowed and scanned the area. The houses were about a half mile apart and most of the farms were just a few hundred acres at best. The GPS unit indicated the address for the Branch house was one tenth of a mile ahead on the right. The patient slowed to a stop on the side of the road. A dark blue pick-up truck was parked in the driveway, next to a front porch. Directly across the road was another house. Both homes were a half mile from the nearest neighbor and another mile from the nearest cross street either north or south. The house on the right, or west side, was a two story, white clapboard, center hall colonial. The house across the road, on the east side, was a single story, red brick ranch with a thick growth of trees parallel to the road, open at the driveway entrance and in front of the house, concealing the property and buildings behind. The west side property was fenced and had very few trees along the road, but substantial growths of trees and bushes separating several fields beyond the house and the few outbuildings on the property.

The light colored sedan cruised slowly toward the two driveways and the mail boxes. The west side box had the name 'Branch' and the number 16732. The east side box had the name 'Ripley', the number 16735. There was also a realtor's sign indicating that the Ripley property was for sale. The patient noted the Realtor's name, Carter & Fitch, and made a quick note of the phone number. At the same time, a man came out of the white house and walked toward the blue pick-up truck. The patient immediately recognized Dave Branch, and sped up past the two properties. The patient turned right at the intersection a mile down the road and another right at the next intersection. "One more pass and I'm outta' here," muttered the patient as the sedan made a U-turn and backtracked toward the two houses. Another drive-by, this time from the south and the patient finished the first of several reconnaissance missions.

The day was young and driving by the residences of the other three men took very little time. Both Dorsey and Nestor lived in town houses on opposite sides of town and Wilkins lived in a development of single family homes east of town center. The patient was finished by noon and stopped at a diner on Lomond Road near the freeway for lunch. Sitting in a booth, having a sandwich and thinking the town houses and the single family homes were not conducive for any kind of workable plan, the Branch farm began to look better and better. The patient decided that a closer look at the farm was in order and thought the property across the road could serve as the key to open that door. A call to the realtor told the patient that the property was vacant and available immediately. The owners were retiring and had moved to Georgia to be near family. "Perfect," thought the patient, and finishing lunch, ordered a second cup of coffee for the ride, then left the diner and drove south.

It was approaching 2:00 pm as the patient pulled into the driveway of the Ripley property and parked. The patient noted that the blue pick-up was still parked in the driveway across the road and Dave was sitting on his front porch watching the world pass by. He noticed the car and saw the driver walk up to the front door. He got into his truck and drove across the road, rolled down the window and said, "If you're lookin' for the Ripley's, they moved out a few weeks ago."

The patient turned around and said, "Hi, my name's Trent Laskin and I'm mostly curious. Could you answer a few questions for me before I get a broker involved?"

"Trent . . ?"

"It's a family name."

There was no sign that Dave recognized the patient and as he stepped out of his truck, he replied, "Okay, sure, what can I tell you?"

"Well, how much land are we looking at here?"

"I think this place is a little bigger than mine. I've got 265 acres and Don Ripley has about 280, give or take."

"Great, that's about the size I'm looking for. Do you know what has been grown here over the last few years?"

Dave thought for a second and said, "Mostly corn, as I recall. Might have done a year or two with alfalfa, but I'm not sure."

"What about the out buildings, are they in good repair?"

"The barn is almost new, maybe two years old. The old one was in bad shape and Ripley used most of his dynamite to bring it down. Next day he was pushin' the rubble into a pile with his front end loader down that slope near the creek. He got a permit to burn it, so long as it was at least 500 feet from the next building. Fire department was here, watching. Made a big party out of it. We was roastin' hot dogs and watchin' the fire all day."

"Sounds like fun."

"Yep, it was. Then a day or two later a truck delivered a load of heavy wood and a cement mixer. Some guys showed up with a big old drill and started digging holes. Well, within a week the new barn was framed out and the siding was delivered. Roofers showed up and in another week, BINGO, he had a new barn."

"Can we see the inside?"

"Don't see why not," said Dave as he led the way.

They crossed the yard to the barn. It was more than three hundred feet from the road and behind a thick stand of trees. The door was not locked and the barn was empty save for several bales of hay and some bags of fertilizer.

"Isn't this fertilizer dangerous, ammonium nitrate?"

"Yeah, if you mix it with diesel oil the right way it could make a hell of an explosion," laughed Dave.

"That's scary, probably should get rid of it."

"Yeah, I guess," said Dave, "I'll take it back to my place and spread it in a field. There were also a few sticks of dynamite left after Ripley took down the barn. They're in a wooden box in here somewhere. Ripley told me that I could have them, but I haven't taken them yet. We used 'em to get rid of tree stumps, but there ain't no more trees on my place that need to come down. So I just left them sticks here. Anyway, you have to get a permit to blow things up, just like startin' a fire, ya need permits." Dave moved on through the barn. He peeked inside another box and said, "Chain, use it to do a bunch of things, kinda' like duct tape, use it to keep horses in a stall, hold fence sections together, all sorts of things, he's got a full box here."

"This is a nice barn, seems to be well built," said the patient, drawing Dave back to the central bay.

"Yeah, these 10 x 10 center columns are set in concrete," said Dave pointing to the four center posts in the barn. They formed a square about 15 feet on each side and rose to the top of the loft, holding up the center of the roof. "Ripley built this place to last."

They looked in the rest of the stalls and checked the water connections. Then Dave opened the main power panel, pointing out the power distribution and available circuits. "You could pull a 220 line off here if you needed it."

They walked outside and Dave said, "Would you like to see the rest of the property?"

"Yes, I would," replied the patient, "The house appears to be in good repair, and that other building, the garage has 1, 2,... 5 overhead doors?"

"Yeah, I think he kept his car in the first one and the others were big enough for some of his equipment and all of his smaller tools. It's connected to the house and he could get out there in bad weather to work on stuff."

"I'll wait until we have the realtor here to check inside the house, but what about the fields and water?"

Dave turned toward his truck, "Hop in, I'll give you the nickel tour." They drove past the barn and over a small stream. "This creek runs a few feet deep and is pretty constant all year. Ripley has a few pump houses where he draws water off for the fields." He continued down the dirt road for almost a mile, "That's it, this property is a big rectangle and the fields all front on this road." He made a three point turn and headed back toward the house. "Do you want to walk the fields?"

"No, thanks, that's not my area. We have someone else who would come out and look after that. But I must say, this is quite impressive and I would like to learn more. Who is the realtor?"

"The sign out front says Carter & Fitch, but if I may recommend someone to represent you, I suggest Bob Dorsey, he's an old friend, I'd be happy to give him a call and tell him you are interested," said Dave.

"I really appreciate that, but first, I would like to check with my main office, be sure that the financial end is in order before going any deeper into this. If you could keep this meeting quiet, when I'm ready to move on this place, I'll call you. Could I get your number?"

Dave imagined a piece of the sales commission coming his way and he responded, "Sure," then wrote down his number on a piece of paper. "There you go. When do you think you may be ready to move on this?"

The patient thought for a moment, "Well, I do have a few other properties to check out, but so far this one is at the top of my list. I'll give you a call next week and let you know where we are."

"Okay, that sounds great, and I'll keep your name quiet until I hear from you."

Trent thanked Dave, got into the silver car, pulled out of the property and headed back toward Vaneksburg. Dave hurried back to his house and called Bob Dorsey. "Bob, somebody stopped by the Ripley place. Might have some interest there."

"Dave, that's great. Who was it?"

"Trent — Oh no you don't, Bob," said Dave. "First, what kinda' cut comes my way for steerin' this fish to you? Let's have an agreement here, old buddy, and none of this two or three hundred bucks for the tip. This is a couple of million for the package and a fee to you around 300 thousand, so let's get serious, buddy."

"Seriously, the total fee might be over 150 grand, maybe more, but half of that goes to the company that listed the property and half to my broker. By the time it flows down to me, I'm lookin' at maybe 10 grand. If I cut you in, it's barely worth it. The chances are that the deal won't materialize and I'll just wait it out and find another buyer. If you wanna talk about two or three thousand, well maybe we can talk about that."

"Five g's," said Dave.

"Two," returned Bob.

"Four," spit Dave.

"I'll do $2,500, and that's it," said Bob with finality.

"I never liked you," said Dave.

"Yeah, yeah, are we good at $2,500?"

Dave was angry, after imagining a score of $100,000, to settle for next to nothing. "Yeah, $2,500."

"So who is the fish, " asked Bob.

"Sounds like some kind of corporate thing. They may want more than just one property, so maybe we should talk about additional sales to follow this one," said Dave.

Bob was seeing Dave's claws digging into his back and didn't like it. "Let's get together and hash this out before we meet with this Trent character. How about tomorrow?"

"You be here tomorrow around noon and we'll talk," said Dave.

"Noon, I'll be there."

*   *   *

The following morning the sun rose a few minutes before 6:00 am. Bob Dorsey was up and having his morning coffee while reading through the description of the Ripley's property. He was going to be ready to answer any questions that might arise. He drove to his office and spent the rest of the morning checking out other properties that might prove interesting to a prospective corporate buyer, then printed out a list with some details on those other properties. As he was reading over the details, Al Goldman walked into the office.

"Good morning Bob, What's cookin'?"

"Mornin' Al, I just got a lead on the Ripley place a few miles south of town," said Bob.

"Hey, that's great, I did the walk through a month ago with the listing agent from Charlie Fitch's office," said Al.

"Well, this lead is not solid yet, but an old friend lives across the road and saw someone looking around, and got the guy's name."

"You never know, it could work out," said Al, "Who is the buyer?"

Bob looked a little uncomfortable, "Don't know yet, I may have to pay my friend for the info, so he's holding back until we talk this morning. All he has told me so far is the guy's name, Trent something. He didn't tell me the guy's last name."

Al scratched his head, "Maybe that is his last name. Trent, hmmm, that could be first or last. Listen, Bob, if you need anything from me, I'll be in all day. Good luck with this one."

"Thanks Al, I'll see you when I get back."

At 11:00 am he got in his car and drove toward Dave Branch's house.

Bob pulled into Dave's driveway at 11:38, saw Dave sitting on his front porch and parked his car. "Mornin', Dave," he called across the front yard. "I'm a little early, there was no traffic on the way here."

Dave grinned as he watched Bob cross the yard, "I just made a pot of coffee, you interested?"

"Sure, no cream, no sugar."

Dave waved him up to the porch and said, "Just getting me a refill," as he walked back into his house. He returned a minute later with two full cups, handed one to Bob and sat down again.

Bob looked across the street at the Ripley's house and said, "Dave, is that your truck over there in Ripley's driveway?"

"Yeah, I'm getting rid of the ammonium nitrate that's in the barn, probably take the last of his dynamite too. That stuff made Trent a little nervous."

"Good move. Hey, on another note, have you been talking to that new cop in town?"

"McLarry? After the first interview at the station, he called me and had a few more questions. Nothing serious, he asked about you and the others, but it was all stuff we had talked about before. He asked about times when we got to the Wharf and did we catch anything when we were fishing. What about you?"

"Same stuff, about a week ago. He was still harping on those meetings at the Hotel. I just stuck to the story. No deviations," answered Bob, "and he asked about the warehouse. Like did I ever go in there." Bob sipped his coffee, "So where did you find this mystery buyer, Trent?"

"This one found me. I should have more info this week," said Dave. "Before we get too deep into this, let's agree on some basics here, Bob. I have a lead that could make you a bunch of money. Maybe it's ten grand, maybe a hundred, so agreeing on $2,500 just doesn't work. I think we should agree on a percentage. If you give me half of whatever you get, that's fair."

"Half!" said Bob, "I've been thinking about this too and I knew you would want more if the price flies way up. So I agree with you, a percentage would work, but not anywhere near half. That's way too much."

Dave thought for a second, "I really like half and half, fifty percent?"

"Remember this is my only source of income. I can't just hand over half of what I earn. Even five percent is a lot. No, I can't do fifty, but I could do five."

"Come on Bob, you could get rich on this deal. You can do better than five percent, you could easily do 25."

The two men argued percentages for about twenty minutes and finally agreed ten percent of Bob's commission should go to Dave. They sat on the porch for another half hour and soon ran out of things to talk about. Bob made some weak excuse and left at 1:15. Dave never gave up Trent's last name.

*　　*　　*

CHAPTER TWELVE
Plotting...

There was another committee meeting the following Wednesday evening. It began with a round of burgers and glass of wine. A few planning items were settled, and then a free-for-all conversation broke out.

"Where is our new friend, the detective?" asked Brent, "I've enjoyed hearing a fresh perspective on the Darryl Zamanski case."

"Probably working on another car accident," responded Barb with a sarcastic smile. "I heard he was given a traffic accident to check out at the hotel. Not a lot of major crime around here to keep him busy."

"He's working on Darryl's case," said Brent, "I don't think it has been touched in almost 20 years and really needs a hard look."

Phil agreed, "I think you are right. Darryl's case should be given the high tech treatment it didn't get back then."

"I would like to see that Branch bastard get what's comin' to him," said Sandy, "Are lynch mobs illegal?"

"Very," replied Mark. "By all accounts, Darryl was a nice kid. I never got to know him, but he sure got the short end of the stick. His case deserves a second or even a third look."

Jim added, "We have to remember this is not a television program. High tech investigations take a long time, you need the right kind of information, like DNA, and the right data base to compare it to, then just maybe you could get some answers."

"What sort of information do they need?" asked Lisa.

"I think Jim is saying that since the crime was committed nineteen years ago, proper samples may not exist and even if all the data was documented and verifiable, you may not get the results needed to make an arrest, never mind a conviction," said Audrey.

Jim looked at Audrey, "Thanks, you're right in tune with the song I'm singing. Short of a confession from any of them or some testimony by a credible witness, they got nothing."

Barb leaned forward, "I've had three glasses of wine and it's all very clear to me, we beat 'em 'til they talk. What about that water-boarding thing, anyone know how that works?"

"Very illegal, Barb," said Mark, "But I do like the way you think."

"So what can we do?" asked Sandy, "I'm certainly not about to jump into bed with one of them to get them to talk. Didn't they use a cattle prod on Darryl? I would be willing to do that to Branch."

"This is all very scary stuff, torture, beatings, cattle prods. We are civilized, we need an intelligent and legal way to get the truth out of them and put it into the hands of the authorities," said Lisa.

The conversation continued for another twenty minutes and the group dispersed. Mark caught Barb before she got to her car, "You are in no shape to drive, young lady. Get in my car and I'll take you home."

Barb thought, "I can drive," then she smiled and said, "Okay."

The next morning Mark drove her back to her car and she went to work.

*　　*　　*

The patient sat in traffic thinking about the Ripley Farm, the barn and the four men. Branch would be the easiest to attract to the barn, but Dorsey would also be drawn in by the real estate deal. It was the other two that could prove problematic. Once they were all there, controlling them would be the next hurdle. "I have to capture them one at a time, and secure them. Lock them up, tie them up, knock them out, drug them," mused the patient aloud, wrestling with the problem and driving back into Vaneksburg proper. "I need more time to figure this out," muttered the patient as the sedan continued north, passing under Route 66 heading north to route 50. Driving east toward Fairfax, a road side sign drew a smile. "Adult Store, 5 miles ahead", muttered the patient with a grin, "I have to check this out."

The patient pulled into a gravel parking area in front of a small, white wood frame building with only one other car in the lot. A neon sign in the window flashed "Open". The patient entered a small space, crowded with mannequins displaying leather clothing, whips, collars and restraints. As the patient browsed the various displays, a middle aged woman in business attire came in from an adjacent room. She looked at the patient and very politely asked, "May I help you?"

"Good afternoon, I'm curious, just lookin' around." The displays of handcuffs and leg restraints sparked the patient's imagination. While looking around at a variety of wares, a plan started to take hold. Turning back to the saleswoman, the patient said, "I'm a teacher at the Community College and have a criminology class where we will be discussing various forms of restraining people. This shop was recommended by a friend as a source for some information I could use for that class."

The woman smiled in a knowing way and asked, "Can you be more specific, what sort of restraints you are talking about?"

"Well, a basic hand cuff and leg restraint combination would definitely be on the list. What do you have that could restrain a very strong individual?"

"What do you mean by very strong?"

"I want this to be as realistic as possible, so whatever I discuss or purchase has to withstand some very strong young men trying to break them. My students are primarily young men with an interest in law enforcement. They would laugh at me if the restraints could not hold them."

The woman led the patient to a corner of the store with several types of restraints. She held up one pair of hand cuffs and said, "These are made by the same manufacturer that supplies equipment to the Fairfax Police Department and these," she said as she opened a box of leg restraints, "are the same make as the hand cuffs, very well made."

As the patient examined the two sets of restraints, the woman asked, "Will you be needing anything else? We carry collars, whips and gags."

The patient smiled, "No, I think these will do. How much are they?"

The woman turned the box over and said, "The leg restraints are $45.99 and the hand cuffs are $54.99. That's $100.98."

The patient interrupted, "You know, it would probably be good to have a few of these. Let's make it two sets."

The woman stopped, turned and said, "Two sets of cuffs and leg restraints?"

"Yes, two sets. It's a big class and my budget can handle that amount."

As they went back across the showroom, the patient looked at one of the mannequins with a ball gag strapped to its head and said, "I'll take a couple of those gags also."

Walking out of the store and smiling, "Taken care of for less than $200, ha," the patient put the purchases in the trunk, got behind the wheel and turned on a smart phone. The internet located another adult store several miles away on Route 28. The patient drove out onto the highway and turned south. "Another set of these toys and then home for a little more planning."

Later that afternoon, sitting at home watching television, the patient started to draw the barn on a tablet, five bays long and three bays wide, "Dave Branch said that the bays were 15 feet by 15 feet." The drawing showed a floor plan with the doors, columns and the six bales of hay. "Hmm, I don't remember, but at least five." Further doodling resulted in the drawing that showed the bales of hay arranged so that the four center columns each had a bale next to it, facing the center of the barn.

"Hmmm, a place for each of them. If I can get them in the barn, one at a time, and force them to sit on a bale of hay, maybe I can get the restraints on them before they realize what's happening." More thinking and more sketching, "There, that may work." The patient had drawn a stick figure sitting on a bale of hay with a rope tying the leg restraints to the building column, another rope around the midsection attached to the column. "That should hold 'em. I'll need to buy some rope tomorrow."

Very satisfied with the plan thus far, the patient leaned back in a large soft recliner and began to doze off. An hour and a half later the patient stirred and through bleary eyes realized that it was almost 6:00 pm. "Time for the news," turning the channels to get to a news program, the patient came across a scene in one of the more popular series where a woman was shocking a villain with a taser, repeatedly. "Oh, that must hurt," a smile broke across the patients' face, "Yeah, that must really hurt."

"That could work, a stun gun. Get them to walk into the barn one at a time, stun them, put 'em in irons and when they can stand again, make them sit on a bale of hay." The patient was pleased and decided to make dinner.

"I can get them all to sit and listen, and they can only talk when I loosen the gags. Oh, this is going to be fun. I'll get them to tell me everything and pass it along to the new detective." The patient strode into the kitchen and began to make dinner. "I'll go back to the barn, arrange the bales and set up the restraints. I will need some rope or wire or duct tape. Chain, Dave showed me a box of chain, that's perfect." The patient sat at the kitchen table, eating dinner and thinking about making the four men confess, "and if they don't, I'll shoot them, one at a time. Maybe the last one will talk, or I'll just shoot him too." The wicked smile broadened.

*   *   *

CHAPTER THIRTEEN
Thickening...

Manassas was a short drive west on Route 66 and south on Route 234 for a few miles. Banner's Gun Shop was in a strip mall on the north side of Rte. 234. The shop owner, Fred Banner, was a pleasant man and happy to help a potential customer learn more about hand guns.

"My father left this to me and I want to be comfortable using it for protection. I hope I never have to shoot anyone," said the patient. "But, I still need to know how it works so I can be prepared."

"Okay," said Banner, "First, have you ever fired this gun?"

"No," replied the patient, "I've had it for several years, but never used it."

Banner took the gun and began to look it over. "Well, it's in pretty fair shape, did you clean it?"

"No," replied the patient, "It's been kept in a plastic bag on a shelf since I got it."

"I'm gonna' wipe it down and check the moving parts, see if it's ready to use. Then, let's get some ammunition, take it into the range and try it out."

Banner finished checking the weapon and returned to the counter with a box of .9mm ammunition. "This is a .9mm Glock 19 Gen 4. The magazine holds 15 rounds and it's pretty common amongst law enforcement. It's also popular for personal protection."

"Would this stop a bad guy?"

"Oh, yeah. This is a very good weapon for self-defense."

The patient listened intently and asked, "Can I try it out?"

"Absolutely," replied Fred as he picked up the gun, ammunition and the magazine. "Let's go into the firing range, and give it a little dance."

He motioned the patient through a door leading into a long room with a glass wall on the far side and an elevated bench seat on the near side. There were tables bolted to the floor in front of the bench and the aisle between the tables and the glass wall was about six feet wide. Recessed lights shone down on each table. Fred looked at the patient and said, "Have you ever used a handgun before?"

"No, not really. I've picked this one up and tried to pull the trigger, but never fired it."

"Okay, sit down and let's cover some basics," Fred said as he placed the Glock on a shelf between them and sat in the adjacent seat. "This is a Glock 19. It is a .9mm semi-automatic weapon that weighs about 20 ounces. It is a weapon, it discharges a projectile, a bullet, at a high velocity following an explosion of gunpowder in the casing or shell of the cartridge." He handed the patient a .9mm cartridge. This is a center-fire cartridge, the primer is in the center of the casing and has to be struck by the firing pin. This cartridge is a shell made of brass, a bullet made from lead, gunpowder and a primer. The handgun has a spring loaded firing pin that strikes the primer when the trigger is squeezed, detonating it, which burns the gunpowder, causing an explosion which pushes the bullet out of the barrel."

The patient felt like a first grader all over again, but did not interrupt the lecture. Rolling the cartridge around, the patient asked, "Is it safe to handle these, I mean could one just go off if I dropped it?"

"Well, that would be very rare. You would have to drop it hard enough to detonate the primer. People are constantly dropping live rounds on the concrete floor and I've never had one go off yet. Now, don't go throwing these little things around carelessly. Rule here is kinda' like Murphy's Law, if it can go wrong, it will."

"Got it, treat them like they want to go off."

"That works. Now, the cartridges or bullets are placed in a magazine. This Glock has a spring loaded device that holds 15 rounds and pushes the next round into the chamber after one is fired. When you have fired the entire magazine, the slide will stay open, like this," he said as he moved the slide backwards.

"Okay," said the patient, now starting to think this lesson might have to be repeated several times. "There's more to this than point and shoot."

Fred grinned, "Yeah, now let's load the magazine." He depressed a single cartridge into the magazine and showed it to the patient. "The second one will push the first one down and so on until you have a loaded magazine. This one holds 15, some hold 10, some 17, different size magazines but all the same size cartridge for this weapon." He put a second cartridge in the magazine and handed it to the patient. "Let's start off light. I will fire the first couple of rounds, then you fire the next."

The patient nodded and Fred continued, "Always point the weapon down the range. Loaded or unloaded, point it down range. Never point it up at the ceiling and never put your finger on the trigger until you are ready to fire. That old cowboy thing about spinning a gun on one finger does not work with modern weapons. Always remember these are weapons, not toys or tools, they are deadly. Are you ready?"

"Yes."

"Okay, it's not loaded and I want you to show me how you will pick it up, and fire it." He walked over to a panel on the wall, opened it and flipped a few switches. The room on the other side of the glass wall lit up, a ventilation system whooshed on and the patient saw a counter run from one side of the room to the other, with dividers about every 3 feet. There was another 6 foot aisle between the glass wall and the counter with another shelf along the glass wall. Fred led the patient toward the door through the glass wall, "The counter is the firing line. Nobody goes beyond the firing line. Nobody puts their hands out into the range, and the partitions between each position are bullet proof. You place your weapon on the counter along with your ammunition and do not load it until you are ready to fire. Take care of setting up the targets and put your other materials aside before loading the weapon."

Feeling like a scolded teenager, the patient murmured, "I understand," and noticed there were 6 lanes lit up and an aisle running the length of the range, beyond which was dark. There were three doors leading into the firing line room and each bore the warning, SAFETY... EAR PROTECTION... SAFETY.

"Now, we are alone here, so let's go in back and look around before we start shooting." Fred slid a card through a reader and the lock on the firing line door clicked. He held the door open and they entered. Each lane was equipped with a pulley system that carried targets out about 100 feet. Fred walked up to the lane numbered 5 and laid the weapon on the counter. Then he attached a paper target with spring clips to the pulley and pushed a button that took the target out to about 15 feet.

"Put on the ear muffs now and listen."

The patient put on the ear muffs and everything went very still, Fred's voice became very quiet, but still audible. He put the magazine with the two bullets already loaded on the counter. "I will fire the first round so that you can hear the noise and see the kick in my hands. Watch closely." Fred checked the placement of the ear protection and said, "Are you ready?"

"Yes, I think so."

"Okay, just stand right here and look past my right shoulder," Fred indicated a place just left of the right partition. He adjusted his own ear muffs and picked up the gun. "Keep your hands down and watch my hands."

"Okay, I'm watching."

Fred placed the magazine in the grip and released the slide, chambering a round. He pointed the gun toward the target, set his feet, placed his right hand with the gun in the palm of his left hand, extended his arms and aimed at the target. "Three, two, one." The sound of the gun discharging was not as loud as the patient had expected and the gun barely moved in Fred's hands. A very slight kick upward was the only movement. "Second shot, three, two, one." The slide stayed in the open position after he fired, and Fred released the magazine, laid the Glock and the empty magazine on the counter, still pointing down range, and looked at the patient. "Okay, you can take off the ear muffs for a second since no one else is here. Whenever you are on the firing line, that's this side of the glass wall, you should wear the ear muffs. Always keep your weapon secured and unloaded until you are on the firing line. Now, it's your turn. Let's see you load the magazine."

The patient struggled with the bullet and the magazine, still leery about an accidental discharge. The first cartridge finally in place, the second presented a new challenge. Pushing the first cartridge down with the second was not as easy as watching Fred. The magazine now loaded with two bullets, the patient indicated, "I'm ready."

"Okay, tell me what you're doing as you do it," said Fred.

The patient picked up the Glock, inserted the magazine and released the slide, saying "Magazine in, now releasing the slide." Pointing the weapon down range, the patient said "Aiming at the target," as the right hand was placed in the left and the gun pointed at the target. "Three, two, one."

Both the sound and the kick surprised the patient. Straining to see a hole near the middle of the target, the patient heard Fred say, "You were a little to the left and low."

Looking low and left, a hole appeared well away from the center, but still on the target. Aiming again at the center of the paper, the patient squeezed off the second round. The slide remained in the open position. "Better," said Fred, "Still low and left, but not bad for a first timer. It's a matter of learning where the bullet will go when you do certain things. It comes with practice. Let's try loading 4 rounds and doing it again."

The patient pushed the magazine release, removed it, and laid it on the counter next to the Glock, still pointing down range. Fred opened the small box of cartridges; the patient took one and pushed it into the magazine with some effort. Fred grinned, "The spring in a new magazine is usually stiff, but after a few cycles, it will become more friendly."

The patient struggled with the next 3 cartridges and finished with a big sigh. "I'm not as strong as I used to be."

Fred nodded and the patient loaded the magazine into the grip, then releasing the slide. "I'm ready to begin."

"Remember, everything moving goes down range, your eyes, the business end of the Glock, the target and the bullets. Everything else stays here. Now plant your feet, right hand in left, point and squeeze. No need to count down, just make sure you are ready and fire when comfortable."

The patient fired the first round, lowered the Glock and looked at the target, "I think I hit it a little to the left and low again."

"Yes, but better again. You're doing very well. Now relax, breathe easy and go again."

The patient fired the rest of the load and laid the Glock on the counter, "Can I do it again?"

"Absolutely, I'm open until 8:00 pm and you can stay as long as you like," laughed Fred, "The more you shoot, the more I make."

They both laughed and the patient said, "I'll get through this box of ammunition and then decide if I want to do another. This is kind of fun."

Thirty minutes later, the patient bought another full box of ammunition. Holding and aiming the weapon had gotten easier by the minute, but the half hour on the range had been an exhausting experience and the patient felt weak. "I'll have to come back again for another round of practice."

"We are open six days a week, closed on Sundays," said Fred, "You come in any time you want and we will keep you busy."

"I will. By the way I am also interested in a stun gun. What do you have?"

Fred pointed across the room, "Let's take a look over here. There are several models I think are the best of the bunch. Of course, they run from $10 up to $100, so you have a lot of choice, but personally I like this one," he said as he pulled the black plastic device from the box. The two prongs looked menacing and he said, "No worries, it's not charged up, see, no battery."

The patient took the device and held it, "How does it work?"

"This baby will penetrate a couple layers of clothing, easily through a shirt and sweater and maybe a light jacket, but it is best applied directly to the skin, like the back of the neck, belly or shoulder. Hold it there for a few seconds and your target goes down in a lump. Gives you plenty of time to get away, or tie him up, whatever."

"How often do you have to recharge the thing, I mean, could I stun five people in a row, one after the other or what?"

"Depends on the battery, a new one will put out several good blasts of four to five seconds each. So I guess if you were to try to do ten bad guys, it could work."

"Well let's hope I never need the thing, but you never know these days."

*   *   *

The patient was back home by mid-afternoon, sitting in front of the television, taking the Glock apart and reassembling it. After an hour of stripping down and reassembling the gun, the patient managed flawlessly. The second challenge was loading the magazines. Each clip held 15 cartridges, but the patient struggled with each cartridge and stopped after 10 in each magazine. The patient gave the weapon a thorough cleaning and wipe down, and placed the unloaded hand gun in a large brief case. The foam filling was carved out and fitted to accept the weapon, two magazines, an additional box of ammunition, four sets of hand cuffs and matching leg irons, the stun gun and a spare battery. The patient leaned back in the recliner, half watched the television and mentally ran over scenarios of stunning and restraining each of the four men.

*   *   *

CHAPTER FOURTEEN
Capture...

By Tuesday evening, four days before the reunion at the Vaneksburg Hotel, the patient had a plan and several alternate scenarios ready to implement. The venue was the Ripley Farm, in the barn, and first target was to be Dave Branch. At least Branch could be dealt with, if all else failed. The plan was simple and that was the beauty of it. The old 'Keep It Simple Stupid' rule or 'KISS' was deemed the best way to success.

The patient called Dave at 5:15 after leaving the Doctor's office in Fairfax and asked if they could meet at Ripley's barn around 6:30 that evening. Dave accepted and the patient started driving in that direction. "Fingerprints, I should be aware of fingerprints." The patient pulled into a drug store, purchasing a box of latex gloves and a bottle of water. Arriving at the Ripley Farm, the patient saw Dave outside the barn, sitting in his truck, smoking a cigarette. The patient pulled up and parked. "Hi Dave, this won't take long. Could we go inside the barn?"

"Sure, the power is still on so we will have lights."

The patient took a briefcase from the front seat of the Focus and the plastic bag from the drug store and followed Dave as he entered the barn. Dave hit a switch and the first bay lit up. He walked to the center bay and as he turned to announce the coast was clear, the patient had set the plastic bag down and held the .9mm Glock in one hand and the briefcase in the other.

"Stay at least that far away," said the patient, "Now walk back to the middle of the barn."

"What the hell is this? A robbery?"

"Shut up, Dave, now sit on that bale of hay," said the patient. As Dave sat down the patient moved behind him and set the brief case down on another bale, opened the case and removed a pair of handcuffs and the stun gun. "In case you are wondering, yes, I do know how to use this little toy, now face the middle of the bay." Dave turned facing away and the patient stepped closer and pressed the stun gun into the back of his neck. Dave stiffened and collapsed on the hay bale. The patient quickly retrieved the plastic bag, opened the box of latex gloves and put on a pair. Then the patient handcuffed Dave, walked around and placed the leg restraints on his ankles. The chain was wrapped around the leg restraints, pulled under the bale of hay and wrapped around the building support, then pulled so that Dave's legs were snug against the bale. Another length of chain was pulled around Dave's waist and again pulled snugly against the column and a third length was used to keep his hands against the column. The patient then drove nails through the chains and into the back of the column.

As Dave started to regain consciousness, the patient was putting the ball gag in place. "Do you recognize me, Dave?"

He shook his head and tried to speak through the gag, but all that came out was angry mumbling and spit.

"Relax, Dave, I just want you to talk to me, tell me what really happened nineteen years ago. Tell me how you and your band of jerks beat and killed my friend. Tell me that, Dave, and maybe I'll let you go, or maybe I'll give you to the police." The patient smiled and walked around the building column, looking at the restraints. "You know what I think, Dave? I think you aren't going anywhere soon, so you should relax and get comfortable. Are you ready to talk yet, Dave?"

Dave was breathing heavily around the gag, sweating and drooling. He nodded his head, implying he was willing to talk. The patient pulled a little tab on the ball gag and the ball came out of his mouth. He shouted, screamed and cursed as loudly as he could. "We were cleared of everything back then, you got no right to do this to me."

"You're right Dave, I have no right to do this, but that's what makes it so perfect. You see, you got away with murder all those years ago and I will never be arrested for this little mistake, or is it a crime. I don't know and I don't care." The patient walked around the column again. "Now, I am going to put this gag back in your mouth, so open wide."

Dave screamed again and clamped his mouth shut. As the patient moved the ball closer to Dave's mouth, he jerked his head forward, trying to bite the patients' hand.

"Not nice, Dave, but I have a solution for everything." The patient walked behind Dave, picked up the stun gun and pressed it against

Dave's back. Once again his body stiffened and fell silent. The gag was replaced, an additional chain added, around Dave's neck and the whole thing nailed to the back of the column.

The patient checked the time, 6:15 pm, then called Bob Dorsey, "Bob, Trent Laskin, I realize the hour is late, but I have to get back to Chicago and I have a few points I'd like to clear up before I go. Could you come out to the Ripley Place? Dave and I are in the barn, talking, and I need you to clear up a few points so we can move this deal forward, and Bob, let's continue to keep this quiet."

Bob was still at his desk when the call came in. He began to doodle on his calendar 'Trent, Chicago, barn.' He gathered a few papers and started for the door as his boss, Al Goldman, saw him.

"Half day today, Bob?" said Al jokingly.

"Hey Al, gotta run. The Ripley deal may be coming around. I'll see you tomorrow," he called over his shoulder as he ran out to his car. He drove a little over the speed limit and arrived sooner than the patient had anticipated. "Trent, you look vaguely familiar, have we met before? I was almost out the door when you called, lucky you caught me. What would you like to discuss?"

"Let's go into the barn, I left my briefcase in there, and I'll tell you what I need."

"Sure, after you," said Bob, still thinking about where they had met previously.

As the patient walked through the door, Bob saw Dave bound and gagged sitting on a bale of hay. The patient turned, faced Bob and held the Glock, pointed directly at Bob's chest. "As I told him, yes, I do know how to use it, now you sit over there on that bale."

Bob was confused and didn't move. The patient pointed the gun at a bale of hay and fired, then said, "Bob, I told you to sit down on that bale. NOW."

Bob looked at the gun, staggered over to the bale and sat down. The patient tossed the leg restraints at him and told him to put them on. He paused and looked up at the patient.

"Or I could just shoot you."

Bob fumbled through the process of putting them on and then the patient threw him the handcuffs and told him to put them on one hand. The patient walked behind Bob as he was placing the cuff on his left wrist and raised the stun gun to Bob's neck. He didn't see it coming and reacted with violent, jerky movements, wetting the front of his pants.

Trussed up, Bob started to awaken. His expression was more fear than pain, mixed with shock and anger. The patient explained Bob could still talk and maybe he would go home tonight. Dave stared at Bob, shaking his head as much as he could. Bob didn't know what to do and began to cry. The patient replaced the ball gag and surveyed the two of them.

"Not so tough without all your buddies around. Well, I'm going to help you out; I'm going to invite Ron and Carl to join us."

The patient walked out of the barn, turning off the lights before closing the doors.

*   *   *

Wednesday morning about 9:30 the patient called Ron Nestor at the car dealership. "Ron, my name is Trent Laskin and I got your name from Dave Branch. He told me you may be able to help me with a few of my cars."

"A few, just how many are we talking about?"

"I only have four here and I'm afraid I can't keep them all. I have several more back in Chicago, all in a storage facility. They are far too valuable to park outside on the street."

"What makes and models are they?"

The patient was in uncertain territory here and answered with, "I have relocated my two Shelby Mustangs, a '56 T-Bird and one of the Corvettes to the barn here. I know I can't bring them all here, the barn will only accommodate ten at most, so I have to either expand this barn or sell a few of the cars. I think in the short term I'll have to reduce my inventory. Dave said that you were pretty good at dealing with antique cars."

"Bring them in and we'll have a look at them," offered Ron.

"Please understand, these are not street cars and I just can't risk any damage by driving them in traffic. It would be so much better if you could stop by here and look them over. If you can handle the sale, we can get the transport truck back here to move them to your facility."

"I don't normally do this."

"Oh, Dave was sure that once you've seen these cars, you would be panting all over them. Would you like to speak to Dave first?"

Ron replied, "Is he there? I've been trying him all morning."

"Hang on," said the patient, and half covering the phone, pretended to call Dave. "Dave, Ron would like to speak to you."

The patient rolled the phone around a bit, waited a few seconds and spoke to Ron again. "Ron, Dave is looking under the hood of the green Mustang; I have to get back inside the barn. Can you come see these cars or should I call someone else?"

Ron paused then said, "You're at Dave's house?"

"No, across the street at the old Ripley place, I just bought it."

"Okay, Trent, I'll come look, but I cannot guarantee that I will buy these cars. Maybe I should bring my mechanic as well."

"Listen Ron, I want to keep these cars under wraps until the security is in place and their new homes are established. I hope you understand. Just you for now."

"Okay," said Ron, "I'll be there in about 45 minutes. The Ripley place, right?"

"Well, technically the Laskin place now."

"Yeah, Laskin."

*   *   *

Ron arrived and saw the patient standing outside the barn. The large doors were closed and the patient asked Ron to park next to the other three cars in front of the garage. "Isn't that Bob Dorsey's car?" He asked as he walked toward the patient and the barn.

"Yes, it is," replied the patient. "Bob is finalizing the paperwork on the property for me. Are you ready for the surprise?"

"Yeah, let's see these cars," said Ron as he pulled open the door and stepped inside. "What the..." As he turned toward the patient he found himself looking down the barrel of the Glock .9mm.

"Join your friends and sit down," said the patient, "On that bale," pointing to another bale of hay. The leg restraints were already in place with one end of the chain nailed to the back of the column. "Sit, or I shoot you. It would be my privilege to put a bullet in your belly, so it's your choice, Ron, you sit or I shoot."

Ron hesitated, as if considering a different move. The patient pointed the Glock at the bale and fired. "That bale, Ron, NOW." Ron's face showed confusion and shock. He started to turn toward the bale and again hesitated. "I'm getting tired, Ron. It would be so much easier to just shoot you. It's your choice." Ron sat on the bale and the patient walked behind him. "Buckle up Ron, I feel like pulling this trigger again just to show you I mean what I say."

Ron shackled his legs and was hit with the stun gun. He went through a process similar to what the others had experienced. "I like this little electric toy," said the patient and continued, "I'll be right back children, you all be good while I am gone."

Immediately placing a call to Carl Wilkins, the patient noted the time was 10:45, and started embellishing the tale that had worked so well to lure Ron out to the farm. "Carl Wilkins, my name is Trent Laskin and I need a security system to protect my collection of antique cars." That was enough to get Carl to the barn by noon. After he parked his car alongside the others, he looked over at them and raised his eyebrows in question.

"Dave Branch, Bob Dorsey and Ron Nestor are all in the barn," the patient answered.

Carl looked at the barn and back at the patient, "What's going on here?"

The patient had one hand in front and the other behind, out of sight, holding the Glock. "Let's go into the barn and we can all talk about it."

Carl looked as if he were about to argue and the patient pointed the gun at Carl. "Please, let's go into the barn."

"Wait a minute, here. What's that?"

"No Carl, listen up, I said go in the barn, NOW, or I will shoot your maggoty ass, and enjoy doing it."

As Carl hesitated, the patient pointed the gun more precisely at Carl's chest. Carl paused, looked at the patient's face and then at the gun, and then back to the face again.

"It's a .9mm Glock 19, and I have used it before. Are you going to 'Make my day', Carl? Are you?"

The door opened and the two walked in. When Carl saw the three men bound and gagged, he spun around and almost knocked the patient to the ground. The Glock dropped and Carl moved like lightning toward it on the floor. The patient had already pushed the stun gun into Carl's back. The charge pulsed and the patient discharged it again. Carl was unconscious before he hit the floor. The patient quickly ran to the fourth bale of hay and picked up the handcuffs and leg restraints. By the time Carl could see clearly and rise shakily to his knees, the patient had regained the Glock and was sitting on another bale of hay watching him. "Get up, Carl, get up slow and get up NOW."

The leg restraints wouldn't allow Carl to stand so the patient told him to crawl on his hands and knees to his designated bale of hay. "I really would like to shoot you, Carl, so just give me an excuse. Now, lie down on your belly."

Carl lay down with his feet touching the bale and the patient unlocked his left leg restraint. "Now, sit up on the hay Carl."

Carl did as he was told, thinking about lunging at the patient if the opportunity presented itself. The patient walked behind Carl and said, "Look straight ahead, Carl, see Dave Branch over there?" As Carl looked at Dave, the patient pushed the stun gun into Carl's neck. He flopped and sagged onto the bale and the patient quickly pulled a chain around Carl's neck and hooked it on a nail in the column. The other restraints were quickly secured and the patient now had all four men bound and chained to posts in the barn.

"Time to rest, gentlemen, rest and think. Think about these four things:

First: Why are you here?

Second: Who am I?

Third: What is happening?

And finally: Will we get out of this?"

The patient paced about the barn, walking behind each of them and holding the stun gun, "Four simple but tough questions."

The four men were unable to respond over their gags. Their eyes followed the patient from side to side, looking worried, wondering what this was leading to, what they were accused of, and what would happen to them.

"Darryl Zamanski," said the patient, "Tell me how and why, then maybe we all go home."

The four men stopped looking at the patient, and started exchanging glances amongst themselves. Dave knew he was the most likely fall guy. He would face the harshest punishment because he was the only one over eighteen at the time of the incident, and he was the one who wanted to hurt Darryl the most. Perhaps he should speak first and secure a favored place in the prosecution; he was willing to roll on the others to protect himself.

Bob was terrified, not capable of splitting hairs and minimizing his culpability. He had spotted Darryl; he had pointed him out to Dave. In his mind, he was the prime mover in this attack. He had never known whether the kicks to Darryl's head and abdomen, or the dozen hits with the cattle prod had been the actual cause of death, but his fear now increased exponentially.

Ron knew their ages at the time mattered, but he also knew they could all have been charged as minors or adults. The main thing was the fact that Dave had been the most violent hitter, and the only one who was eighteen. Yes, Ron had used the cattle prod, but so had Bob; he felt he could deflect most of the blame onto the others.

Surely the worst would be the arrest and Carl believed most of their coerced confessions would be thrown out. It seemed like it might be a draw; they might not even be charged and if they were, the cattle prod might be a problem. He could put most of that on Ron and Bob. Dave actually had kicked Darryl much more than he had. Then he began to wonder about leaving town if this went public. It was a small town, there'd be gossip and remaining in Vaneksburg could become uncomfortable. Perhaps moving to a new city and finding a new job. He might actually have to work and he found that mildly amusing, but irritating.

The patient went to the middle of the bay and looked at the four, "You murderous scumbags all took part in killing Darryl and now it's time to pay up. I'll give each of you a chance to speak, one at a time.

Dave wanted to be first, but the patient wanted him to be last. Carl was given the nod, his gag pulled out and after a little coughing and spitting, he looked at the patient. "I think that I remember you now. You were..."

"I am not the subject here, Carl. You and your boys here are the subject, and what you did back then."

Carl stiffened at the accusation, but still felt sure he was safe, no jury could convict him of any crime. "I forgot your name, but I remember your face."

The patient tapped Carl with the stun gun, to remind him of the unpleasant feeling. Carl glared and opened his mouth to speak, "You and Z were tight."

The patient gave him another short stun and shoved the gag back in his mouth, then turned to Ron Nestor. "Ron, would you like to say something intelligent?"

Ron nodded and the gag was pulled out. "You sure you have the right group of guys here? What makes you think any of us had anything to do with that kid?"

"I've had nineteen years to think about it, Ron. Yes, I have the right group and each of you had a part in beating Darryl." The patient held the gag ready to put back in Ron's mouth when he gathered spittle in his mouth. "Swallow," said the patient holding the stun gun about three inches away from Ron's neck. He swallowed and the gag was put back in.

Bob was shaking when the patient gestured toward his gag and asked the question, "Are you ready to talk?"

The other three all watched and wondered how much Bob would give up. He was the weak link, if anyone would crack, they knew it would be Bob.

Bob nodded and the gag was pulled, "I don't know what you're talking about." The gag was pushed back into his mouth.

The patient looked at a cell phone, noting the time was after 3:00 pm. Looking at Dave, who appeared eager to talk, the patient paused to think. Since the others had refused to give in, the patient assumed Dave would fall into line. "He needs more time to mull things over in his head and I'm running out of time," muttered the patient, then turned and started to walk away. "Tired, people, I am getting very tired and this is not going in a direction that makes me happy. I have a doctor's appointment in an hour, so I am going to let you think about this overnight and I will see you in the morning, or maybe the afternoon. I haven't decided yet." The patient walked out of the barn, turned off the lights and fastened a padlock to the door.

* * *

Dr. Schrader was in his office as the day wound down and the patient called while making a turn onto Lomond Road and confirmed their appointment. "I am running a little late," said the patient, "I may be a few minutes off schedule."

"No problem," said Dr. Schrader, "Are you keeping busy?"

The patient almost laughed, "Just being a little bad, doing something I never would have tried six months ago."

"Any changes since last your visit?"

"The headaches are getting a little worse and I am beginning to feel a little unsteady after standing for a while, but I'm still getting around and looking forward to the reunion this weekend."

"Be careful, don't overdo it and we can talk about your meds when you get here."

"Okay, I will see you in an hour."

The ride took less time than anticipated and the patient arrived before 4:00 pm. While sitting in Dr. Schrader's waiting room, the plan for the four men in the barn continued to evolve. Getting them to talk and turning everything over to Detective McLarry seemed noble, but somehow impractical. "I should just shoot the bastards," muttered the patient as the door opened and Dr. Schrader overheard the last six words.

"Now, just what kind of trouble are you plotting?" he asked laughingly.

"Oh, it's nothing. Just a few old acquaintances that seem to have gotten away with everything they ever tried."

"Well, by all means then, just shoot the bastards."

They both laughed as they went into the exam room.

*   *   *

CHAPTER FIFTEEN
The last meeting...

All eight members showed up at the Vaneksburg Tavern for the last meeting before the reunion date. "Glad this is the last meeting," said Jim, "I could go broke feeding this crowd." He laughed, looked out at the dining area and waved Carol into the room. "Full house again tonight," he said to the group, "I guess that means we get dessert also."

They laughed at Jim's joke and Barb said, "Let's get through the business and open it up to whatever."

Carol walked around the table checking on the dinner orders. She paused behind Sandy, "Cheddar and tomato?" Looked at Mark, "Extra fries," Then behind Brent, "Hold the onion. Barb, lettuce and tomato?" She stopped behind Lisa and said, "Well done?"

Lisa looked up and said, "Could I do a salad instead?"

Jim nodded his approval and Carol moved on to Audrey. "How about you, honey? You look like you could use a burger with everything?"

"I'm not that hungry, could I do a salad too?" replied Audrey.

Jim nodded again and Carol went back to the kitchen.

Sandy opened with "Phil and I have contacted almost everyone on our lists. So, as of Monday, we have 34 definite yeses, 12 maybes, 14 refusals, 5 cannot be located, 8 have not responded and 3 have passed away. Phil, have you got anything beyond that?"

"Actually, yes. I finally heard from Tom Kline, he's a yes and Beverly Marshall is now Beverly Knowles and she is a yes."

"Great, so we are 36 positives and with partners, that's 72." Barb looked across the table, "Audrey, can we do 72?"

"Sure," replied Audrey, "The tables can seat 8 each and we asked for 10 tables to be fully set. That would allow us room for another 8 people with the numbers we have now." She paused, "Oh and they could set up as many as six more tables, if needed."

"Jim," said Barb, "Are we good with the numbers?"

"Yes, everything's fine there. I met with the head chef and we are on the same page. We can serve as many as we seat."

The rest of the meeting went smoothly and with the reunion business finished, the group turned to dinner and conversation. Eventually the topic of Darryl came up and Jim suggested that the committee invite Ian McLarry to join them. The group seemed to agree. Ian would have a chance to meet a number of people who knew Darryl and maybe he would pick up some valuable information.

"So, where is this investigation now?" asked Phil.

"Well," said Barb, "Our new detective has questioned each of the four jerks several times and he isn't letting up. I don't think he is getting the kind of information he needs, but the chief apparently calls him a bulldog, once he bites down, he doesn't let go."

"But he still doesn't have enough to move forward," asked Phil. "I wonder if there's anything we could do, like talking to others from that class, what was it, '94, and see if they can remember anything."

Barb said, "I wish we could do just that, but I'm afraid we might ask the wrong question or push the wrong button and screw the investigation up."

Sandy was on her second glass of wine and said, "I'm all for shooting 'em. The bastards killed Darryl and have been walking around free for almost twenty years. I say shoot the sons of bitches."

Mark added, "Sometimes, I think that is the answer too, Sandy. But then we would be the same as they are, murderers, and that makes me reconsider. There has to be a way to get justice for Darryl and for the community as a whole. This was a crime, not only against Darryl, but against us all. The criminals should be brought to justice."

Brent sat quietly, listening. Then Lisa said, "Just what can we do? I mean legally. Can we drag them in here one by one and beat the answers out of them? I think not. Can we try to gain information from them in normal conversations? I think conversations like that may be hearsay, or whatever the term is for a conversation that is not witnessed or recorded. I think we're stuck being the eyes and ears that pass along information we learn to Detective McLarry, and not the hands that drag information out of the suspects."

Mark leaned in and said, "You know, the story as I recall it had, like, ten guys fishing at the Wharf all evening. Now two of them are dead, one has moved to California, we know where the four jerks are, that leaves three people that were supposedly at the Wharf with that group when Darryl was attacked. I think their names are Joe Baines, Ben something and Paul Burger. Where are they today?"

Brent put his hand up and said, "I think Joe Baines is a Pharmacist at the Target store in Leesburg. I could talk to him."

"Maybe the detective should do the talking," suggested Audrey, "We should keep it all legal."

"Agreed," said Brent. "What about the other two?"

"Ben Grayton," said Jim, "And Paul Burger. Let's put a list together and hand it to Ian."

"I'll call him," said Barb.

"It's kinda' late, isn't it?" asked Sandy. "He's probably home with his feet up, not thinking about this at all."

"Then I will leave a message," said Barb as she opened her cell phone and pushed a number.

"You have him on speed dial?" mused Jim.

"No, this is the main number for the police station. Hello, could I speak to Detective McLarry? Sure, I'll hold. He's still there."

The group waited silently, "Hi, Ian, this is Barb Nessman. Oh, I'm fine, we were just finishing up our meeting and were talking about the investigation. We thought we should tell you about the other boys at the Wharf that night." She paused as Ian spoke. "Oh, you have," she said listened again. "Ian, I told you, you are my source." Barb listened for a few seconds and looked deflated. "Well, we tried, thanks, Ian. Oh, by the way, we want to extend you an official invitation to our reunion on Saturday. You and a guest, your wife or," she paused. "Oh, okay, just you then. Okay, see you."

Sandy said "Well?"

"He's single," replied Barb.

"No, what about the others?" said Sandy.

"He has spoken to Joe Baines and said it went nowhere and he has a line on the other two, but is not expecting much from them."

"And?" posed Lisa.

"And he is probably walking in the front door right now," said Barb.

"That was quick," said Phil.

"Well, the police station is right across the square," said Jim. "He drops in a couple of times a week for lunch or dinner. I'll have Carol send him back here when he comes in."

The conversation continued for a few more minutes and Ian walked into the room. "Good evening all, I didn't mean to break into your meeting tonight."

"You're always welcome here, Ian," said Barb.

"Listen people, I really wish there was something to report, but we are kind of in a lull. These things don't always fall into place and you often have to stay with it for an extended period. We may not have much today, but tomorrow is another day and sooner or later, something will surface and we will be off and running again."

Carol walked into the room with a tray and asked Ian where he was sitting.

"Anywhere, and thanks."

She put his plate and drink on the large table and left the room. Then Jim approached and said, "Listen here, my burgers are the best in this town, but even mine will not be very good if they get cold. Sit and eat."

The group laughed, Ian sat at the table with the others and listened to the conversation as he ate, pausing only to tell Sandy, "No, you can't just shoot the bastards."

* * *

CHAPTER SIXTEEN
The Inquisition...

The patient filled a new prescription that promised greater relief from the increasingly intense headaches. Walking was getting more challenging, though not painful, but long walks were out of the question. Now that the four men were secured in the barn, the level of physical activity on the patient's part was going to be limited. "I can question these guys while sitting on the bale in the middle. I don't have to wrestle with them or lift anything heavy. Just poke them with my little stun gun or hit them with a stick," muttered the patient while driving to the Ripley Farm.

The sun was up and the day looked fresh and promising. A very pleasant day was in the offing, without a cloud in the sky. The patient hoped the beautiful weather was a good omen that the plan for the four men in the barn would go smoothly. As the silver Focus approached the Lomond Road address, the patient noticed a pick-up truck pulled to a stop on the shoulder in front of the Ripley place. The Focus turned into the driveway and stopped. The patient opened the car door and wondered how to handle this intrusion as a man left his truck on the road and approached.

"Good morning," said the patient, "Can I help you?"

The man seemed a little nervous and blurted out, "This place for sale?"

"Well, actually, I'm here for that very purpose. I've made an offer and the realtor assures me it will be accepted."

"Oh, okay," said the man, "Can I ask, how much land is included?"

The patient remembered the conversation with Bob and said, "The front part with the house is five acres and there are about 273 plantable acres. Then the access roads, barns, outbuildings and two pastures cover another 12 acres, for a total of 285 acres. They had planted corn for the last few years and boarded four horses."

The man paused, "285 acres, that's more than I thought. Is the house in good shape?"

"Yes, it's only about thirty years old, newer kitchen, oil heat, a five car garage, newer barn, a lot of positive features. It was expensive, much more than we wanted to spend, but we are looking forward to getting the team together to start the planning. That's what we are doing today, planning. I think I may be a little late, so if you will excuse me."

"Oh, sure," said the man. "So you have a deal all signed?"

"Right after the meeting this morning. The financing is all arranged and we are ready to move on this site. After all, it is May, almost June, so we may have missed the opportunity to get two full plantings in this year."

"So maybe you will change your mind and not buy?"

"That has already been discussed by the corporate people, they want this property and as I said, they are anxious to begin the planning."

The man seemed a little discouraged and turned to walk away, "Thanks, anyway."

The patient remembered the other part of the conversation with Bob, "There are two other properties, each one around 200 acres, down this road about 4 miles and again about 12 miles. I haven't looked at them but heard they are similar to this one."

The man paused, listened and nodded, "Thanks, I'll have a look at them right now." He was in his truck and moving within a few seconds.

At the same time, the neighbor to the north, Paul Jansen, was collecting his mail and saw a man standing halfway up Ripley's driveway. The man appeared to be talking to someone, but Paul couldn't see who. Then the man turned and went back to his truck and drove away. The neighbor looked at his mail and walked into his house.

The patient turned, looked at the fence and gate. "I'll padlock the gate, that'll give me more privacy and keep most people out of the back."

*   *   *

The patient opened the barn door and entered. The odor of human waste was apparent, but not as bad as it would be in 24 hours. "Oh, did we have an accident? Well, I'm not cleaning you up and I'm not loosening the bonds either, so you can just sit there in your own filth. I'm here to ask a few questions and let you four talk." The patient walked around behind the men, checking their bindings. "You boys been trying to escape? Your wrists are cut up and bloody. Please, gentlemen, do not struggle. You'll just make things worse. If you would just 'fess up, I could call the police and leave you to them. Don't talk, and I'll have to start shooting you. Maybe in the foot, or the leg, maybe in the gut, or in the head. I could just stand at the door and start shooting, see what I hit that way. It's your choice."

The patient produced the gun. "Now, I'm not an expert but I can hit targets as big as you, easily. Wanna see?" The bale in the middle of the bay was easily viewed by each man. The patient looked around for a target and spotted a wooden box with red writing sitting on a shelf. "Dynamite, perfect." The box with the last four sticks was set on the bale. The patient lifted the dynamite out of the box and walked back to the door, placing the dynamite on the shelf near the door and then took aim at the box. The first shot was wide and low. The patient walked back to the central bale. The sound in the barn seemed very loud. "I have always been low and left," admitted the patient. "Let me adjust and shoot again. Should I get you guys some ear protection? Naw, this is so much more fun. I might hit one of you, but, oh well, so, no ear protection."

The second shot ripped through the lower corner of the wooden box. The patient approached again. "Did I hit any of you? No? Maybe I'll try again." The patient looked in the box and feigned a surprised look, "Oops, missed one." The patient took the dynamite box over to the shelf, pretending to place the rest of the dynamite in the box with the first stick. "I should find another target."

The patient walked around the barn looking at the various items left behind. "There's more chain here, and some small tools, a hammer, a jar of nails, some hinges, good stuff," laughed the patient, and put the chain near the door along with the hammer, nails and hinges. "I almost forgot, you fellas have not had breakfast. But that's okay because I have a treat for you." A short walk to the Focus and the patient came back with small bag of bagels and four bottles of water. "Eat up, 'cause that's all you're going to get 'til you talk and the cops show up." The patient pulled the gag from Carl's mouth. As he was trying to say something, the patient squirted water into his mouth and then pushed a bagel between his teeth. "Eat, you filthy pig, eat the whole thing 'cause that's all you get until tomorrow."

Carl choked down the bagel and water. The food and water was forced and he did not resist. Hunger and thirst overrode anger and mistrust. Finished, Carl started to say, "You can't do this to us, I know my rights."

The patient tapped Carl with the stun gun and the ball gag was reinserted. The patient went to Dave next. "You understand if you step out of line with me, I will stun you, stop feeding you and shove the gag in again."

Dave tried to nod and the patient pulled the gag. The bagel was put in his mouth and he ate. Water was squirted in and he drank. "Very good Dave, now tell me about Darryl."

Dave cleared his throat and tried to talk. His voice was raspy, almost unintelligible. "I didn't do nothing to that little--"

The stun gun was held in place longer than necessary and the gag replaced. Dave was out cold and would not see or hear the next two men as they fearfully ate, drank and refused to talk. All gags replaced, the patient went to the car and returned with four brown paper shopping bags. One on each head and the patient took the dynamite box over to the garage. The first door next to the house was not locked and easily opened. The patient put a blasting cap in the middle of the bundle of four sticks and tied them tightly together. A little wire, an alarm clock and a battery were placed in the wooden box. The chain was wrapped around the inside of the box and the nails were sprinkled around on the chain. The wire cutters were used to snip the chain in enough places so that the longest piece was about two feet long. Everything at the ready except for the battery connection to the alarm clock and the patient walked back to the barn. The box was placed on the central bale equally distant from each of the men. "You little boys think about talking to me tomorrow, or I will take a few more shots at the wooden box. Be good now and I'll see you in the morning."

As the patient drove out of the driveway, the neighbor next door noted the silver car leaving the Ripley Farm, but thought nothing of it as he got into his truck.

The patient drove back to town and greeted Jim at the tavern. The two sat at the bar, drinking and talking for an hour. "Well, it's getting late and I have things to do tomorrow, so I'm gonna' run," said the patient.

Jim reached for the tab but the patient got it first, "Jim, I've got this."

"No you don't."

As the patient paid the tab and walked out, Jim noticed a slight limp.

*   *   *

The Friday before the Reunion was another beautiful day, cloudless, with the temperature climbing into the 70's. Barb herded her class out to the school yard at Thomas Jefferson Elementary and watched them run around, leaning against the chain link fence facing West Center Street. A small voice interrupted her concentration on a tune she was trying to remember. She startled, "Hey, Audrey, not working today?"

"No, I tied up all the loose ends at work last night and drove out here this morning, ready for the weekend."

As they were chatting, a little girl with mud on her sun dress ran up, "Ms. Nessman, I got mud on me."

"Don't worry, honey, your mom has had a lot of practice washing little mud spots." The little girl grinned and ran back into the playground.

"One of yours?" asked Audrey.

"Yeah, and I love them all." The bell rang and Barb said, "Time to go in, back to beating intelligence into these little monsters."

"Ah, you love them all."

"I do, I really do." She paused, "What are you up to today?"

"Just wandering around, remembering. I haven't visited much lately. But I'll see you tomorrow. Is there anything that needs doing before the cocktail hour begins?"

"I think we are good, but check in with me tomorrow. I should be at the hotel by noon."

"Well I'm already booked there for the weekend, so whatever you need, I'm ready."

The two separated and as Audrey walked toward the center of town, she saw Sandy and three other women coming out of the Bowling Alley. They waved and Sandy ran across the street to catch up with Audrey.

"Hey Aud, wait up, I can't run like I used to," called Sandy as she stumbled up on the curb.

Audrey flinched at Sandy's misstep, "Are you alright?"

Sandy rubbed her ankle, "That's twice this week I've done that," she said with a twisted grin.

Audrey teased, "Didn't you used to run cross country?"

"Yeah, way back when dinosaurs roamed the earth," replied Sandy, "Where you headed?"

"Well, I took today off and I'm walking around, just remembering things. What about you?"

Sandy started breathing easier and replied, "Well, I thought I would grab a little lunch, then run home and shower since I have an overnight shift at the hospital. Wanna join me for lunch at the tavern?"

"Sure, but this time it's another salad for me, those burgers are great but too much."

The two friends walked across the square and saw Ian McLarry talking to another man in front of the police station. Sandy giggled, "He's single, you know."

Audrey looked over her shoulder at Ian, smiled, looked back and said, "No, I didn't know."

Lunch was full of speculation about their classmates, "I wonder how she looks today. Fifteen years makes a big difference - new babies, jobs, marriages, friends. That can really hang years on you," said Sandy, "Oh, look who's coming."

As Audrey turned to see who Sandy was referring to, Ian walked over to their table, "Hey ladies, mind if a rusty old cop joins you?"

Sandy lit up, "Please do."

Audrey smiled and said "Hi."

Ian sat and ordered a burger, "These things are addictive, I love 'em." He looked at Sandy and said, "So what drags you two in here today?"

Sandy practically burst, "I saw Audrey walking in the street heading this way and we decided to have a little lunch. By the way, detective, how goes the investigation?"

"You must have really liked this Darryl. You're going to a lot of trouble to try to put the bad guys away after 19 years."

Sandy responded, "I don't have a family like some others do, I mean, they're all gone. I'm out here alone. Audrey and the others are the closest thing I have to family. So Darryl was, well, he was one of us, and damn it, he deserved better. I deal with life and death every day at the hospital and I can't tell you how many times I have thought how nice it would be if Dave Branch or Carl, or any of them, were the accident or emergency victim. I am that sure they killed him." Her eyes started to fill.

Ian was about to say something and Sandy continued. "I want to shoot the no-good bastards."

"Sandy, you can't do that," repeated Ian, "That would be bad. You would be stooping to their level."

"Sometimes a little bad can be a good thing," she said as she turned toward Audrey.

Audrey said, "I wish we knew for sure they were guilty. I mean, I'm sure, but you probably need proof. Can't you do that waterboarding thing to make them talk?"

Ian grinned, "They might talk if we tortured them, but evidence gained illegally would be thrown out, of course. So, if we got a confession under duress, the confession would be useless."

"But then we would know," said Audrey.

"True, but then we couldn't punish them," said Ian.

"We could testify we have known all along they were guilty and kept quiet because we were afraid. Now we are older, wiser and no longer living in fear of their retaliation, we have come forward," said Sandy.

"No," said Ian, "I want a rock solid conviction. I'm looking for that little piece of the puzzle that leaves no question about their guilt."

"You don't want to cheat even a little?" asked Sandy.

Ian looked at the two, "As a cousin once told me, 'We don't just want someone we could convict, we want the guy who actually did the deed'."

"How close are we really, Ian?" asked Audrey.

"I am convinced these are the guys, but I don't have the proof that would allow me to arrest them."

"What if one of them did talk, without torture?" asked Sandy.

"That would change the dynamic and we could probably proceed. But there are so many variables; the 19 years, their ages at the time, the lack of physical evidence, memories of what happened, the list goes on."

Sandy said, "So they will probably get away with it."

Ian said, "Look, it's not an easy thing to accept, but all we may get out of this is the knowledge they did it. They could get off with very minor sentences."

Audrey said, "Because they were minors?"

"Yeah," said Ian with a disgusted look on his face. "Except Dave Branch, he was 18 at the time."

*   *   *

The patient was full of questions on the drive south. "Am I doing the right thing?" "Do those men have rights that I have violated?" "Can any real justice come of this?" "Should I just shoot the bastards and be done with it?" "Will people hate me when they find out what I have done?"

The Focus turned into the Ripley farm, the patient opened the gate, got back in the car, drove into the open yard, closed the gate again and walked slowly to the barn. There was a stick, the size of a walking cane, lying on the ground. The patient picked it up and continued toward the barn. "Perhaps a little beating will loosen their tongues." A wicked smile appeared on the patient's face as the padlock opened and the patient entered the barn. A waft of air leaving the barn through the door told the patient that another day of stewing in their own waste did indeed smell much worse than the previous day. Choking down a cough, the patient approached the center bay. The four men were still bound, gagged, sitting on bales of hay and bleeding from any number of minor cuts and scratches around their wrists and throats.

"Well, gentlemen, you had a whole day to think, now, are you ready to talk?" The patient went first to Dave Branch and slowly pulled the paper bag from his head. His face was covered in sweat, and mucus leaked from his nostrils. His eyes were bloodshot and slightly swollen and his breathing labored. The patient pulled the gag from Dave's mouth and said, "Well, tough guy, wanna tell me something that I already know?"

Branch coughed and spit, his voice raspy and low, every word slurred and accompanied by another cough, drool or spit, "Who are you? Why are you doing this?"

"Don't you recognize me, Dave? Well, that hurts my feelings. You don't want to hurt my feelings, it upsets me." The patient pointed the stick at Dave's face, "A little whipping may straighten you out." As the patient finished speaking, the stick swung around and hit Dave below his shoulder. A tear welled in his eye and an expression of defeat and surrender crumpled his face. Two more swats with the stick produced nothing more. "Are you going to talk to me now, David Branch?"

"What do you want me to say?"

"Dave, Darryl was my friend and a nice boy. You, on the other hand, were not a friend and not a nice boy. I know you killed him, you and your little gang beat him to death and I want to hear each of you say it, say you did it. Say you killed him. Tell me how and why. That's all. Maybe then we can all go home."

Dave tried to speak but he coughed so violently that he vomited instead. The patient stepped out of the way and turned toward Carl, whacking him with the stick and pulling the bag off his head. "Are you ready to talk, Mr. Wilkins?"

Carl's face looked much the same as Dave's, covered in sweat and spit. As the gag was pulled from his mouth, he cleared his throat and eyed Dave, still spitting out the last of his vomit. "No matter what we say, none of this will stand up in a court," he choked out. "If I say we did it, it was under duress." The stick struck Carl in rapid succession three times and the gag was pushed back in place.

Bob gave in immediately, "Yeah, we pushed him around a little, punched him a few times, but we didn't mean to kill him. Just push him around a little," as he started to cry.

The patient hit him with the stick, saying, "This is a little pushing around; Darryl was beaten, kicked and poked with a cattle prod, you disgusting piece of crap." The gag was put back in and the patient turned to Ron. His bag was removed and the gag pulled out. The patient said, "Well, your turn. Talk to me." Ron was silent, dazed. The patient hit him twice with the stick and, exhausted, sat on the bale in the middle of the bay. Ron stared straight ahead. No reaction.

"Okay, we will do this again in the morning," said the patient breathlessly. "I'm tired and I have a big day tomorrow, so you little boys can ferment overnight again. I think I will bring my gun with me tomorrow. I need practice and you four make such terrific targets."

The bags were left off and the gags all replaced. The four men stared at the patient, horror stricken, wondering if they would ever get out of this mess. They were now eager to say whatever the patient wanted to hear. They had all decided that talking was smarter than maintaining silence. Three of them knew being minors at the time of the incident meant Dave Branch would take the biggest share of the blame and punishment. A year, maybe three, max, in jail and then they would be out. Even jail was starting to look better than this barn. Carl tried to capture the patient's attention by twisting and grunting.

The patient turned, looking at Carl, "Do you have something to say, Carl?"

Carl grunted and spit, so the patient pulled the gag out of his mouth and he cleared his throat. "If we say what you want to hear, will you let us go?"

124

"Of course, Carl. I am not an animal, like you four. What do you want to tell me?"

"Like Bob said, we didn't mean to kill him, it just happened."

"Carl, he was beaten with a club and electrocuted."

"It was a piece of a pallet that broke off and those two used an old cattle prod they found," Carl responded nodding toward Ron and Bob.

"And you, Carl, what did you use to beat him?"

"Nothing, I just pushed him a little."

Dave was trying to talk through the gag, practically foaming at the mouth. The patient pulled the gag out of his mouth. "You hit him as much as we all did, and you kicked him too," he panted.

Carl tried to yell at Dave, but just coughed and spit before the patient could get the gag back in his mouth. Dave was now screaming, "You ain't gonna' dump this all on me. You were kicking him in the head."

The patient tapped Dave with the stun gun and pushed the gag back into his mouth, then turned to Bob and Ron. "So you two used the cattle-prod on him, eh. That was not nice, boys. You probably joined in on the beating too." As the patient spoke, the stun gun tapped Bob and Ron, not enough to knock them out, just enough to hurt them and make them strain against their bindings.

The patient looked at the four and said, "Like I said, I have a big day tomorrow, but I'm tired, so I will come back in the morning to finish this little adventure." The patient picked up the wooden box and carried it out the door, locked it and walked over to the garage.

*   *   *

CHAPTER SEVENTEEN
The Reunion...

The patient woke at 6:30 Saturday morning, turned on the coffee pot, retrieved the morning paper and relaxed on the bed, browsing the front page. The morning brought several concerns for the patient. First, the worry that someone would stumble upon the four men captive in the barn. Not only would they go free, the patient would be in danger of arrest. Second, the worry someone would miss one of the men, and start a search. The police would look to the other three for information, and four missing men would guarantee a larger, more focused search. That would be problematic, to say the least.

Carl Wilkins was married, but going through a divorce and his wife probably wouldn't care if he stepped out for two or three months. He had disappeared several times over the last year, so leaving unannounced for a few days was nothing new. The patient saw a silver lining in that situation; if Carl turned up dead, perhaps his wife could collect some insurance.

Ron Nestor was in a casual relationship, still single and living alone, so no one would miss him for a couple of days.

Bob Dorsey was very close to his mother, but her mental acuity had deteriorated so much lately, she seemed very frail and vague. Half the time, Bob didn't think she even recognized him. No one else was close to Bob so that would probably be okay.

Dave Branch lived alone and nobody liked him. If reported missing, the search might not start for a week or two. The patient laughed at the thought.

But, what to do with them now? Let them go? No, they would never be punished. Turn everything over to the police? No, all of the evidence had been obtained illegally and therefore was useless. "I should just shoot them, or use the dynamite and blow them up." The patient started the Focus, smiled and said aloud, "I like that. I think I will use the dynamite. I hope there's enough."

Smiling and driving out to the Ripley Farm, the patient thought about the final plan; the men, or more accurately, the four murderers, blown up. They would be gone, destroyed, and they would have been punished for what they had done all those years ago. The patient was driving about a half mile north of the Ripley farm, thinking, not paying attention to the surroundings when a car started to pull out of a driveway. The driver waited for the patient's car to pass and fell in behind the patient. As the Focus pulled into the Ripley Farm, Paul Jansen wondered if that might be his new neighbor. He couldn't see through the tinted windows to the driver. He wanted to stop and chat, but didn't have time right then, so he continued on down the road and the patient drove into the open area behind the house, parked, turned off the car engine and walked into the garage. The wooden box rested on a work bench. The patient realized, "This is what I really wanted to do in the first place."

It took very little time to wire the alarm clock to the battery and the blasting cap. The patient laughed out loud several times while placing all the pieces of chain, nails and hinges in the box. The wooden box and the cover were soon wrapped in newspaper found at the end of the workbench. A roll of tape was found in a drawer and the wooden box and cover was quickly taped. The patient thought for a minute before picking up the wrapped box and walking into the barn.

"Good morning, gentlemen, I hope you slept well." The wooden box was placed on the bale in the middle of the bay and the patient walked in a big circle, checking the bindings on each wrist and ankle. "I've brought you four a little gift. We'll open it tonight around eight, when the party really gets going. I have invited someone very special to join us."

The four men were not happy about this announcement. Who was the special guest? What was in the box? They each tried to get a few words out, but the patient ignored their sputtering and spitting protests, walked to the wooden box and opened the lid. The four men couldn't see inside the box, but the patient checked that everything was in place and the alarm was set for 8:05, less than 10 hours away. The lid was replaced and the patient turned toward the door, "I'll see you all very soon," then laughed and was gone.

The men were scared now. Scared beyond anything they had ever experienced. This person, they now recognized, had them chained to posts, shackled and gagged for, oh, how many days now? And, eight PM this evening was hours, long, hot, miserable hours, away.

Dave was coughing as he strained against the chain around his neck. He wondered, "The beatings, the gun, the box, what was in the box? Where was all this going? Are we gonna' be killed or turned in to the cops?"

Bob leaned back against the column. He was defeated, completely beaten. He wondered, "The guest, who was the special guest? Maybe it was that new cop, the one with all the questions. Maybe it would be another psycho ready to punch them, or kick them, or beat them with a stick or poke them with a cattle prod, as they had done to Darryl."

Carl pulled at his bonds thinking, "Confess, all we have to do is confess and we all go home." He relaxed, then thought again, "Yeah, sure, confess, and we get a bullet in the head." As he once again strained at his bonds, he thought, "Maybe we go to jail, maybe the cop is coming to pick us up and take us to jail. We should dump it all on Dave. That kid was his problem, not mine."

Ron tugged at his chains, he could see the others straining against theirs and he knew the chains wouldn't break. He relaxed and watched the others continue to struggle. He thought about Darryl and accepted his fate. "We killed that kid and now his friend is gonna' kill us," he sputtered with a laugh, through his gag.

*   *   *

CHAPTER EIGHTEEN
Reunions ...

Barb and Mark inspected the speaker's podium and checked the projector showing photos from their years in high school. Sandy and Lisa were looking at each table, checking the number of seats and the set ups. Audrey sat at the DJ's table going through the music and reviewing the speakers list. Everybody checked on someone else and everything seemed to be ready. The five met near the door and stood looking at the room.

"We're as ready as we are gonna' be," said Barb.

Audrey smiled and said, "I think we did a damn good job."

The others looked at Audrey, she had always been such a quiet little person and the sudden burst of enthusiasm surprised them.

Barb looked at her watch, "It's almost 2:00 o'clock, we should run home and get ready."

Four o'clock rolled around and the five were back at the main ballroom, dressed and ready to meet and greet their classmates.

The reunion activities at the hotel began on time. Several waiters began to circulate with glasses of wine, platters of cheese and crackers and other assorted hors d'oeuvres. Ian walked in through the main doors and was greeted by Barb, "Ian, so glad you could make it. I thought you might want to meet a few more people from the class of '97."

"Barb, I really appreciate this."

"Not a problem," said Barb, as Mark approached with two drinks. "Oh, thanks, Mark, can you show Ian where our table is located. We have Sandy and her date, Jeff, Phil and Eileen, and Audrey. That leaves one open seat, so Ian can join us."

"This way, detective," said Mark as he turned and started across the room. They approached an empty table near the speaker's podium and

Mark extended his hand, "Pull up a chair and I'll get you a drink, name your poison."

"I'm good with soda water and a twist," said Ian.

"Okay, be right back," said Mark as he turned and saw Sandy, "Hey, Sandy, we're right over here," pointing toward Ian and the otherwise empty table. He stepped toward Sandy and the tall man with her, "Hi, I'm Mark Lindstrom."

Sandy responded, "This is Jeff Marshall, we work together."

The tall man smiled, extended his hand and said, "Mark, Sandy has mentioned you several times. Nice to put a face and name together."

"And this is our new Detective in town, Ian McLarry," said Sandy.

"Detective, Sandy has mentioned you also," said Jeff, offering his hand.

"Please call me Ian," he said as he shook Jeff's hand.

Sandy put her purse on the table next to Ian and looked at Jeff, "A glass of white wine?"

Jeff said, "You sit, I'll get the drinks."

Sandy sat next to Ian, "So detective, anything new?"

Mark spoke up, "Sandy, let's wait till the others get here and Ian won't have to say it twice."

Jeff returned with two glasses of white wine and sat down next to Sandy. "Detective, Ian, Sandy talks about you and this investigation constantly. Has there been any solid progress? I mean, after twenty years, the physical stuff at the site must be gone and witnesses' memories will have faded considerably. Makes this a real challenge for anyone in your shoes."

"Little bits and pieces. Something remembered here and there differently from the original statements just may give us a wedge to pry it open. That's primarily what I'm after."

Barb walked up to the table, "Does everyone here know Audrey?"

Jeff and Eileen both stood and introduced themselves. "I heard what you just said," commented Audrey, looking at Ian. "Perhaps we should all be quizzed again?" Barb ushered her to the seat next to Ian.

"Each conversation can bring new material to the fore. You never know when someone will slip and give up new information or when an unknowing witness may say something that brings two pieces of a puzzle together. People remember things in several ways and sometimes recalling an incident can bring up something that was missed before. You have to understand, with respect to this investigation into the four men you have labeled as the killers, their alibis are based on the word of six other men. Their stories may not be as strong as they were when the incident occurred," said Ian, "The problem is that two are dead and one moved to California, leaving only three. I've talked to the local ones face to face and called the guy in San Diego. Their stories are all still pretty much the same as they were back then."

Barb grinned, "So is the bulldog losing his grip?"

Ian looked at Barb, "I will find out who has been talking out of school, but I don't give up at the first little bump in the road."

Jeff cut Sandy off as she was about to say something, "Ian McLarry, that name rings a bell with me. I participated in a study at the Cleveland Clinic in 1999 and 2000. There was a child abduction case that was solved after 9 or 10 years and the detective from Cleveland Heights was a Jim McLarry. Any relation?"

Ian grinned, "Yeah, that's my cousin. We have a big family and the prime occupation seems to be law enforcement or the military. Why do you remember that case?"

"My younger sister was 12 when the little girl from Cleveland Heights was abducted. They both had blond hair, blue eyes and based on the pictures in the paper, they could have been twins, a few years apart, but they looked almost exactly the same. But, the scariest similarity was the name, Annette. That's my sister's name also."

Barb stood, said she was going to introduce Ian to as many people as she could, took Ian by the arm and led him about the room. Each introduction led to a brief conversation and all seemed to point in the same direction. Darryl was a very nice kid and his murder was tragic. The room, like the community at large, was divided. There were two camps, one suspecting Dave and his gang and the other believing it was, "Someone passing through town, not one of us."

When the dinner bell rang, everybody returned to their tables. Ian was elated. He had met and talked to more people than he could remember.

Sandy finished another glass of wine and held the empty one out toward Jeff and smiled. Jeff took the glass and set it on the table, "Let's have dinner before we have another drink."

Sandy frowned and turned toward Ian, "So what have you learned so far, detective?"

"I have learned you have some very nice friends and I'm going to enjoy living here in Vaneksburg."

Sandy persisted, "What about the case, what about Darryl?"

"I hope you all appreciate that the investigative process is long, boring and often frustrating. That said, everything I learn about the people surrounding the events of 19 years ago can help me better understand the overall case and allows me to fit the pieces together like a 1,000 piece jigsaw puzzle. At first the pieces don't make sense. Then, as a few fit into a group, sometimes they fit into the overall scheme, sometimes they don't. But a new angle can materialize. That's why everything is so important. No little bit of information is too small. After a few possibilities take shape, an event can be verified, then a series of events, all held together by the insignificant, nondescript pieces that pull two or more clusters together. Finally, there is enough of the overall puzzle assembled to see the picture. We, as investigators, rarely get all the pieces and in this case, I am still collecting as many little bits as I can. This could go on for quite some time before we reach a conclusion."

"Well said, detective," said Audrey, "When do you think we will be able to see how the picture is developing?"

"Why don't we meet at the Tavern on Wednesday and I'll give you an update."

Jeff smiled and said, "May I join your group on Wednesday?"

Sandy looked at Jeff and hugged his left arm. Barb said, "I think that's a yes."

*   *   *

Around 8:05 the closing speeches at the reunion wound down and the DJ was setting up his music system. Back at the Ripley place, an alarm sounded inside the box on top of the bale of hay in the barn. It was pitch black, and the four men could see nothing, but that didn't stop their imagination from running wild with lots of scary possibilities. Carl was the first to panic. He strained at the cuffs on his wrists, kicked at the irons on his ankles and pushed on the chains around his neck and waist. The others heard the same noise and they all started to pull, twist and struggle as it became apparent the patient had not returned, but something big was about to happen. Each of them fought to find freedom and each was rewarded with bloodied wrists, ankles and necks.

The alarm was still ringing when the men saw a brilliant white flash of light...

* * *

Barb introduced several speakers and gave a short speech herself about the changes to the school since their graduation. Then, in closing, before the music and dancing, she said "We should all raise our glasses to toast those who could not join us tonight, and those who have passed away."

As the crowd raised their glasses, the names of people who were not there were remembered. Among those names was Darryl Zamanski. A brief silence, a short drink and Barb looked at Mark, "Now, how about a little music. Let's get this party started."

The speeches were done and the cash bar opened. As the music began to play, people migrated from table to table around the room. Several couples ventured out onto the dance floor and were soon joined by more.

Ian was sitting at the table, engaged in conversation with Jeff about working with Sandy, "What do you do at the hospital, Jeff?"

Sandy put her wine glass down and answered before Jeff could, "He's an emergency room surgeon."

Ian looked at Jeff, "Dr. Marshall, I presume?"

"Jeff, please," responded the surgeon, "In the ER 'Dr.' works, away from there, my name is Jeff."

Sandy stood and put her hand on Jeff's shoulder, smiled and looked at the dance floor. He looked at the others at the table and said, "Excuse me," stood and walked Sandy to the middle of the floor.

Mark took Barb's hand as she returned to the table and ushered her to the dance floor as well, then Phil followed suit with Eileen, leaving Ian and Audrey at the table. After a minute, he said, "You have a great turnout here for a small class. There must be a hundred people here."

Audrey smiled and said, "One hundred and six responded with a yes. That includes their partners, of course."

"What about you, Audrey, where is your partner?" As soon as he said it, Ian regretted his words. He realized, belatedly, his words sounded intrusive, not the right thing to say to a single woman. He looked at her and wondered, where was her mate, her special friend? Surely she had someone. She was attractive, young, bright and very nice. He stood and held out his hand, "Shall we dance?"

They made a very attractive couple. Ian was tall and strong looking, while Audrey was petite and pretty. As they started to dance, the music softened, Audrey frowned and the DJ said, "You guys look altogether too happy to sit down, so we're gonna' play this again." He started the music over, so Audrey smiled and held onto Ian. As the music continued, Audrey leaned into Ian as close as she could. As the music played, Audrey seemed to stumble a few times and Ian thought his big feet were going the wrong way. As he tried to apologize, Audrey looked up, smiled and said "My fault." They danced very slowly in a small circle along with everyone else.

When they returned to the table, Ian's phone rang. He pushed the answer button, "Chief," he paused and listened, then "Okay, it's almost 9:00, where are you now?" He moved his phone to his left ear, took out a notebook and a pen and wrote down an address. "Okay, I have everything I need in the car, Yeah, I'll be there as soon as possible." He pocketed his cell phone, looked around the table and said, "Please excuse me, I have to check something out. I'll be in touch." Then he looked at Audrey, smiled and said, "Thank you for the dance." Then he hurried out the door.

Barb leaned over to Audrey and whispered, "You're blushing, my quiet little friend. Is something happening here?"

"Oh Barb, don't be silly. He's very nice, but I'm heading back to Fairfax in the morning. I may never see him again."

Jeff looked at Sandy, "My beeper, Sandy, I have to go."

"Jeff, what's going on, both you and Ian?"

"I don't know, probably nothing to worry about, traffic accident on 66 maybe," responded Jeff.

Sandy's beeper sounded in her purse, "Looks like we're all needed for this one." She looked at Barb, "Hey, this has been great, but we have something going on at the hospital. Like Jeff said, probably an accident on Rte. 66. That could draw a crowd." Sandy and Jeff left together. Jeff dropped Sandy at her apartment and continued on to the hospital. Sandy changed quickly, jumped in her car and headed for the hospital.

*   *   *

The patient knew then the dynamite had exploded and there were four men in a barn either dead or wishing they were. It would not take Ian long to eliminate the majority of the suspects. Everyone on the committee would be on the list, and that would include the patient.

"At most, I have only a few months left. Maybe I should just call Ian and confess," thought the patient. "Then again, maybe I should just let people wonder." A slight laugh and the patient thought about death, "If there is a heaven, I may not get in. If heaven exists, does that mean hell also exists? Maybe that's where I'm headed, along with those four bastards. Then again, maybe I did the right thing and I will be in heaven, with Darryl."

* * *

CHAPTER NINETEEN
The scene...

This was the first time Ian had used the siren on his police car since arriving in Vaneksburg. He pulled out of the hotel parking lot, turned right onto Vaneksburg Road, left on North Sixth Street, right on Lomond and drove six miles south arriving at the Ripley farm two minutes before nine. A pair of Virginia State Troopers had blocked off the driveway, forcing Ian to brake to a stop. He showed his ID to the trooper, "Detective McLarry with the VPD," he stated tersely.

The trooper waved at his partner and one of the cruisers backed up to allow Ian passage. "Go ahead, detective, pull your vehicle onto the lawn on the right, we want to keep an alley open to the barn area."

Ian put his creds in his breast pocket, displaying his badge, "Thanks." He parked and walked toward the gate where he encountered another officer, one of his. "Steve, where is the chief?"

"Hey, detective, I think he is over there where the tent is being set up," said the officer.

Ian found the chief in conversation with a fireman standing next to two officers spreading out a ten by ten pop-up tent. The fireman was wearing normal civilian clothing, a heavy fireman's coat, helmet and gloves. As Ian approached, Chief Bowen turned to face him. "Ian, have you met our Fire Chief, Stan Morton?"

Morton had taken off his gloves and now removed his helmet, saying, "Detective, my pleasure. I wish we were meeting over a cup of coffee. Normally, we have so few incidents. But that ain't gonna' happen now. So, welcome detective, glad to see you."

Ian extended his hand, "We'll get to that coffee soon, Chief. Right now why don't you brief me on what is going on here?"

"We'll take it from the top, detective," Morton said as he opened a notebook. "At 8:34 this evening we received a call from one Paul Jansen.

He lives about half a mile north. He reported hearing a loud noise between 8:10 and 8:15. He went outside and didn't see anything. Decided to run over here because he knew the Ripleys had moved a few weeks ago and the place was vacant. He drove into the driveway, parked, walked through the gate and back toward the barn. Saw the damage to the barn doors and smelled something burning. He called us immediately on his cell phone, said the barn looked like something had exploded in there. He knew Ripley had used dynamite to remove stumps and probably had some left over. Figured that it must have blown up. He couldn't figure out why it blew, just that it might have.

As we mobilized, we notified Chief Bowen we had a possible explosion out here and he notified his team. I assume that's when you were called. We arrived on scene at 8:40. These two state troopers were both relatively close by and they showed up about two minutes after we did." He looked at his notes again, "Yeah, they arrived at 8:42 and offered to lend a hand. Crowd control was not an issue, but the scene is, well, Hell, there was an explosion. The inside of the barn is a mess. Our guys may have disturbed some evidence in our initial site check, we put down a few small fires and started looking for victims and checking out the structure. The power is out in the barn so we have a few portable lights rigged inside and out. We're setting up two overhead lights now so we can illuminate the scene. Ned, you want to add anything?"

Chief Bowen stepped in closer, "We called in the auxiliary forces and they're showing up one at a time. They'll take over the perimeter, maintain crowd and traffic control and relieve the troopers of those duties. The two fire vehicles and an ambulance are parked in front of the barn area. We found four victims so far and they are all dead. The bodies are mostly intact, but burned and messy, so we're looking for any bits and pieces that may have been blown off. The four victims were chained to the posts in the center bay. Stan thinks that COD was the blast wave, but we'll get that confirmed from the ME after he has checked them out. We also notified the hospital to standby for at least four victims."

"Thanks, Chief, did you relay the condition of the vics, and what about press, have they gotten wind of this yet?"

"Well, we don't know if we have found all the victims yet and the paramedics need to make that determination. As for the press, hell, they'll be here soon enough. I should get a statement ready. I'm not going to release any names until we have positive IDs on all four victims and we've notified their next of kin."

Ian looked at the barn and said, "Four victims?"

Chief Bowen stepped closer to the barn, "Yeah, four so far."

The fire was out, but the smell of burnt wood, oil and flesh hung in the air. The Fire Chief approached Ian and Bowen, "Ned, you and your guys can have access to the site, but we'll be picking up bits and pieces through tomorrow. The frame of this barn is slightly damaged, but appears stable. I recommend nobody tries to move any heavy objects inside. They could probably rebuild this thing using the same framing. Amazing."

Ian stepped toward the Fire Chief, "Chief, what do you think happened here?"

Morton took a few steps away from the barn, turned, removed his helmet and said, "I'm not sure yet, but somebody was really pissed off at these four guys."

"Four, you're sure there were only four of them?" repeated Ian.

"Yeah, all chained to posts in the middle of the barn, sitting on a bale of hay. Detonation was in the center of the four. The blast tore them up some. We've found a few pieces of the bomb. My guess is dynamite. Folks out here used it to remove tree stumps. The fella that called it in, Jansen, he guessed it was old dynamite. My guys are scratching around for anything we can find. So far, the few bits of red paper and sawdust would be consistent with dynamite. We also found a few pieces of a wooden box scattered around in there," said Chief Morton.

"Maybe by tomorrow we'll have something to reconstruct. Come daylight we'll be able to see better outside, if it doesn't rain," said Ian.

"Thanks," said Stan, "Where are you from?"

"Pittsburgh," Ian returned, "Born and raised in Monroeville, just north of the city."

"You ever deal with bombs, or any other explosives?"

"Pittsburgh PD, ten years. You see a lot of different stuff in a big city and we had our share of people blowing things up. I took a few classes on explosives. Personally, I've only encountered one situation with a pipe bomber."

"Did you get close to the pipes?"

"Yeah, a little too close. We put the pipes in a container one at a time and as the bomb tech wheeled them out to the detonation box, the damn thing went off. The blast threw our man back a few feet and he caught a couple of metal pieces. One grazed his right arm and one hit him in his left thigh. He was lucky, everything healed and he got to wake up the next morning, still alive. I escorted him to the blast box. I carried a heavy shield, but the blast still shook me."

Chief Morton shook his head, "I think we are beyond the explosive stage here. No live devices, no booby traps, just bits and pieces."

Ned and Ian both started to ask at the same time, "Is it safe to go in?"

Stan nodded, "The barn weathered the blast pretty well, some siding was blown out but the structural part seems intact. The four victims were each 5 to 6 feet from the blast, facing it. They were chained to the posts and sitting on bales of hay. The pressure wave at 6 feet was not only enough to kill them, but do some significant physical damage as well. There are parts of them scattered around the barn."

Ian looked at Chief Morton, "Dynamite, you figure it was dynamite?"

"Right now that's the working assumption. All we have to go on are pieces of red paper, sawdust and bits of a wooden box."

"How much dynamite would it take to do this kind of damage?"

"Good question," mused Stan, "That's beyond my level of expertise. We need an explosives tech to do a more detailed analysis. I think the dynamite was old and may have leaked most of the nitro, so maybe one, two or more sticks. Each one could have been a full 8 inch stick or shorter, I really don't know."

Ian looked at Ned, "You ready to go inside?"

Stan said, "Be careful and stay alert, it's a mess in there. I mean, you are gonna' see four bloody things that were human beings a few hours ago. Now, well, just be prepared for the sight."

"Thanks Stan," said Ned, "Ian, I'm right behind you."

Stan was right. In each of the four corners of the central bay a blood soaked mass was unrecognizable as a human being. The point of detonation appeared to be positioned in the middle of the bay. Ian wondered if the four victims had seen the dynamite. Did they know what was happening? Did they know why it was happening? He looked at Ned, "We may need help on this one, Chief."

Ned looked around and back at Ian, "Yeah, I don't even know where to begin. Let's get outta' here and talk about this." He turned and began to walk out of the barn.

Ian continued to scan the floor, "Hey chief, we should get a search warrant to enter the house and all the other buildings on the site. I assume we don't need one for the barn." He saw a piece of a wooden box in a corner, walked over and photographed it from several angles. Then he went back to the center and photographed the point of detonation and each of the victims from that vantage point. As he was photographing some blood and bits of flesh on the wall behind one of the victims, he felt his stomach clench and his gorge rise. "Time out," he muttered and carefully made his way outside again.

The tent had been erected and was set up as a field office for the investigative team. Ned and Stan were standing nearby with bottles of water. Ian approached and Bill Atkins immediately handed him a chilled bottle.

"Need something to get the taste out of your mouth, Ian?" asked Bill.

"Thanks, Bill," he said. "What do you make of all this?"

Bill pulled his coat a little closer and hugged himself protectively. "I think it's Dave Branch in there. His house is just across the road and the Ripleys moved out a few weeks ago. He normally would be out here trying to see what was going on but nobody has seen him."

Ian put his hand on Bill's shoulder and guided him away from other ears. "Bill, I have no idea who's in there, and we don't want to speculate. Dave could have gone into town, or to a movie or over the hill and through the woods to granny's house. He might still show up"

Bill was a little pale and pointed toward the garage near the house, "That's Dave's truck, the blue one and I don't see him walkin' around."

"The blue one is Dave's?"

"Yeah,"

"Bill, run the plates on the other three vehicles over there. I guess I assumed they belonged to the guys working this scene. And Bill, let's keep everything quiet until we know what's going on."

"Okay," he said and made his way back to his cruiser.

Ian started to walk toward the four vehicles parked in front of the garage. He stopped and looked at the ground. It was dry dirt, like a baseball infield. Tracks were everywhere, tire marks and footprints.

Ned approached Ian, "Hey, are you okay?"

"Chief, yeah, I'm fine. Look at the tracks on the ground. Have the crime scene techs been over here yet?"

"I have no idea. Whose cars are these?"

"Yeah, we need to know who parked those cars. The fire department came in their trucks, the troopers blocked the entrance almost immediately, your car and mine are out on the front lawn. Bill Atkins said that the Ripleys moved out a few weeks ago, so, who owns these vehicles?"

"Let's get this area taped off and call in the plates."

Ian was making notes in his book and said, "Bill is running the plates now, should have something in a minute or two."

Ned gave Ian a thumbs up and started toward his car, "I'll get the tape."

Bill returned in a few minutes with Chief Bowen. Both men had a roll of yellow crime scene tape. Bill flipped open his note pad, "Ian, the cars are registered to David Edward Branch, Myra Jean Nestor, Robert Foster Dorsey and Wilkins Security Systems." He flipped the notebook closed, put it in his pocket and looked at Ian.

Ian looked up at the stars, thinking about the reunion committee and their conviction that these same four men were responsible for Darryl's death. He felt slightly sick and a chill ran up his spine. He looked back at Bill, "Okay, that's our lead, now let's follow through. Bill, you said Dave Branch lives across the road."

Bill started to move, "I'll go bang on his door, be right back."

Ian scratched his head and started to look at the ground again. "I hope I'm wrong." He was looking at the ground and photographing assorted tire marks and footprints when Bill came back from Dave Branch's house.

"Nobody is home," said Bill.

Ian looked up, glanced across the road, then back at the markings in the dirt. "Bill, let's keep this whole area behind the house clear until morning. These tire and footprints are important."

Bill walked to the fence line and ran a yellow tape to the corner of the house, sectioning off the four cars parked near the garage and the dirt area in front of the garages.

Ned, Bill and Ian all realized immediately the significance of those four names. "Whoa, we gotta keep this quiet until we know more," said Ian. "Bill, we need to secure the site overnight, daylight will be here in a few hours and we need to be back out here to examine the ground thoroughly."

"Not a problem," said Bill, "We have about twelve auxiliary officers here now. They will maintain the perimeter and, if it's okay with the chief, I will stay on site till you guys get back in the morning. I was going to be on traffic overnight anyway."

"You got it, Bill," said Ned Bowen. "Ian, I'm gonna' grab a few hours of shuteye and be back here in the morning with my Sherlock gear. I expect the Feds will show up then and take over the site. Access to the FBI lab will be a huge advantage. What our lab lacks, their lab can provide. As soon as the sun makes an appearance, so should we."

"I'll be here," said Ian, "But I ain't wearing a funny hat."

*　　*　　*

Jeff arrived at the hospital and met Dr. Franklin Markham in his office. "Good evening, Frank, what's all the commotion about?"

Dr. Markham looked tired, he was in his seventies, and this job was making him feel even older. Retirement was on the forefront of his mind lately and this case was so horrific, it might be the last straw, the one that would push him to sail off into the sunset and spend the rest of whatever time he had left fishing or reading. Jeff, on the other hand, was young and had a lot of years ahead of him. The medical examiner's job was his, if he wanted it. "Jeff, come on in. We have a dandy here. Apparently, three or four victims were in an explosion about 6 miles south of here. According to the brief call from the site, they are all dead. Officers at the scene are still looking around for others, and the med techs are staying until they are sure everybody has been accounted for. I'd like you to take this one, it's going to be rough and I'm too damn tired to take it on."

"Sure, Frank," replied Jeff, "Tell me more. You said there were three, maybe four, victims?"

"Yeah, three or four at least, and the team is checking the site to see if there are any more."

"The state medical examiner in Manassas will have the lead if he wants it, or he might let us handle it here. The local police will be here tonight and back out at the site in the morning, gathering all the information they can get. They have a new detective from Pittsburgh, accustomed to rougher scenes than we usually see out here in the sticks."

"I met a new detective at the reunion this evening. His name is McLarry, nice guy. I look forward to working with him."

"You may want to go out there and have a look around either now or in the morning."

"If there's a chance that the team will be bringing the victims in here in the next hour, I'd be better off staying here now. Then, I'll hit the site in the morning, in the light of day."

"Okay, Jeff. You know your way around the morgue; it's at your disposal for the duration of this case. Can you bounce back and forth between the ER and here?"

"I'll make it work, Frank. Right now I want to contact the team and see where they are."

Back at the Ripleys' barn, the four bodies were tagged and bagged and all unidentifiable bits were photographed, mapped and collected for future identification. Ian had more yellow tape strung around the immediate area and positioned the auxiliary force around to keep the curious clear and out of the area. The hospital team loaded their van and Ian escorted them back to the hospital.

* * *

CHAPTER TWENTY
The investigation begins...

The Medical Examiner's van arrived back at the hospital just after 10 pm, and the victims were taken directly to the morgue. Jeff was there talking to Sandy as the gurneys were wheeled in. Ian parked in a space reserved for police and followed the gurneys into the morgue. "Jeff, will you be performing these autopsies?"

"Wish I was, Ian, but state law mandates any death from violent causes or homicide, be investigated by the OCME. I'm going to fill out a bunch of paperwork, try to identify the victims, make a preliminary investigation into the cause of death and then probably send them to Manassas for autopsy at the state facility. I would like to be there to assist if I can, but that will be determined later."

Ian thought for a minute, "So what can I do to help you out?"

"Do we have names yet?"

"Yeah," said Ian, "And that brings up a little problem."

Sandy had gone back to the ER and Ian looked around for other people that could overhear. "Jeff, these four men have been the prime focus of my investigation into a nineteen year old case."

"Yeah, Sandy has told me."

Ian put his hand up, "Let's not talk specifics right now. I'm going to record every conversation with people that could be suspects and that includes the entire reunion committee, and I don't want to have any questionable procedures."

"Ian, I don't envy your position. I do understand where you're coming from and I will cooperate in any way necessary. Do you want to set up interviews with us all together or individually?"

"Jeff, I appreciate that, but I'm not sure you will be included in that grouping."

"You should know that Sandy and I are very close and we have had a number of conversations where she has opened up."

"Again, I hear you, Jeff. Let's keep it all above board. When could you come into the station and give a deposition?"

"With or without Sandy?"

"I have to interview you separately, but the same day is okay. Listen, I know this is uncomfortable, but," he hesitated.

"Ian, don't apologize, you do what you have to do. I've seen this kind of situation on television and in the movies, and I have seen murder victims before. Not to worry, I think we're all professionals and we all understand what to expect."

"Thanks, Jeff," Ian walked over to one of the gurneys, "Do you have name tags?"

Jeff opened a drawer, pulled out a few tags with strings attached, picked up a pen and said, "I do now."

Jeff opened the first body bag and Ian noted the smaller plastic bag inside containing a wallet, watch, ring, necklace and a pair of glasses. "This one is tentatively identified as Branch, David Edward."

Jeff wrote the name on a tag and placed it on top of the bag. "We will clean these guys up before we put the tag on the victims' big toe." Jeff walked to the second bag, opened it and Ian said, "Wilkins, Carl James," Ian turned around and looked at the third bag as Jeff filled out the toe tag. Jeff opened the third bag and Ian said, "Nestor, Ronald Foster." Again Jeff made notes and they walked over to the last bag, Jeff opened it and Ian said, "Dorsey, Robert Allen."

Jeff and Ian looked at each other and shook their heads. This one was going to get messy.

*　　*　　*

Early Sunday morning Ian drove back to the Ripley Farm. The site was still secured by Bill Aikens and the team of auxiliary officers. He parked in front of the house again and walked to the tent being used as a field office. Ned Bowen and two other men he didn't know were in the tent.

"Ian, I'd like you to meet Paul Danvers and Dan Harshaw, FBI special agents assigned to this case," said Chief Bowen.

Ian extended his hand and greeted both men. "My pleasure, gentlemen."

Dan Harshaw looked at Ian and said, "I know a cop in D.C. named McLarry, any relation?"

Ian nodded, "Martin McLarry, Yeah, we're cousins."

"You have other cousins in Cleveland too?" asked Harshaw.

"A few," replied Ian, "I have a big family."

"How about a crusty old Marine at Quantico."

Ian grinned, "You mean Lucas, another cousin."

"I know him, he's a hand-to-hand combat instructor," he paused. "Oh yeah, I'll never forget him."

Paul interrupted, "Let's get back to this case, you two can catch up later if you want, but right now we're focusing on this crime scene."

Ian did not appreciate Danver's attitude and puffed up to his full height, "I shot film here last night, but thought it better to continue in the daylight. I also picked up a few bits and pieces and bagged them, they are in storage at the station. I started a log, listed everybody I could identify who has been on site, including civilians, fire and police, both local and state. We have a very rudimentary timeline starting about 8:00 pm last night. Your arrival on site will be noted. I noted a number of tire tracks and footprints near the garage and the vehicles parked there, we'll be photographing those today."

Danvers looked at Ian, "The state boys were here? Who was first on the scene?"

Ned cleared his throat, "We were, Bill Aikens was patrolling out this way when the call came. He turned around and arrived here in a matter of a few minutes. The State guys arrived a few ticks later and the rest of our team came after that. This is our scene."

Harshaw walked after Ian as he turned and headed toward the vehicles and the garage. "McLarry, look, Paul may be a little rigid, but he's a good man. We want to cooperate, not alienate."

Ian stopped and looked at Harshaw, "You guys can be as hard-ass as you like, I know we have a job to do and we're in this thing together. Right now I want to finish what I started last night and get you two back to your cozy little offices in Quantico. I'll keep you in the loop, but don't expect me to bow and scrape when you pass by, or run to get your coffee. Are we clear?"

"I think we are, Detective."

Ian continued to the taped off area and scanned the numerous tracks and footprints. He noticed a track that appeared to be on top of the others and followed it to an apparent parking place. As he was looking, Harshaw spoke, "What do we have?"

"Tire tracks that look to be set down over the others. The vehicle apparently was parked here behind the house and made a circular turn, crossing the others tracks as they left." He pointed at the marks in the dirt as they turned toward the fence and the driveway leading out. He set down numbers for each shot and placed a metal carpenters square next to and across the tire tracks, photographing as he talked, getting several angles on each of the four tracks as they made the turn.

Harshaw watched as Ian took pictures and spoke into a recorder with each shot. Ian walked back to where he thought the unknown vehicle had been parked. He looked closely at the ground and smiled when he found a few footprints. Ian laid the carpenter's square on the ground and shot a set of thirteen shots capturing five good impressions.

Harshaw said, "You've done this before?"

"Yeah, a few times," replied Ian.

"Here in Vaneksburg?" asked Harshaw.

"No, I've only been here a few months. I did ten years as a street cop in Pittsburgh. Saw a lot of things we don't normally get here." He took a measuring tape off his belt and stretched it across the tire track, then photographed the tape from above each impression. "I need to get some plaster impressions of these tire treads and the footprints," he muttered.

Harshaw said, "I've got some casting stuff in my car, I'll get it," and he hurried back toward the front of the house. He returned a few minutes later with a tool box and a pail. "We'll need some water," he said as he turned toward the house and located a hose bibb near the door. "Have we got warrants to enter the house yet?"

"We got permission from the realtor to enter any structure. I think he is coming out here today to give us keys for the house and garage. He should be here anytime now."

Harshaw filled a gallon jug with water and came back to the prints Ian wanted to cast. "I think these are the best of the bunch," he said, pointing at two prints. "The others are too scuffed to be any good. These look like a size 10 or 11 man's shoe, could be one of the victims or could be our perp."

Harshaw nodded, "These look good," he replied as he sprayed the prints with polyurethane and started to open the plaster frame. Ian took a few extra pictures of the impressions and they cast the two footprints individually.

"Okay," said Ian, "Let's get those tire treads." The two men worked together and looked for other impressions in the dirt. They found a few footprints coming from each of the vehicles and then, surprisingly, several prints indicating two people facing each other. Ian again placed his carpenter's square on the ground and photographed the scene from four directions at different angles. "How much plaster do you have?"

"Enough to get these," replied Harshaw.

"I have one set of size 10 or 11 and another set a lot smaller," puzzled Ian. "I wonder."

Harshaw looked closer at the small prints, "A woman perhaps, or a kid."

"We can check the tread patterns and see where that leads us." murmured Ian, loud enough for Harshaw to hear.

Harshaw stood up, "Not a problem. We have a database that covers shoe prints. Should be a quick read. I'll be able to tell you the manufacturer, the size and whether it's a man's or a woman's shoe." Harshaw wiped his hands on a damp towel, "If we can find a few prints in a row, measure the stride, we might be able to estimate the height of the wearer."

"Every little bit helps," said Ian.

"I know, detective, and we're here to help."

*　　*　　*

"Ian, the realtor is almost here. Do you want to search the house or get started on the barn?" asked Ned.

"I'll take the barn," Ian replied and walked in that direction, looking at the ground.

Unfortunately, the footprints near the barn were trampled by the fire fighters and the tire tracks from before the incident were pretty much wiped out by emergency vehicles and first responders. Ian began by photographing a full picture of the barn from a distance. He circled the barn shooting from every side and several different angles. He got close-ups of the damage to the doors and the siding. Once inside the barn, he walked the perimeter, shooting toward the center. As was the case outside, footprints from before the explosion were wiped out by the blast wave and subsequent activity.

An hour into his investigation of the barn, Ian decided to take a break. He walked out to the tent and found a folding chair, sat down and opened a bottle of water. Ned entered the tent and said, "The realtor just left. We went into the house and nothing seems to be disturbed. Checked the garage and found that someone had used the workbench to assemble and package the bomb. I lifted a few prints and found some short hair samples. Those could be from either our unsub or the previous occupant of the house. What did you find in the barn?"

Ian emptied a brown paper shopping bag full of small plastic evidence bags onto a table in the middle of the tent. Each bag was numbered, labeled and sealed. "Well, Chief, I found some fragments of a wooden box, bits and pieces of an alarm clock, a 9 volt battery, some wire, tape, newspaper and what appears to be a red paper commonly used in dynamite manufacture. Then there is this," he said as he held up another small plastic bag containing a bullet, "This is one of two I found. I also found three shell casings, could be more out there, but I think we should look for gunshot wounds in the victims."

Chief Bowen added, "Jansen, the neighbor, said Ripley used dynamite to remove stumps, and had a few sticks left over and offered them to him. Jansen said they were in a wooden box in the barn with some blasting caps. He guessed there may have been 3, 4 or 5 sticks. He's pretty sure they were 8 inch lengths. So that matches what we found."

Ian was looking at his notes and said, "I'd like to talk to Jansen, is he here?"

"I'll have someone get him, he just lives next door," said Chief Bowen.

"Next door is a good half mile away. Not much between here and there except those trees. He may have seen or heard something. I'll go to him." Ian glanced back at the barn, "How many sticks would do this much damage?" He thought for a minute, "Size, type, age, all factors in dynamite blast wave analysis. Chief, could we get the Feds to work that end and we handle the rest, it is our case, right, on our turf?"

As Ian was asking, Danvers came into the tent. "What do we have thus far?"

Ian looked at Danvers and said, "I have to list all this stuff in a recovery log, then I intend to go back into the barn and continue my search. After I finish cataloguing what I find we can discuss what has been collected."

"Look, McLarry, maybe we got off to a bad start."

Ian cut him off, "Yeah, maybe, but I don't have time to crawl around behind you, so if you plan to help, then help. If you plan to get in the way, I'll move you aside. Right now I could use an opinion on how much force the blast generated. How much dynamite would be required to generate that force and was the dynamite Ripley left in the barn sufficient to do the deed? We don't know yet how old the dynamite was, we don't know exactly how many sticks there were. You guys are supposed to know about that kind of stuff. So if you want to help, chew on that." He picked up his bottle of water, drank what remained and tossed the empty into a trash barrel. "Now if you'll excuse me," he opened a laptop computer and began cataloguing the evidence on the table.

Danvers looked at Harshaw and said, "Let's find out where and when Ripley got that dynamite. He moved south, but we should have a number for him. I gotta call Quantico," and he walked out of the tent.

Harshaw turned and followed Danvers. Ned leaned in close to Ian, "You plan on killing these two Fibbies or lettin' 'em do their job?"

"That big one pissed me off, Chief. This case looks like it's going to involve some people I've come to know and like. I'm going to be stepping on a lot of toes and I don't want a sloppy investigation to put them in jeopardy. I can work with just about anybody, but I will not tolerate some arrogant SOB trying to push us around. I ran into that sort of thing up north and it never helped an investigation."

"Okay, Ian, let's finish this job before the waters get too muddy."

"The FBI will soon figure out this is a straight forward revenge killing and not their cup of tea. I think they will soon move on to other cases."

"What do you have against the Feds?"

"Not a thing, it's just Danvers rubbed me the wrong way right off the bat. You don't stand your ground, stake your claim, these guys will walk all over you. Seen it happen a lot. But I promise to play nice. Hell, Chief, I got cousins and friends in the Bureau," said Ian.

Danvers walked back into the tent, "Just talked to Ripley, who says there were 3 eight inch sticks and probably three blasting caps. The stuff was almost two years old and might have leaked some nitro, so the blast force may have been reduced. He got it from a removal outfit that was going out of business and they didn't watch the inventory very closely. He probably shorted a couple of four stick loads and kept the odd ones in that box in the barn."

Ian heard him and said, "Okay, if we assume there were 3 eight inch sticks, could they do this much damage or would the un-sub have added to the load?"

Danvers said, "Okay, we will have to diagram the site here."

Ian interrupted, "Here are my diagrams and notes from yesterday," and handed Danvers a thin three ring binder with several pages of sketches and notes. "The photographs have all been loaded into our database, so they can be accessed here in the station or on your system back at Quantico."

"Not bad, McLarry," said Danvers, "Not bad."

*   *   *

Later that afternoon, Ian was preparing to leave the site when Bill Aikens came into the tent. "Hey, Ian, I'm here to secure the site until morning."

"Bill, I'm sorry you are stuck out here in the middle of nowhere."

"No problem, I would rather be here than on the highway looking for people speeding through our little chunk of heaven. Most of them are from the DC area, very few are from around here. By the way, a fella stopped out front a few minutes ago, asked what was happening and wanted to know if the farm was still on the market."

Ian shook his head, "Police cars, emergency vehicles, obviously something major is going on and this character wants a tour."

Bill said, "He's not from around here. Said he stopped by the other day, Thursday, and some lady said she was going to sign the purchase papers that day."

"A lady, did he describe her? Or her car?"

"I gotcha covered, Ian. I didn't ask about the car, but you can," said Bill, "He's just outside the gate, waiting for you."

Ian stood and headed toward the gate, turned and said, "Hey, Bill speaking of folks from around here, do you know Jansen, the neighbor one property north?"

"Paul, hell, yeah. A good friend. What's up?"

"He called this thing in, maybe he saw something else we don't know about. I want to drive over there and talk to him. You wanna come with me?"

"Sure, Ian." Bill took out his cell phone and entered a number, "Paul, are you home?" He looked at Ian and smiled, "Put on the coffee, son, I am bringing a detective with me, and we are gonna' grill you."

"Grill?" said Ian.

"He's a good friend and makes decent coffee."

Ian turned toward the gate again, "First let's talk to our newest friend here at the gate."

Bill called a man over, "Come on in for a minute. Can we ask you a few questions?"

"Sure, officer, what kinda' questions?"

Ian opened his notebook, "Real easy questions. First, what is your name?"

"Ross, Ross Hendricks."

"Okay Ross, my name is Detective Ian McLarry, Officer Aikens and I are with the Vaneksburg Police Department. There was an incident here yesterday and we're trying to figure out what happened."

"Okay," said Hendricks, "How can I help you?"

"You told the officer that you stopped here the other day. Is that correct?"

Hendricks shuffled a little and said, "Yeah, it was Thursday, and I was looking around for places to buy. I was on my way to a possible property a little south of here when I saw the sign and a car in the driveway."

Ian made notes and looked up at Ross, "The person you saw, was it a man or woman?"

"A woman, but I didn't get a good look at her, she was way over there," Ross pointed at the gate, "And I was down by the road. Sun was bright and she was mostly in shadow."

"So you couldn't pick her out of a line-up?"

"No, but she was not tall, kinda' thin. Couldn't tell what color her hair or eyes were, but it was definitely a woman."

"What did you talk to her about?"

"Don't remember exactly, but she told me it was 285 acres total. She said the house was in good shape, about thirty years old with a new kitchen."

"Is that everything?"

"Pretty much, oh, and she said there were two other properties a few miles down the road," said Ross, pointing south.

"That's it?"

Ross looked around as he thought and said, "She said something about corporate folks anxious to get this place planted and how she was going to sign the papers that morning."

"Corporate," said Ian, "she knew a number of details about this place."

"I thought she was the real estate agent at first, or maybe had been dealing with one," said Ross, "Anyway, she told me about two other properties down the road and that's where I was headed when I saw all the commotion here. Maybe it's cold, but I thought maybe her deal fell through and this place might be available again."

Ian looked at Ross and said, "I can't address the sale of this property. You'll have to deal with the realtor on that, but this is now a crime scene and nobody is getting their fingers in this dirt until we have completed the investigation and we have released it. Could take weeks - or months."

Ross looked around the property, then back at Ian, "I'll just talk to the realtor. The location of this place is much better for my kids. I can wait until you guys are done." He turned and walked over to the realtor's sign, wrote down the phone number, noted the address, then turned back towards Ian and Bill, "The officer has my name and contact info, are we done here?"

Ian looked at Ross, "Not quite, did you see the car she was driving?"

Ross cocked his head, looked toward the gate and said, "Yeah, it was one of those little compacts, a Toyota or something. Silver, four doors, that's all I remember. Couldn't see the plates, not even the colors, coulda' been pink and green or blue and white, I really don't know."

"Okay," said Ian, "We're done for now. I may call you with more questions."

"Anytime, detective. Hopefully when you come see me again, it will be here," said Ross as he gestured toward the red brick ranch and turned toward his pick-up.

Ian looked at Bill, "Takes all kinds." He closed his notebook, looked north toward Jansen's house and said, "Let's move."

They drove in separate cars so Ian could continue back to the station when they were done. Bill arrived first and stood on Paul's front porch while Ian parked. "Ian, this is Paul Jansen."

They shook hands and Paul said, "Come on in, I just brewed a pot of coffee."

The three men sat in Jansen's kitchen and Ian began, "Paul, you called the event next door into the station, and I wonder if there is anything else you may have noticed that might help us figure this thing out."

"Nope, nothing comes to mind. I was inside when I heard the noise. It sounded like a kind of boom and a little shudder. I came out on my deck and saw a little cloud lit up by the moon, kinda' hangin' over Ripley's barn. I went on over and seen the doors messed up, smelled somethin' burnin' and called 911. Never went in the barn, just called it in and waited out here. Came home after the fire trucks and cops arrived, you guys didn't need me in your way."

"Did you notice anything unusual over there in the last several days?"

"Nope, every coupla days somebody slows down and looks at the 'For Sale' out front , but that's it."

"Anybody ever get out and take a closer look?"

"As a matter of fact, yeah. I saw a fella in a pick-up stop and walk up toward the house last week, Wednesday or Thursday, but he came back out a few seconds later. Got in his truck and keep on going."

"Was he alone?"

"Coulda' been someone else in the truck, too far off to be sure. He turned around when he was leavin and looked to be talkin' to someone back up by the house. Couldn't see who it might have been, trees in the way."

Ian made a few notes, "Wednesday or Thursday?"

Jansen thought for a second, "Let's see, it was Thursday, I think."

"Okay, that's good information, can you think of anything else?"

"Hmm, Oh yeah, when I came back a little later to head out, a car came out of Ripley's driveway. Don't know if it was just turnin' around or if it had been there a while."

"Did you see the driver?"

"Nope, just noticed the car, 'though I couldn't tell you the make and model. Could have if it was still 1960, but it ain't. It was about the same size as my Chevy Cruze, one a them little cars."

"What else, color, plates, tinted windows, 2 door, 4 door, anything else that you remember."

"Plates, no, if they were out of state I might have remembered but I'm guessing they were Virginia plates, dark blue letters on white. Color, silver or grey, I guess. I don't remember the doors, but most are 4 door so I think that's what I saw, but not sure. Tint, yeah, the windows were dark."

Ian sat up straight and closed his notebook. "This is all good information. If anything else comes to mind, please call me," he said as he handed Paul his card, then turned toward Bill. "Bill, I gotta get back to the station. Give me a call in a few hours and we can bounce a few ideas around." Ian stood, shook Paul's hand and said, "Paul, thanks again."

*   *   *

Sunday evening the patient answered the phone and talked for twenty minutes to a relative. The relative lived in Colorado and was the closest family the patient knew. They hadn't seen each other in several years and were never very close, but they were family. The patient's condition was discussed in general terms and the relative understood time was growing short. That evening they talked about the relative's children, who would both be in college at the same time in a few years. Then the patient said, "I have just revised my will and would like you to have a few of the family things. Also, I won't need my car soon and it's all paid off. So I'm going to put the title and a key in the mail to you. You can drive it or sell it, but it will be yours as soon as you receive this letter."

The relative was thankful for the car and wondered what the family things might be, perhaps photos, or some furniture that had been in the family for some time, maybe some jewelry.

"Thanks, I'm not sure what to say. I will try to carve out some time in the next few weeks to visit."

The patient was pleased the car would be helpful to the relative and did not elaborate on the condition that would soon bring the terms of the will into effect.

*   *   *

CHAPTER TWENTY ONE
Interviews: the doctor and the nurse...

Ian was sitting in Chief Bowen's office at 8:30 am Monday. The two men were having their morning coffee and a bagel, and discussing the upcoming interviews with the Vaneksburg High Reunion Committee. Ned set his mug down on his desk, "It looks like we could have a few hundred suspects from what I hear about those four boys."

"Let's hope this round of interviews will bear some fruit and we won't have to read off the same questions to that many people," replied Ian. "I don't like the thought, but I have to admit, the reunion committee is at the top of the probable list right now: four women and three men. I would really like to clear each one of them, but, well, I just have a feeling some of them are involved."

"You have narrowed it down to seven suspects?"

"Seven possibles for the initial go round, but there is evidence it might be a woman. The reunion committee seems to believe these four victims were guilty of killing Darryl Zamanski, 19 years ago. They've been pretty vocal about their suspicions, so I have to put them at the top of the list. Some of them may have worked together. I need to quiz them all to see where their stories lead me."

"Are you sure you can be objective here, Ian?"

"Chief, I know you are going to be following this case as closely as you can. I expect that. This is my first real investigation with your department and if our situations were reversed, I would stay as close as possible without getting in the way. I'll probably make a few mistakes along the way and I hope you'll be right there to steer me in the right direction."

"Ian, I trust you and don't think I have to lead you through this thing."

"Not lead, Chief, watch, watch, and make sure I am doing my job."

Bowen picked up his glasses, leaned forward and said, "When is your first interview?"

"In about 15 minutes, with the nurse and the doctor."

* * *

Sandy and Jeff arrived at the station just before 9:00 am. Ian met them and asked Sandy to talk to Chief Bowen while he talked to Jeff. "Are we suspects?" she asked as she and Ned went into his office.

Ned smiled and said, "You and I are just talking as two old friends. Ian will handle the interview with you and answer your questions."

In the interview room, Ian told Jeff to pull up a chair, "I am going to ask you a series of questions to establish your whereabouts when the bomb was detonated, where you were during the day leading up to the time of the incident and where you were after. There are also a few basic questions that cover several other points of interest. So are you ready to begin?"

Jeff held out his hands and said "Sure, let's get to it."

Ian placed a small tape recorder on the table, sat across from Jeff, opened his notebook, turned on the recorder and began, "This is Detective Ian McLarry; it is Monday, May 28, 2012 approximately 9:15 am. This conversation relates to the investigation into the deaths of four people, David Edward Branch, Carl James Wilkins, Robert Allen Dorsey and Ronald Foster Nestor." He looked at Jeff and said, "Are you ready to begin?"

Jeff sat up straight and answered, "Yes."

"Please state your name," began Ian.

"Jeffrey Steven Marshall."

Ian had a list of questions prepared and checked off the first answer, adding Jeff's middle name in the margin. "Your occupation?"

"I am an Emergency Room Surgeon at Gradison Road Hospital," he replied.

"Your address and phone numbers?"

Jeff answered and Ian continued, "Where were you on May 26, 2012 at 8:00 pm?"

"I was attending a high school reunion with a friend."

"Can you please identify that friend? "

"Yes, her name is Alexandra Lansing."

Ian checked off another answer, "Were there others present at that reunion?"

Jeff paused, thought and answered, "Yes, approximately 90 people plus the hotel staff."

"Can you name anyone that can verify your presence at the Hotel at 8:00 pm on the day in question?"

"Yes, Barbara Nessman, Mark Lindstrom, Phil and Eileen Kline, Audrey Redding and Ian McLarry."

Ian grinned at the sound of his own name, "What time did you arrive at the Hotel?"

"We arrived at about 4:00 pm."

Ian noted the time of arrival, shifted in his chair and continued, "Where were you earlier that same day, between 8:00 am and 4:00 pm?"

Jeff thought for a second and responded, "I was on duty at the hospital from midnight Friday until noon on Saturday, then I went home, got there about 12:30 plus or minus and took a nap. I set my alarm for 3:00 pm, got up, stood in the shower for a few minutes and dressed for the evening. I got to Sandy's place at about 3:45 and she was ready to go. We got to the Hotel at 4:00, again plus or minus a few minutes."

Ian wrote down the times, then said, "What kind of car do you drive?"

"I have a 2009, BMW 328," Jeff grinned, "I love that buggy."

"What color is it?" asked Ian as he noted the cars' year, make and model.

"Silver."

Ian checked a box on a spreadsheet with his notes, "Do you own a second vehicle?"

"Yes, I have a Harley I don't drive nearly enough."

Ian wrote down the motorcycle information, looked up at Jeff and asked, "What time did you leave the hotel?"

"I received a call from my answering service at approximately 8:45 PM, informing me an emergency required my presence at the Hospital."

"Did you leave at that time?"

"Yes, both Sandy and I left about two minutes later."

"And you went to the Hospital?"

Jeff paused about a second and replied, "Not directly, I dropped Sandy at her apartment on the way, and arrived at the hospital a few minutes before 9:00 pm."

"Are you aware of an incident that occurred at 16735 Lomond Road on Saturday May 26, 2012 at approximately 8:15 pm?"

"Yes, there was an explosion in a barn, and four individuals were in the barn at the time of the explosion."

"How did you become aware of this incident?"

"I was called to the hospital to provide emergency response for that incident. The condition of the four victims had not been officially determined at that time and my presence in the emergency room was necessary in case anyone required treatment."

"Has the condition of the four victims been determined?"

Jeff looked at the floor and replied, "Yes, all four victims are deceased."

"Has a time of death been determined?"

"The liver temperatures taken at the scene and repeated at the hospital indicated that the time of death for all four was the same."

"What time was that?"

"I don't have any notes with me, I believe the time of death for all four was approximately 8:15 pm on May 26, 2012."

Ian noted the times, "Have you determined the cause of death?"

"The Code of Virginia requires any death resulting from violence or homicide be investigated by the OCME, the Office of the Chief Medical Examiner, if they choose. The nearest office is in Manassas, Virginia. The four bodies may be transported to that location in Manassas for autopsy, if the OCME requests. When that office has determined the specific cause of death, the information will be transmitted to the Vaneksburg Police Department."

Ian left the recording equipment on and continued, "Thank you, now I want to ask you about the last several weeks."

"Okay," said Jeff with a deep breath.

"Did you have any conversation with any individual in the last several weeks about any of the four victims of that explosion prior to the incident?"

"Yes, my friend and I discussed these specific four men on several occasions," said Jeff.

Ian checked another box on his spreadsheet, "In what context did you discuss these individuals?"

"A number of people believe these four men to be the perpetrators of a murder that occurred about 19 years ago."

Ian noted the time reference, "Who was the victim of that murder?"

"The victim was Darryl Zamanski," he replied.

"Who is the friend and what was the context of those conversations?"

"My friend is Sandy Lansing and the conversations centered on what we could do to get these four men arrested and put in jail."

"Did any scenarios involve the killing of these four men?"

"No, not seriously."

"Please explain," said Ian.

"My friend Sandy knew the victim, Darryl Zamanski, and felt for years those four men were responsible. Apparently a number of people felt that way. During several conversations, Sandy said, 'Why don't we just shoot the bastards,' but she was just frustrated, it was not as a serious proposal to actually shoot anybody."

"Have you heard others issue similar statements about these four men?"

"Once or twice, but I don't remember who said what."

"Had you ever met any of these men prior to the incident in the barn?"

"Not that I remember. I treat lots of people in the ER at the hospital, and it is possible. I may even have treated one or more of them, but I do not recall."

"Did you have any knowledge of the barn incident prior to its occurrence?"

"No, I did not."

Ian put his hand on the recorder, "Thank you, that ends this interview. I will likely have more questions in the future. The time is 9:35 am."

"Okay, call any time."

Ian said, "Thanks, Jeff." They walked out to the reception area and saw Sandy was still in Ned's office.

*　　*　　*

Ian stepped into Ned Bowen's office, "Sandy, would you come with me, please?"

Sandy followed Ian and Jeff replaced Sandy in Ned Bowen's office. "Pull up a chair," said Ned, "And let's talk."

Ian closed the door to the interview room. "Sandy, I hope you understand this conversation must occur and I have to consider the entire class of 1997 as suspects until I can whittle it down to one person."

Sandy nodded knowingly, "Jeff and I talked about this and we understand, you have to check out everyone as a cop, whoever did this, broke the law, killed those people."

"Let's sit down and run the interview by the book, are you ready?"

"Yeah, let's do it."

Ian turned on his recording device and repeated the same opening statement, "The time is now 9:42 am, please state your name."

Sandy was excited about the upcoming questioning and she replied, "Alexandra Lansing."

"Your occupation?"

"Emergency Room nurse at Gradison Road Hospital."

"Where were you on May 26, 2012 at 8:00 pm?"

"I was at the Vaneksburg High School Reunion, class of 1997, at The Vaneksburg Hotel."

"Were there others present at that reunion?"

"Yeah, about a hundred people."

"Who can verify your presence at the Hotel at 8:00 pm on the day in question?"

"Jeff Marshall, Audrey Redding, Barb Nessman, Mark Lindstrom, Phil and Eileen Kline, and you."

"What time did you arrive at the hotel?"

"Jeff and I got there around 4:00 pm."

Ian wondered about this woman, could she have murdered these four men? He looked at Sandy and asked, "Where were you between 8:00 am and 4:00 pm on Saturday?"

Sandy looked puzzled, "Home. I worked the noon to midnight shift at the hospital on Friday and I went home after and slept until almost 10:30, went to the store to pick up some stuff and headed over to the hotel to give Barb a hand with the prep for that night,"

"How long did you stay at the hotel?"

"I don't know, maybe 2:00. We went to the tavern around noon for lunch, and then back to the Hotel."

"Who is we?"

"Barb, Audrey and me."

"Did you walk over or drive?"

"I drove. Barb was nervous about being away from the preparations for too long and Audrey was looking tired, so I drove."

"What kind of car do you drive?"

"I have a Ford Fusion."

Ian checked another box on his spreadsheet and asked, "What color is it?"

"It's grey."

He made another note, "Do you own a second vehicle?"

Sandy shook her head, "No."

"What time did you leave the hotel?"

"Around 9:00 pm both Jeff and I were 'beeped'. We were needed at the hospital as soon as possible. Jeff dropped me at home first and he went on to the hospital. I changed into some scrubs and drove in, got there before 9:30."

"Are you aware of an incident that occurred at 16735 Lomond Road on Saturday May 26, 2012 at approximately 8:15 pm?"

"Yeah, there was an explosion at the Ripley Farm in the barn and four guys were killed."

"Do you know these four men?"

"I know them, but we weren't friends. We didn't talk or go to the same parties."

"Prior to Saturday night, were these men the topic of conversations in which you were involved?"

"Yes, several times. Actually, more than that. Jeff and I talked about them and Audrey and I had lunch one day last week and we talked about them."

"Sandy, have you ever made a statement that implied you wished to harm any of these men?"

"Undoubtedly. The first time I met you, I said Dave Branch should be dead, something like that. And more than once, thinking about the way Darryl was murdered, I have said we should just shoot them, Dave and his buddies, or run them over with a truck. But that was frustration talking."

Ian made a note and looked at Sandy, "Who is Darryl?"

Sandy looked confused, then noticed Ian pointing at the recorder and she replied, "Darryl Zamanski was a very nice boy we started high school with. He was killed the first month of our freshman year of High School. He was a great kid. A lot of us felt those four men in the barn were the ones who beat him to death."

"Sandy, did you have anything to do with the capture, restraining or killing of any of these four men?"

"No, I did not."

"Are you aware of any individual who may have been involved in the killing of these four men?"

"Seriously, no, I am not, but these four guys got away with murder and a lot of people I know would pin a medal on their killer rather than see them arrested."

"Thanks, Sandy. That concludes this interview. I may have more questions in the future."

"Anytime, Ian."

"It is now 9:58 am," said Ian as he turned off the recorder. Then he walked Sandy back to the reception desk and found Jeff reading a magazine. "Hey, Jeff, where did you put Chief Bowen?"

"He's talking to a couple of FBI guys in his office."

Sandy said. "Is that it for now, Ian? I mean, do you think we are done with the interview?"

"Probably not. As an investigation progresses, questions arise, information is gathered and more questions arise. I'm sure we'll be talking again."

"Who's next?" asked Sandy, eagerly.

Jeff took Sandy's hand, pulled her toward the door and said, "Ian, we're leaving now. Call anytime," as he guided Sandy out of the building.

Ian shook his head, grinned and walked back toward Chief Bowen's office. The two FBI agents were there and Ned waved Ian in.

"Ian, we have a little more background on the dynamite. It seems dynamite can begin to lose its punch over time. If it sits too long and all the conditions are right, the nitro may bleed out. Freezing can also have an effect. Anyway, as a result, Quantico cannot definitively state what force was generated by the explosion. They can give us a range based on average numbers for three 3/4 inch by 8 inch sticks, about five or six years old, and then again assuming four sticks."

Ian made a note in his book and said, "Did we get anything on the restraints, four sets of handcuffs and leg irons?"

All three looked at Ian and shook their heads. "Okay, I have several more interviews lined up and more to come later. Right now I want to get the whole Reunion Committee on record. I'm about to call the realtor for the Ripley Place and Bob Dorsey's office. Maybe someone can tell me the name of this potential buyer. I'll see what I can find out about the restraints too." He looked at the FBI Agents and said, "You guys let me know the results of the dynamite examination, and anything that pops on the tire or shoe prints," he turned and walked out of Ned's office.

*   *   *

CHAPTER TWENTY TWO
Interviews: the teacher...

Ian repeated the same opening statement in each of his interviews that afternoon. Barb Nessman came into the station at 3:15. Monica showed her into the conference room, called Ian and brought Barb a bottle of water.

Ian came into the room, placed the recorder on the table and said, "Hey Barb, how are you today?"

She smiled nervously and said, "Okay, I guess. I just got out of school and came right over."

Ian said, "I appreciate that. You've had a full day already and I only have a few questions for you." He smiled, "Okay, just relax and tell me the truth and everything will be okay. Are you ready to begin?"

"I guess."

Ian turned on the recorder, opened his notebook and looked at Barb, "This is Detective Ian McLarry, the time is 3:22 pm, Monday, May 28, 2012. This interview is being conducted at the Vaneksburg Police Department regarding an incident that occurred on Saturday, May 26, 2012 at 16735 Lomond Road." He looked at Barb, "Please state your name."

"Barbara Nessman."

"What is your occupation?"

"I'm a school teacher at Thomas Jefferson Elementary."

"Where were you on May 26, 2012 at 8:00 pm?"

"I was at the Vaneksburg High School fifteenth year reunion at The Vaneksburg Hotel for the class of 1997."

"Where were you earlier that day, from 8:00 am till 8:00 pm?"

"At 8:00 am, I was having breakfast and looking through the newspaper. Then around 9:00 I went to the dry cleaners and picked up a few things. Around 10:00 or 10:30, I drove over to the hotel to start checking on the preparations. I had lunch with Sandy and Audrey around noon and ran home about 2:00 to get ready for the evening. Mark and I returned at 4:00 PM. We were there for the rest of the evening."

"Were there others present at that reunion?"

"Yes, we had a great turnout, approximately 94 people."

"Can you name any others that can verify your presence at the Hotel at 8:00 pm on the day in question?"

"Yes, if I list the people at our table, that would be Mark Lindstrom, you, Audrey Redding, Phil and Eileen Kline, Sandy Lansing and Jeff Marshall."

"What time did you arrive at the hotel?"

"I was there several times during the day, getting things ready, but Mark and I arrived at about 3:30 for the event."

"Did you drive?"

"No, Mark picked me up."

"What kind of car do you drive?"

"I have a Dodge Caravan."

"What color is it?"

"Red, dark red, almost maroon."

"Do you own or have access to a second vehicle?"

"No, not really. Mark lets me drive his truck sometimes."

Ian looked at Barb with a curious look on his face, "His truck?"

"Yes, I bought several large pieces of furniture and Mark has let me use his pickup to move them."

"What time did you leave the hotel?"

"After 12:00 midnight, we got back to my place around 12:30."

"We?"

Barb sat up straight, "Yes, Mark and I," she said proudly.

Ian smiled, "Are you aware of an incident that occurred at 16735 Lomond Road on Saturday May 26, 2012 at approximately 8:15 pm?"

"Yes, there was an explosion in Mr. Ripley's barn."

"Are you aware of any injuries resulting from that explosion?"

"Yes, I heard that four men were in the barn at the time of the explosion and they are all dead."

"Do you know these four men?"

"Yes, well, more accurately, I believe they are the four bullies we have discussed several times over the last few weeks."

"Please explain that last statement."

"Alright, over the last nineteen years, Darryl Zamanski's killing has been the topic of conversation and speculation in this town. When the reunion committee began holding meetings to plan the event held on Saturday, we frequently finished our meetings with various topics of conversation. Darryl was probably discussed most often. Then, you contacted me and asked if you could meet the committee and have a few minutes with the members to discuss an old murder case, Darryl Zamanski. That's when the discussions became more lively. We thought your investigation might lead to the arrest and conviction of Darryl's killers."

"Okay Barb, do you recall when the first meeting occurred and where?"

"I thought you might ask that," said Barb as she removed a note from her purse and unfolded it, "Wednesday, April 25th we met at the Vaneksburg Tavern." Barb smiled and looked at Ian.

Ian grinned and continued, "Barb, who was present at that meeting?"

Barb opened the paper again and said, "Everyone did not attend all the meetings, and my notes are a little sketchy, but I wrote down Lisa Harkins, Phil Kline, Audrey Redding, Brent Coyle, Sandy Lansing and Mark Lindstrom. Oh, and, of course, Jim Schuster."

"And yourself?"

Barb smiled and said, "Oh yes, and me."

"Barb, the four men you mentioned, please tell me their names."

Barb's face darkened as she cleared her throat and said evenly, "Dave Branch, Carl Wilkins, Ron Nestor and Bob Dorsey."

"You believe those four men to be the ones who killed Darryl Zamanski nineteen years ago?"

"Yes, I do."

"And you believe those four men were in the barn when it exploded?"

"Yes, I do."

"Barb, have you ever made a statement that implied you wished to harm any of these men?"

"Yes. Frequently."

"Did you have anything to do with the capture, restraining or killing of any of these four men?"

"No, I did not."

"Do you have any knowledge of any individual who did participate in any way in the killing of these four men?"

"No, I do not."

Ian closed his notebook and paused, "Barb, could I get a list of the attendees at the reunion?"

"Sure, would you like a list of the entire class?"

"I already have that, but a list of attendees would be very helpful."

"I'll fax it to you this afternoon when I get home. Oh, by the way, I brought you a few photos from the reunion," said Barb as she opened her purse and took out an envelope. "I'm not the best photographer, but you might enjoy these." She handed him the envelope.

Ian smiled, "Thanks Barb, that concludes this interview, but we may have more questions for you in the future. It is now 3:45 pm." He turned off the recorder and leaned back in his chair, "Are you alright, Barb?"

"I'm okay, it's just, just that, well, we talked about getting those four guys and now, somebody has killed them and I guess we are all suspects, the whole committee."

"Look, Barb, I have to consider a lot of possibilities," he said, opening the envelope. The pictures were primarily of him and Audrey and a few other people at the table. He flipped through the photos and looked at Barb, "You should also keep in mind the possibilities are nearly endless. It may be one of you folks on the committee, but it could also be someone we have not identified yet. The point is, I will dig into this mess and include people I think could be responsible and exclude people not involved. So, sure, you are a suspect and I have your statement you were not involved. That's a start. Let me do my job and," he smiled, "If you did it, I'll get ya. Just as sure as if you didn't, I'll clear you. You are the only one who knows for sure if you were involved, and soon I will know."

She relaxed, smiled and said, "Thanks Ian, so you're not going to give me the third degree, or whatever the old movies used to call it?"

"Nope, no water-boarding, no rubber hoses, no good cop - bad cop interrogation. We'll talk again soon and I'll know a little more. Soon I'll know enough to put some pieces together. Whoever the bad guy is, I'll get him, don't worry."

*   *   *

CHAPTER TWENTY THREE
Interviews: the restaurateur ...

Ian made several phone calls and scheduled three interviews for later that afternoon. Jim Schuster would be first at 4:00 pm, followed by Mark Lindstrom at 4:30 and Lisa Harkins at 5:00. He also arranged for Phil Kline and Brent Coyle to come in that evening. Audrey Redding had returned to Fairfax, so Ian called her at home and left a message.

Jim Schuster walked across the town square from the tavern and arrived at exactly 4:00 in the afternoon. "I'm here to see Detective McLarry," he said to Cindy.

"Sure, Jim, I'll give him a call and let him know you're here." She rang Ian and said, "Detective, Jim Schuster is here to see you. Shall I put him in the conference room?" She hung up and said to Jim, "He will be right out, would you like some coffee?"

"That would be nice," responded Jim.

Monica walked in the front door and Cindy said, "Perfect timing," as she stepped out from the reception desk and led Jim to the small conference room, "Cream and sugar?"

"Oh, thanks, I'll take it straight up," said Jim as he took a chair and sat down.

Cindy was walking out as Ian came into the room, "Coffee, Detective?"

"Thanks, Cindy, sure," he sat across from Jim at the table. "Jim, thanks for coming in. This is going to be a routine interview. I have to talk to everyone who may be able to shed a little light on this investigation."

"I understand, Ian, I guess the whole committee is on your list and probably a bunch more."

Cindy returned with two cups of coffee and placed them on the table. She turned and closed the door behind her.

Ian placed the tape recorder on the table and said, "Are you ready, Jim?"

"Ready as I'll ever be, Ian."

Ian turned on the recorder and began, "This is Detective Ian McLarry; it is Monday, May 28, 2012 approximately 4:15 pm. This interview relates to an investigation into the deaths of four people, David Edward Branch, Carl James Wilkins, Robert Allen Dorsey and Ronald Foster Nestor." He looked at Jim and said, "Are you ready to begin?"

Jim sat up and answered, "Yes."

"Please state your name," began Ian.

"James Matthew Schuster."

"Your occupation?"

"I am the owner and operator of the Vaneksburg Tavern."

"Where were you on May 26, 2012 at 8:00 pm?"

"I was at my fifteenth high school reunion."

"Were you there with anybody?"

"Yes, my wife, Megan."

"Were there others present at that reunion?"

"Yes, but I don't know how many, I guess around 100."

"Can you name others that can verify your presence at the Hotel at 8:00 pm on the day in question?"

"Sure, I was at a table with Brent and Carol Coyle, Lisa Harkins, Terry Bascone and Bob and Linda Maddox."

"What time did you arrive at the Hotel?"

"We arrived about 4:15 that afternoon."

"What kind of car do you drive?"

"It's a Caravan, a mini-van."

"What color is it?"

"It's blue, light blue and faded."

"Do you own a second vehicle?"

"My wife uses the Explorer."

"What time did you leave the hotel?"

"We were there until about 10:30 pm when we heard about the bomb at Ripley's. The fun seemed to die out when the news filtered through the crowd."

"Did you leave at that time, 10:30?"

"Pretty close, we talked for a bit, said goodnight to several people and left. It might have been after 11:00 when we finally got out."

"Where did you go from there?"

"We went home and I took the baby sitter home, so I got back around midnight, more or less."

"Where were you earlier that day, from 8:00 am until 8:00 pm?"

"What time did you leave the tavern?"

"It was around 4:00. The game had just started and I listened to it as I drove home."

"Who was playing?"

"Oh, the Nationals were in Atlanta. I got home, changed and we hustled over to the Hotel. Caught a few more minutes of the game in the car. Got to the hotel, checked on the food prep and the rest of the evening was mine."

Ian relaxed for a second, "Who won?"

"Nats, 8 to 4. Good game, and I missed most of it."

"Are you aware of an incident that occurred at 16735 Lomond Road on Saturday May 26, 2012 at approximately 8:15 pm?"

"Oh, yeah, like I said, the news hit the hotel around 10:00 or 10:30."

"Do you know what happened?"

"We heard the barn at Ripley's Farm blew up and four people were inside when it went."

"Do you know who the four people were?"

"Yeah, Branch, Wilkins, Dorsey and Nestor."

"Has the condition of the four victims been determined?"

"Yeah, all four are dead."

"Okay, now I want to ask you about the last several weeks."

"Okay," said Jim.

"Did you have any conversation with any individual in the last several weeks about any of the four victims of that explosion prior to the incident?"

"Several conversations, with the other committee members at our weekly meetings."

"In what context did you discuss these individuals?"

"These four guys killed Darryl Zamanski back in '93 and we all wondered what could be done about it today. That was almost twenty years ago."

"Did you discuss any scenarios that involved killing these four men?"

"Well, sometimes one of us might say something."

"Please explain."

"Twenty years ago somebody beat a friend of ours to death. Since then, no arrests, no suspects, no nothing. We are sure the four guys who died in that barn did the deed, but we didn't have proof. So we talked about how to get them today."

"What do you mean by 'Get Them'?"

"Well, today DNA evidence is much stronger than it was twenty years ago. Maybe one of the four has talked to someone about what they did. Hell, whatever could get them arrested, charged and convicted."

"Had you ever met any of these men prior to the incident in the barn?"

"Yeah, back in high school, plus I've seen them around town over the years. I guess they knew me and I knew them but we weren't friends."

"Did you have any knowledge of the barn incident prior to its occurrence?"

"No."

"Do you know anyone who was involved in the planning or execution of the barn incident?"

"No."

"Thank you, that ends this interview. I'll probably have more questions in the future. The time is 4:35 pm."

Ian turned off the recorder, "Jim, thanks for coming in and talking to me."

"Not a problem, Ian. I guess this bombing will take precedence over Darryl's murder investigation."

"No, not really. The two are probably connected and I have to look at the victims, determine a motive and find the perpetrator. So, the Zamanski murder is very much in play. It may be the strongest motive I have found so far, and I have to suspect the eight people who put that motive front and center."

"Well, that number might just grow very quickly to include half of our graduating class, hell, it might include half the town. That case divided people into several camps. Those who were sure Branch and some of his buddies did it, those who figured it really was someone passing through town and a smaller group who had no opinion. Feelings ran pretty high for a while and eventually the dust settled. I guess I was in the group that was sure those guys were guilty at first and as time passed, I became less sure and more in the no opinion group. When we started to have the committee meetings, all those old feelings resurfaced and I jumped right back into the group that was sure Branch and friends were guilty."

Ian looked at Jim and asked, "Do you want to change any of your statements from our conversation?"

"No," said Jim, "Just be aware there are a lot of people that are probably not broken up over the Branch Bunch being blown up."

"Does that apply to the eight committee members?"

Jim stood and looked at Ian, "It does to this one." He turned and walked out of the conference room.

Ian watched Jim leave the building and paused, thinking that he had just stepped on his friend's toes. Next up was Mark Lindstrom, due in the office at 4:30. Ian needed a minute to clear his thoughts. He wandered back to his desk and stared out the window.

*　　*　　*

CHAPTER TWENTY FOUR
Interviews: The Mechanic...

Mark Lindstrom showed up at 4:45 and apologized for being late. His garage was a short walk from the police station and he walked in still wiping his hands on a red rag. "Hey, Monica, I'm a little late, is Ian still here?"

Monica smiled, "Yes, he practically lives here. He was running a little late too, so your timing is right on." She showed him into the conference room and said, "I'll get Detective McLarry, would you like a cup of coffee?"

Mark put his red rag in a back pocket, sat down and said, "Coffee sounds terrific."

Monica turned, walked over to the break room and saw Ian pouring himself a fresh cup. "Detective, Mr. Lindstrom is in the conference room."

"Thanks, Monica," he said, looking a little tired. "Did you offer him anything?"

"Yes, I'll bring it right in."

Ian grinned, finished filling his mug and walked into the conference room, "Good afternoon, Mark, did I pull you away from anything?"

"Just finished mounting a few new tires, it was a perfect time for a break. Those things get heavier every year."

Ian grinned, placed the tape recorder on the table, turned it on and said, "Are you ready to begin?"

"Shoot."

Ian turned on the recorder and started, "This interview is being conducted in the Vaneksburg Police Station on Monday, May 28, 2012. It is 4:55 pm."

"Please state your name," began Ian.

"Mark Lindstrom."

"Your occupation?"

"I'm a mechanic at the gas station around the corner on North First Street."

"Where were you on May 26, 2012 between 8:00 am and 8:00 pm?"

Mark paused, "I got to work around 8:30 that morning, stayed until about 3:00 plus or minus, went home and scrubbed up. Got over to Barb's about 3:45."

"Barb?"

"Yeah, Barb Nessman. Then we drove to the Hotel"

"Were there others present at that reunion?"

Mark paused, thought and replied, "Yeah, Barb told me the number, but I forget. Something like a hundred people."

Monica opened the door, walked in, placed a cup of coffee in front of Mark, and looked at Ian as if to ask if he needed anything. Ian shook his head and Monica left the room, closing the door quietly behind her.

Ian continued, "Can you name any others who can verify your presence at the Hotel at 8:00 pm on the day in question?"

Mark picked up the cup and said, "Yeah, Barb, of course, Sandy and Jeff, Eileen and Phil, and Audrey and you. We were all at the same table for dinner."

"What time did you arrive at the Hotel?"

Mark sipped his coffee, then put the cup down on the table and said, "I picked Barb up around 3:45, and we got there a little before 4:00."

"What kind of car do you drive?"

"I use my pickup truck mostly, but that day I drove my Mustang."

"A Mustang," Ian smiled, "what color is it?"

Mark had a look of pride as he replied, "The Mustang is blue, Midnight Blue," and he lifted the coffee for another sip.

"And what color is your truck?"

"Green, a dark military green," he said putting the coffee cup back down.

"You were driving your Mustang that day?"

"Well, I drove my pick-up to work in the morning and after I went home and scrubbed up, then I drove the Mustang."

"What time did you leave the hotel?"

"We probably left around midnight. Barb wanted to make sure everything was taken care of properly."

"Where did you go from there?"

"We went to Barb's place."

"Are you aware of an incident that occurred at 16735 Lomond Road on Saturday May 26, 2012 at approximately 8:15 pm?"

"Yeah, it really shook Barb up, she was kinda' quiet the rest of the night."

"All night."

"Yeah, all night. She felt better in the morning and was buzzing around with a cup of coffee, turning the channels on the television, trying to get more info on the barn thing."

"Did you know the four men who were killed in that blast?"

"I knew two of them, they had been in the station for different things like oil changes, state inspections. They all might have been in the station over the years, but I had no reason to single them out."

"Did you go to Vaneksburg High?"

"Yeah, graduated in '91. Those boys were a few years behind me and I never paid much attention to them."

"Did you know Darryl Zamanski?"

"No, he was in grade school when I graduated, I never met the kid."

"When did you start seeing Barb?"

"It was after I got back from the Gulf. I joined the Navy right after high school, did 14 years and checked out in 2005."

"What did you do in the navy?"

"Mechanic. I did a tour in the Gulf and worked on an aircraft carrier. Then, I was stationed in Norfolk and started working on some of the big stuff at the base. Wound up doing oil changes in the motor-pool and decided I'd had enough. So I came back here."

"How did you meet Barb?"

"At a council meeting. I was curious and went just for kicks. She was there, all fired up about some zoning thing and I liked what I saw. As it turned out, she had lost her husband and nobody was going to replace him. Part of her attraction to me was the fact that I was in the Gulf the same time as her husband. We never met, but when she found out I was there, she stopped in the gas station and asked a bunch of questions. We talked, her more than me, and we just kinda' grew together."

"Do you know anything about the capture, detention or killing of the four men in Ripley's barn?"

"No."

"Did you have a conversation with anyone about these four men and their possible involvement with Darryl Zamanski's killing?"

"Yeah. We talked about it at every committee meeting."

"Please be specific, who was present at those meetings?"

"Barb Nessman, Jim Schuster, Sandy Lansing, Lisa Harkins, Audrey Redding, Phil Kline, Brent Coyle and you attended a number of the meetings."

"Can you characterize the conversations regarding the four men in question?"

"Sure, we all felt those were the guys responsible for Darryl's death and the group talked about different ways to get them arrested, or at least keep them in the spotlight. Barb was pretty vocal about how the four of them got away with murder and when she gets her back up, well, something was going to happen."

Ian scratched a few notes and said, "Something, like?"

Mark was lifting the coffee cup as he said, "Not like killing them, more like starting a protest with placards and marching around city hall. She is not a violent person, doesn't even like contact sports. No, she wanted them arrested, not blown up."

"Did any of these conversations ever go as far as open threats against the four men?"

"I guess the others were more adamant about getting those guys. I was an outsider looking in. I mean, I never knew the kid like they did, so until I started getting close to Barb, it didn't mean much to me."

"Did you have any part in the capture, confinement and/or killing of those four men?"

"No,"

"Are you aware of any other individual involved in the capture, confinement and/or killing of the four men?"

"No, I am not,"

"Mark, is there any statement you would like to make about this incident?"

"No, not that I can think of."

"That concludes this interview. I may have further questions for you in the future. It is now 5:22 pm." Ian leaned back in his chair and let out a deep sigh, "This is the fun part of the job," he said sarcastically. "I get to beat up on my friends."

"Hey, Ian, we understand where you're coming from and this is not the most comfortable set of circumstances for any of us. But, you have a job to do and I think the entire group respects that."

"Thanks, Mark."

*　　*　　*

CHAPTER TWENTY FIVE
Interviews: the retailer ...

Lisa Harkins arrived a few minutes before 5:30, sat down in the reception area and picked up a magazine. She nervously flipped the pages and looked around the room at the same time. Ian came out to the waiting room at 5:30 and spotted her. "Hi, Lisa, come on in to the conference room and we can talk."

Lisa stood and followed Ian into the conference room. "I don't know what I can tell you, Ian."

Ian noted her trepidation and reassured her, "Lisa, this is a standard process. We have to talk to everyone who is even remotely related to an incident. You may have seen or heard something that will help us figure this thing out. Just relax and let me ask you a few questions. You may be surprised what you know that could help us here." She sat in a chair erect, tense as Ian continued, "Would you like a cup of coffee, or water?"

Lisa almost cried, "No, thanks."

Ian placed the recorder on the table, said, "Lisa, relax, I'm not going to hurt you." She sat back in the chair, still clenching her purse in her hands and biting her lower lip. "Now, are you ready?" asked Ian.

"Yes, I suppose," her voice quiet and reserved.

Ian pushed the button on his recorder and quickly asked, "Please state your name."

Lisa paused, "Lisa Marie Harkins."

Ian quickly asked the next question before Lisa could think about being scared, "What is your occupation?"

"I manage a specialty clothing shop for women in the Vaneksburg Mall."

"Where is the mall, Lisa?"

She relaxed a bit and said, "On Vaneksburg Road next to Route 66."

Ian sensed her breathing easier, "Where were you on May 26, 2012 between 8:00 am and 8:00 pm?"

She looked slightly confused, "Saturday, I was home in the morning. I went to the mall around noon and back home. That night, we were at the Reunion, at the hotel."

"Who were you with at the reunion? "

Lisa again confused, "Terry Bascone, you met him."

Ian smiled and nodded, "Who else could verify you were there?"

Lisa looked at Ian, "Brent and Carol Coyle, Bob and Linda Reynolds, Jim and Megan Schuster, we were all at the same table."

Ian nodded again and continued, "How many others would you guess were present at that reunion?"

"Oh, Barb told me, but I don't remember, I think 90 something."

"What time did you arrive at the Hotel?"

Lisa was calming down and said, "I think we got there a little after 4:30."

"Did you drive to the hotel?"

"Terry drove."

"What kind of car do you drive?"

"I have a Toyota Corolla."

"What color is it?"

"It's grey."

"Do you own a second vehicle?"

"No."

"What time did you leave the hotel?"

"About 11:30 or 11:45."

"Where did you go from there?"

"We stopped at the Tavern for a while."

"And then?"

"Terry took me home."

"Are you aware of an incident that occurred at 16735 Lomond Road on Saturday May 26, 2012 at approximately 8:15 pm?"

"The bomb thing, yes."

"Did you know the four men who were killed in that blast?"

"Not really."

"Lisa, did you have anything to do with those men being in that barn on that night?"

Lisa sat up straight, "No, Detective McLarry, I did not."

"Do you know anyone who had anything to do with the four men being in that barn?"

"No, I do not."

"Lisa, that concludes the questions I have for you. Would you like to say anything about the incident?"

She took a deep breath, and said, "I guess it's a terrible thing they got killed, the four of them, but they killed Darryl and they deserved it."

"Do you really feel that way, they deserved it?"

Lisa slowly looked up at Ian, her eyes saying she was angry, her voice flat and deliberate, "Yes, they deserved it, and I wish I had done it."

*   *   *

CHAPTER TWENTY SIX
Interviews: the veterinarian ...

Phil Kline arrived at the station at a few minutes after 5:45, and told the officer at the reception desk he was there to see Detective McLarry. "I'm a little early, supposed to be here at 6:00."

"No problem," said the officer, "He's in with someone else right now so if you would like to have a seat, I'll let him know you're here."

Phil walked slowly around the reception area, looking at the plaques and photographs on the walls. As he turned to check out another wall hanging, Lisa walked into the reception area, "Hi, Phil, are you the next victim?"

"I guess I am," said Phil.

Ian appeared and saw Phil, "Hey, Phil, are you ready for a merciless grilling?" he said, smiling at Lisa.

"Okay, bad cop, bring it on," said Phil sarcastically.

Lisa hurried out the door more relaxed than when she arrived. Ian led Phil to the conference room and asked him if he would like coffee or water.

"Nah, I can take the heat without any liquid."

Ian smiled and placed his recorder on the table. As they both sat down, Ian said, "Are you ready to begin?"

Phil smiled and said, "Now we get serious?"

Ian said, "Yes we do," and as the smile left his face, he pushed the record button. "Please state your name."

"Phillip James Kline."

"What is your occupation?"

"I am a Veterinarian; my offices are in the 300 block of East Center Street."

Ian continued, "Where were you on May 26, 2012 between 8:00 am and 8:00 pm?"

Phil answered, "Last Saturday night, the Reunion, at the hotel. I was at work most of the day, from 7:30 to about 4:30."

"Who were you with at the reunion?"

"My wife and I were at the table with Barb and Mark, Sandy and Jeff, Audrey and you."

Ian nodded again and continued, "How many others would you guess were present at that reunion?"

"I don't know, about a hundred."

"What time did you arrive at the Hotel?"

"I left my clinic around 4:30, went home and cleaned up. I guess we got to the hotel around 5:30, give or take."

"Did you drive to the hotel?"

"Of course."

"What kind of car do you drive?"

"It's a Jeep."

"What color is it?"

"Red."

"Do you own a second vehicle?"

"Eileen drives the Honda."

"What color is the Honda?"

"Silver, or grey."

"Do you ever drive the Honda?"

"Naw, I prefer my Jeep."

"Do you know where Eileen was that day?"

"No, I know she went to the mall for some things, and the grocery store."

"What time did you leave the hotel?"

"A little after 11:30, but before midnight."

"Where did you go from there?"

"We went home."

"Are you aware of an incident that occurred at 16735 Lomond Road on Saturday May 26, 2012 at approximately 8:15 pm?"

"Oh, yeah."

"Did you know the four men who were killed in that blast?"

"Yeah, but not well."

"Phil, did you have anything to do with those men being in that barn on that night?"

"Nope, I didn't."

"Do you know anyone who had anything to do with the four men being in that barn?"

"Nope."

They rehashed the conversation from their meeting at the tavern and Ian finally said, "Okay, Phil, that concludes the questions I have for you. Would you like to say anything about the incident?"

"Not really, I guess I don't feel bad about them being killed because I believe those four guys killed my friend Darryl nineteen years ago."

*   *   *

CHAPTER TWENTY SEVEN
Interviews: the architect ...

Brent Coyle arrived at 6:45, 15 minutes early. Phil had just finished and was walking out to his car as Brent pulled into the parking lot. He waved at Phil and parked in an open spot near the entrance. Ian greeted him at the door and they went directly to the conference room.

"Please state your name."

"Brent Coyle."

"What is your occupation?"

"I have an Architectural Practice in Leesburg."

Ian continued, "Where were you on May 26, 2012 at 8:00 pm?"

Brent answered, "Saturday evening, we were at the Reunion, at the hotel."

"Who were you with at the reunion?"

"My wife and I were at the table with Lisa and Terry, Bob and Linda and Megan and Jim."

Ian nodded again and continued, "Tell me how many others were present at that reunion?"

"Around a hundred."

"What time did you arrive at the Hotel?"

"I was working at home until 2:30, we did a little shopping, got home around 4:00, had an afternoon cup of tea, dressed and came to the hotel. That would have been around 5:00, give or take a few minutes."

"Did you drive to the hotel?"

"Yes."

"What kind of car do you drive?"

"It's a Lexus."

"What color is it?"

"Silver."

"Do you own a second vehicle?"

"Carol has a van, a mini van."

"What color is the van?"

"Blue, almost royal blue."

"And Carol is?"

"My wife."

"What time did you leave the hotel?"

"A little after 11:30."

"Where did you go from there?"

"We went home."

"Are you aware of an incident that occurred at 16735 Lomond Road on Saturday May 26, 2012 at approximately 8:15 pm?"

"Certainly."

"Did you know the four men who were killed in that blast?"

"Yes, but not well. I did a project for a client who was working through Bob Dorsey to obtain a property several years ago. All four were a few years ahead of me in high school and I don't think they knew I existed."

"Brent, did you have anything to do with those men being in that barn on that night?"

"No sir."

"Do you know anyone who had anything to do with the four men being in that barn?"

"No."

Again they covered their initial conversation from the hotel and Ian finished with, "Brent, that concludes the questions I have for you. Would you like to say anything about the incident?"

"No."

* * *

CHAPTER TWENTY EIGHT
Leg Work ...

Audrey Redding had returned to Fairfax, so Ian called her at home and left a message. She returned the call within an hour and said, "My time is pretty much mine to manage, let me open my calendar. I have a few appointments tomorrow, Tuesday, but I can be available any time on Wednesday after 10:00 am. Does that work for you?"

"Sure, Audrey," he said as he remembered holding her close on the dance floor, before the phone call calling him to the scene, "How about 11:00 in the morning?"

"Wednesday morning, 11:00 am, Detective, you are now on my schedule."

"Great, I look forward to it and please call me Ian."

* * *

Tuesday morning began with Ian heading for the break room and his first mug of coffee. As he poured water into the coffee machine for a fresh pot, Cindy approached, handed him a fax and said, "For you, Detective."

"What's this?"

"It's the list from Barb, of the attendees at the reunion," replied Cindy as she turned and went back to her desk.

Ian read the names and noted the signature at the bottom of the note, 'Barbara Nessman', then he paused and looked at Cindy as she reached her desk, "From Barb," he mumbled to himself. "Not from Ms. Nessman or Barbara Nessman, just Barb." He grinned, rinsed out his mug and waited a few seconds as the fresh coffee dripped into the pot.

Ian's first call was to Charlie Fitch, the realtor of record for the Ripley Farm. They talked for a minute and set an appointment for 11:00 that morning. Then he called Bob Dorsey's office and asked for his supervisor. A man answered and identified himself as Al Goldman. Ian set a time to meet with Goldman in his offices at 9:30 and opened his notebook. He outlined a line of questioning he might use for each of the men he was meeting that morning and thought about talking to Cindy about leaking police business out of the office to friends. He decided to wait, picked up his coat and walked over to Ned's office.

"I have a few interviews lined up this morning, wanna join me?"

Ned looked up, "Are you on to something?"

"Who knows, Chief, there are answers out there just waiting for the right questions," said Ian.

Ned leaned back in his chair, "Wish I could go with you, but we have other things happening here. Let me know how it goes."

Ian went to his car and drove across town to the Crandell Agency, Realtors. Al Goldman welcomed him into the office and showed him to a conference room. "I assume this is about Bob and the others," said Al. "Bob was a good man and this has really shaken up a few folks around here."

Ian opened his notebook and looked at Al, "I know this is not the best time for you and your staff, but we need to jump on this now from a law enforcement perspective. Information changes over time and things are forgotten, so we want to ask the questions now while memories are still fresh."

"I understand, detective, what can I tell you?"

"When was the last time you saw Bob?"

Al thought for a second, "It was Tuesday afternoon; he was at his desk checking on his latest deal, about 4:30, maybe 4:45. I left the office and I haven't seen him since."

Ian made a note and said, "So he was not in on Wednesday, Thursday or Friday?"

"I would have to check the sign in sheets for those days. I was out quite a bit of that time. We are very flexible and are constantly running to meetings with buyers and sellers, checking on new properties, all sorts of activity. Bob was in charge of his own time, so it would not be unusual for him to be gone for several days in a row." Al thought for a moment and said, "Let me bring Sarah in with the sheets. Bob could have popped in any number of times." He stood and walked out to the reception area, returning a moment later with an attractive young lady carrying a three ring binder. "Detective, this is Sarah, she is our receptionist and can show you the sign in book. I'm going to check with the others in the cubicle area, see if anyone saw Bob last week."

Sarah sat down and opened the binder to the previous Tuesday, "Bob signed in that morning and was here when I left, but didn't sign out." She slowly leafed through the next few days and said, "No, he didn't sign in or out the rest of the week."

"Thanks, Sarah," said Ian as Al returned to the conference room.

"Nobody recalls seeing him since Tuesday afternoon, but not everyone is here at the same time except for our regular Monday morning meeting." said Al. "I can check with each of them as they come in this week and let you know what I find out."

"I appreciate that," said Ian, "But I would like to quiz everybody myself, as there are several questions I have for each of them."

"Sure," replied Al, "When would you like to start?"

"Now would be good," said Ian.

Al stood and moved toward the door, "I'll get you a list of everyone in the office and let you know who is here now."

"Thanks Al, that'll be a big help."

Al walked out of the conference room and Ian began to formulate interview questions for the employees. Al returned in a few minutes with a list and one nervous looking person in tow.

"Detective, here is the list and Ken Porter would like to be first, as he has a meeting this afternoon with a new client and doesn't want to miss it."

Ian said, "Sure, send him in."

Al gestured toward the man standing at the door to come in and turned again toward Ian, "I went to Bob's desk and his calendar has a name scratched on it for Tuesday evening." He handed the book to Ian and said, "Looks like it says 'Trent'. I think it's the name of the guy who was interested in the Ripley property. It looks like they had a meeting somewhere Tuesday night." He paused, adding, "I didn't look into Bob's work station, or his desk, he may have something else there, but I didn't want to disturb anything. That's for your people to check."

Ian leafed through Bob's appointment book and noted a meeting with 'Dave' at the river with the notation "Fishing". He looked at Al, "Perhaps I will take a look at his work station, after I talk to the people available now."

"Ken, this is Detective McLarry," said Al as he turned and walked out of the room. Ken Porter was the first of seven interviews from the office, but very few facts came to light.

"When I saw Bob on Tuesday he was very excited about a prospective sale a friend of his had told him about. He got a call around 6:00 or 6:15 that evening, maybe later. We were about to lock up the office and head home. Bob answered his phone and lit up like a Christmas tree, waved at me and said 'See you tomorrow', then continued talking on his cell phone and headed back to his desk. That's the last time I saw him."

"Do you know who the call was from?"

"No. I just left, didn't listen to his conversation, maybe I should have."

Ian paged through his notebook, "Tell me, Ken, what do you remember about the Darryl Zamanski murder in September of '93?"

"Nothing, I only moved here about five years ago. That was old news by then and most people around here seemed to think it was someone, like a vagrant, just passing through town, a robbery, right?"

"That was one theory at the time."

"Yeah, I heard some talk about it being some guys Bob used to hang out with, but I thought they were cleared. Anyway, I can't see Bob doing anything like that, he was a nice guy."

"I only met him recently," replied Ian. "In order to figure out who did this, we need a motive. It could be any number of people, for any number of reasons. I have to look at everything that could be a motive, as remote as it seems."

Ken looked at Ian and said, "Well, good luck, detective, I wish I could tell you more, but that's all I know."

Ken left and Ian talked to six more people from the Crandell Agency. The opinions were consistent, Bob was a nice guy, nobody knew any reason someone would want to hurt him, much less kill him. Ian found Al and asked to inspect Bob's office. It was a cubicle with a desk, file cabinet, bulletin board, book shelves and assorted office items, including a calendar. Ian sat at Bob's desk and began with the calendar, starting at the beginning of the year. He quickly paged through the days until he got to Saturday, April 28. The notation said "Dave, fishing at Wharf, 10 am." Ian grinned, that date was the day after he interviewed the first three of the victims. "I wonder what they talked about?" he mused. He spent another 15 minutes browsing through Bob's desk and was out the door at 10:50, heading for the Carter & Fitch agency two blocks away.

* * *

Charlie Fitch met with Ian and told him there hadn't been any serious interest in that property for over a month. "I was about ready to give Don Ripley a call, start talking about reducing the asking price. Instead, I had to call him for a very different reason."

Ian handed Charlie a business card and asked, "Have you had any contact with someone by the name of Trent?"

Charlie looked at the card and answered, "About the Ripley place, no. I am handling the Ripley's farm myself and I don't recall anyone by the name of Trent. I'll check my e-mails and the project folder, see if the name pops up. Come on into my office and we can take care of this right away."

Ian followed Charlie into his office and almost immediately a young girl came in with a mug of coffee for Charlie and asked if Ian would like coffee, tea or water. Ian accepted a cup of coffee as he sat across from Charlie, waiting and watching while Charlie searched through his computer, the coffee filling the gap.

"Nope, nothing, no Trent mentioned in any communication or in any of my notes. Sorry, detective, but we don't seem to be helping."

"Not at all, just knowing this name is unknown to you means something. You've been very helpful." Ian stood, shook Charlie's hand and left. Driving back to the station, Ian's cell phone rang.

"Detective, Charlie Fitch here. I was talking to my secretary after you left and she told me the only caller on the Ripley place in the last month was another realtor from Fairfax. Said she might have an interested party for us."

"A woman?" asked Ian.

"Yep, she asked a few questions and said she would call again if it went somewhere. She hasn't called back."

Ian pulled over to the curb, "Did you get a name?"

"No, it was just a simple inquiry, she asked a couple of questions and hung up."

* * *

Ian sat in his car for a few minutes, thinking about the little bits he had collected so far. He arrived back at the station just before noon and assembled his notes. The restraints were his next focus and he began by checking as many places online as he could find that might handle handcuffs in the immediate area. Cindy asked if she could help with his search and Ian accepted.

"What are we after, detective?"

"Our perp bought four sets of wrist and ankle restraints, probably an unusual purchase, so that's what we are asking about. Then I have to find those gags, a red rubber ball and a strap with a buckle. I guess I'll be visiting some of those 'Adult' stores."

"I've seen them, but never gone in," Cindy blushed, "Really, never went in. There is one up on Route 50 I pass once in a while. Go up Lomond to 50, turn right and it's a few miles on the right side. Big sign, you can't miss it."

"Wanna go with me?" Ian laughed.

"No way," replied Cindy. "You're on your own there."

It was almost 2:00 pm, Tuesday afternoon when Ian arrived at the first adult store on his list. The front door was open and he wandered in. As he browsed the show room, a young man came in from a back room. "Good afternoon, may I help you find something?" asked the young man.

Ian took three photographs from his coat pocket, "Do you carry any of these items?"

The young man sensed at once Ian was not a customer, but probably was a cop. He looked closely at the photos and noted the manufacturer's impression. "Over here, officer," he said and led Ian to a different counter. "These two are made by the same manufacturer," he said as he handed the photos of the handcuffs and leg restraints back to Ian. He opened a counter door and took out a box with a pair of handcuffs and found another with the leg restraints. "Are you just looking or are you buying?"

"Right now, just looking," replied Ian.

"If you are buying, we have a reduced price for law enforcement," offered the young man.

"Thanks, what about the ball gag?"

"That item is over here," he said and led Ian to a nearby counter and pulled out another box from a shelf.

As Ian looked closely at the handcuffs, leg restraints and gags, the young man asked, "Is there anything else I can show you, officer?"

Ian replied, "I have a few questions. First, have you sold many of these recently, like in the last 10 weeks?"

The young man walked over to the door leading to the back room, "I'll have to check on the computer. Please come this way." He led Ian to a small office in the back where he turned on a computer and scrolled through a number of options. He highlighted 'Purchases' and looked at the sub menu, highlighted a few more items and said, "Yes, we have sold over a dozen in the last eight weeks."

"Any of those purchases for four sets?"

The young man searched and said, "No, but I have two purchases for two sets of handcuffs, one three weeks ago, and the other from seven weeks ago."

"How much are these hand cuffs?" asked Ian.

The young man pushed a few more keys and said, "List price is $35.99 for that model."

"What about the leg restraints and the ball gags?"

The young man continued his search, "I have one purchase for two leg restraint sets. They list at $32.99 and two ball gags, at $24.95 on the same day as the handcuffs. Of course if you were to buy all three, I can cut the price a little more than the 20% discount."

"What date was that?"

"That was May 4th."

"Friday, May 4th. And do you have a customer name for me?"

The young man dove into the computer again and said, "No, these were all cash purchases, no credit cards, no names."

"Okay, do you remember who was in the store on that day and bought these items?"

"Well, first, I don't work on Fridays. I have class, so you should talk to Shirley."

"Who is Shirley?"

"She's the owner, usually here during the week."

"So where is she?"

"Not in today, she went to Colorado for her son's wedding this weekend."

"And she will be back when?"

"She is on the schedule for Monday, so I guess by then."

"Thanks, I'll be back."

*   *   *

The patient drove the silver Focus into a used auto dealership in Loudoun County, walked up to the receptionist and asked, "Do you buy used cars?"

"Yes, we do," answered an approaching salesman. "If you have a few minutes, we can have our staff evaluate it and give you a number that will be good for thirty days."

"I don't want to buy another car, just thinking about unloading this one," said the patient, holding up the keys.

"Not a problem," said the salesman, "Which one is it?"

"The silver Focus," replied the patient, pointing through the window toward the parking lot.

"I see it. Give me the keys, I'll have our team check it out and be right back."

The process took about 20 minutes and the salesman came back with a single sheet of paper. "Here you go," he said, "And as I said before, that price is good for thirty days."

The patient paused, thinking and said, "Thanks, this is a good price for that car, I'll think about it, maybe come back next week."

"If you want to go ahead with a sale, bring in the title and registration and we will be happy to sell you another car, or give you money and a ride home."

"That sounds altogether too easy."

"Yeah," said the salesman, "And the next time you want to buy another car, you remember us and come here before some other dealer."

The patient grinned knowingly, "Okay, when I am ready to buy another car, this will be my first stop."

*   *   *

Ian had a list of five shops he intended to visit. His next stop was in Falls Church and then he headed back toward Manassas through Tyson's Corner. The fourth stop on his tour was on Route 28 and it proved valuable. Ian entered the shop and went directly to the handcuffs and leg irons.

As he was looking for the specific model, an older gentleman approached and asked, "Can I help you?" He was a short, slightly overweight man with thinning grey hair and very thick glasses.

"I have a few questions," said Ian as he opened his badge wallet. "I'm with the Vaneksburg PD."

The old man squinted and focused on the badge, "Does that say Detective?"

"Yes," said Ian, "My name is Ian McLarry and I'm a detective with the Vaneksburg Police force."

"Haven't been to Vaneksburg in years, my wife, rest her soul, she liked that square in the middle of the town, liked to walk around and look in all the shops. I just sat on a bench and let her have her day poking in the stores."

"Let's start with your name and position here."

"Sure, Joe Kelsey, and I own this store."

Ian took out the pictures of the restraints, "I'm trying to find where someone bought a couple sets of these several weeks ago."

The old man took the photos and moved into a better light. He held the photos about three inches from his face and said, "Yep, we carry these. You want to see some?"

"Actually, I was hoping to get the name of the customer."

"Bought these?"

"Yes, about three or four weeks ago."

"Well, let's look in the computer," he said as he moved toward a small cubicle in a corner of the shop. "Let me see that picture again," he said, then hummed a non-tune as he entered information into the computer. "Hmm, I've had several sales in the last couple of weeks, got one on the last day of April, three sets of handcuffs and ball gags. Here's another one, May 2nd, handcuffs and leg irons, and another on May 3rd, handcuffs; May 4th, cuffs, two pair, leg irons, two pair and ball gags, two. I kinda' remember this one, nice lady, college teacher as I recall. Said she needed them for a class she was teaching."

"Cash or credit?" asked Ian.

Kelsey tapped a few keys on the computer, looked at the screen, "Cash, I remember now she had a budget and they gave her cash," said Kelsey as he turned toward Ian.

"Do you remember anything else, a name, where she taught school, her height, hair color, anything like that?"

Kelsey paused, thought and said "Well, let's see, she had dark hair, I can't see too good and don't know if it was brown or black, it was short and dark, that's all I remember about the hair. Her eyes, I couldn't tell ya. Height, I'd guess about five-five or six. Weight, my wife told me a long time ago never to guess a woman's weight. I really don't have a clue but there wasn't much to her, small woman." he laughed.

"That's it?"

"She smelled nice, not like some women who pour on a gallon of 'Eau de something', this girl smelled nice, soft and her voice was clear, like she was in charge of something, but nice."

"What about the school where she taught?"

"Don't know. She said it was in Fairfax, could be GMU or NOVA, whatever else is up there?"

"Okay," said Ian. "I may come back if more questions come up."

"Stop in anytime, be happy to help if I can," said Kelsey.

Ian drove back to the station and thought about the information collected thus far, female, about 5'6", short dark hair, teacher, smelled nice, in charge. He ran through the information several times trying to imagine who fit those specifics.

*   *   *

Wednesday morning Ian arrived at the office early. He wanted to build a profile of the suspect before his meeting with Audrey. The factors to be considered: someone who knew Darryl, a basic physical description, information about occupation, vehicle driven, and of course, any criminal record that might exist. He discovered both Sandy Lansing and Mark Lindstrom had minor infractions from several years ago, but nothing significant. Lisa and Barb had excessive traffic violations. Phil, Brent, Jim and Audrey were clean, no record.

The limited descriptions from Jansen would eliminate some people and the discussion with Kelsey narrowed it further. The committee members were the first round, but Ian fully expected his search to expand beyond the committee. His next target would include the alumni at the reunion, a list of nearly 50 people.

Ian was reviewing paperwork when his phone rang. Agent Danvers said, "Good morning, Detective, we have a little more information for you."

Ian opened his notebook and said, "Ready when you are."

Danvers began, "The timing device was an inexpensive windup alarm clock. The alarm was apparently set for 8:15 and since this clock doesn't know am from pm, it must have been set within twelve hours of the event, so your window is 8:00 am to 8:00 pm."

"That helps," said Ian, "Now what about the dynamite?"

"The lab guys are looking at the residue we collected," replied Danvers, "They're still saying the window on this is wide open. You said it yourself, age, size, leakage. With the damage observed, they figure four 8" sticks, based on Ripley's and Jansen's input. They feel the perp didn't add to it, just went with what he had available."

"Got it," said Ian, "Thanks, I'll send you a write-up on the interviews and everything else we have."

"There's more," said Danvers, "The tire treads you cast and photographed are Michelin, P215/55R16. They fit a number of vehicles. The track dimensions are tricky, they're good for a Ford Focus."

"Definitely a Focus, or is that still open? We don't know if the tire tracks were left by our perp or someone else, but it's all good info, thanks again."

"Okay, McLarry, I'll look at other cars, but the Focus looks good for those tracks. The dimensions are right and the tires are standard issue with that car. I'll continue to feed you anything additional that comes our way. Good luck with your interviews," said Danvers and he hung up.

Ian walked into Chief Bowen's office, "Good morning, Chief, I just got off the phone with Danvers. Got some more logs for this little fire. Now, I want to check on the road from the Hotel down to the Ripley farm, see if there is a camera pointed at the street, maybe caught the perp driving past."

"Cameras?"

"Yeah, like an ATM or a gas station, anything that may have caught our guy driving by in a silver compact, like a Cruze or a Focus."

"On Saturday?"

"Yeah, between 8:00 am and 8:00 pm."

"Are you gettin' close to something?"

Ian grinned, "Let's see where all this goes, then maybe."

"Are you going out there now?"

Ian checked his watch, "No, I have an interview with Audrey Redding at 11:00, after that I'll check into the cameras on Lomond."

"Great, let me know how it works out."

* * *

CHAPTER TWENTY NINE
Interviews: the realtor...

It was almost 11:00 am and Ian went out to the front desk to check with Monica. As they were talking, a white Cadillac pulled into the parking lot. Ian watched as the car parked and Audrey opened the door. She entered the building and Ian greeted her and led her to a conference room just off the reception area. "Nice car, Audrey."

"It's a lease car," she replied just above a whisper, "One of the perks of the Real Estate business. I often have to chauffer clients around, and I write it off at tax time. Plus, I get a new one every year."

"That must save you a nice chunk of money."

"This is my first one, got it in November, so I guess the next one will be ready in about six months."

Ian grinned, "Yeah, I have a company car too, but mine is a few years old and they expect me to drive it into the ground. But the real perk is cheap gas, I don't get tickets and they fill all the bullet holes for free."

They laughed as they walked into the conference room. Ian excused himself to get his notebook. "This won't take long," he said, "The least I can do is buy you lunch when we finish."

Audrey smiled, "I'd like that."

Ian returned, placed his small recorder on the table and said, "Would you like some coffee before we start?"

"Sure," replied Audrey.

Ian left and came back within a minute with two cups of coffee. He turned on the recorder, sat across from Audrey and began, "This is Detective Ian McLarry; it is Wednesday, May 30, 2012, approximately 11:15 am. This conversation relates to an investigation into the deaths of four people, David Edward Branch, Carl James Wilkins, Robert Allen

Dorsey and Ronald Foster Nestor." He looked at Audrey and said, "Are you ready to begin?"

She answered in a clear voice, "Yes."

"Please state your name," began Ian.

"Audrey Redding."

"Your occupation?"

"Real Estate sales."

"Where were you on Saturday, May 26, 2012 at 8:00 pm?"

Audrey smiled, "At the Vaneksburg Hotel attending a class reunion."

"Do you recall what time you arrived?"

"Well, I was staying at the hotel that weekend, so I arrived on Friday afternoon and stayed until Sunday about noon."

"Where were you between 8:00 am and 8:00 pm on Saturday?"

"Saturday, I slept in a bit because I was going to be at the Reunion until midnight. Woke up around 9:00, had coffee and read the newspaper, went down to the ballroom and helped out with the preparations and went back to my room to clean up and dress for the evening. I think I arrived at the party around 4:30 and was there all evening."

Ian made notes and continued, "What kind of car do you drive?"

"It's a company car, a Cadillac CTS," replied Audrey.

"What color is it?"

"It's white, or cream."

"Do you own a second vehicle?"

Audrey paused, "No."

Ian looked at Audrey's eyes and asked, "Are you aware of the events that occurred the evening of May 26th at 16735 Lomond Road?"

Her eyes turned down and she answered, "Yes, well, I heard there was an explosion and some men were injured, killed."

"Did you know any of these men?"

Audrey looked up again, "Well, we were in high school at the same time, for a year or two, but I was never close to any of them."

"Did you have anything to do with the capture, detention or killing of these men?"

Audrey's face reddened, she took a deep breath and said, "No detective, I did not."

Ian looked at Audrey as she slowly shifted in the chair, "Do you know anyone who did participate in the capture, detention or killing of these men?"

Again, Audrey seemed unsettled, "No, detective, I do not."

Ian was now uncomfortable. He liked this woman. He wished he didn't suspect her, but she was acting a little strange. And she was a woman realtor from Fairfax. He recalled his conversation with Charlie Fitch. That made him wonder about her real involvement. "Audrey, you seem uncomfortable. Is there something I should know, something you are not telling me?"

She bowed her head again and cleared her throat, "You've met with our committee several times and you know we all felt those men killed Darryl back then, in high school."

"Yes, and now they are dead and I have to find out who did it. I want to find Darryl's killer and I also want to find the person who killed those four men."

"Do you think I did it, that I killed them?" Her eyes watered and she began to say something and stopped. Then she looked up and said in a very clear voice, "They were bad men, very bad, and they killed Darryl. I'm glad they are dead."

"Audrey, I don't know who killed them. It could be you or any number of others. My job is figure it out and allow the legal system, the courts, to sort out the consequences. Should I ask you again, did you kill them?"

Audrey wiped away the tears and sat up straight. "I wish I was big enough and strong enough to have put them all in that barn and shackled them. I wish I had killed them, but I was with you when they died, you and all those other people at the reunion. Perhaps it was someone just passing through town."

Ian looked at her and thought about those words, 'somebody just passing through town'. "Perhaps, but unlikely," he said. The interrogation covered the reunion meetings at the Vaneksburg Tavern, the speculation about Darryl's encounter with high school bullies, specifically Dave Branch, and the events just prior to Darryl's death. Finally Ian said, "I may have other questions for you in the future. The time is 11:42 am. That concludes this interview."

They walked back out to the reception area and Ian said, "Are we still on for lunch?"

"It's a little early, but we could walk around the square and look in a few shops," said Audrey.

"That would be very nice," replied Ian. He signed out and the two walked to the town square. Audrey looked in every window and paused at most with Ian standing next to her. Finally after a half hour of window shopping, they arrived at the tavern. Audrey was tired and seemed to have difficulty breathing.

"Are you alright?" quizzed Ian.

"Oh, it's just a little cold and my allergies are fussing at me. The cool air in the tavern is a relief."

Lunch was brief and pleasant. Audrey thanked Ian and he walked her back to her car. She hesitated, looked at him, smiled and got in her car to drive back to Fairfax. Ian stood in the parking lot watching the white Cadillac disappear around a corner. He wondered about the petite woman he had just interviewed and taken to lunch. "Too nice and quiet, too small, wrong car. Maybe dinner next time," he muttered to himself. He walked back into the station reflecting on Audrey's voice, noting how it became more commanding when she got angry.

*   *   *

CHAPTER THIRTY
Evidence...

Ian reviewed his notes from all the interviews, made a few adjustments and leaned back in his chair. As he was mulling over the meeting with Audrey, Ned came into the office.

"Ian, how was your interview with the Redding woman?"

"Sometimes the least possible scenario fits the questions. She is all wrong for this bombing, but then again, I have a way to go and more people to consider."

"What's next on your schedule?"

"Lomond Road. There may be an ATM or two with a security camera pointing in the right direction. The perp was probably at the scene between 8:00 am and 8:00 pm and at the Hotel that evening."

"That's a 12 hour span, Ian. Can you narrow it down any?"

"Yeah, if I assume the perp was at the Reunion, I can cut it off at 4:00 pm, but I'll be looking at the whole 12 hours even if I find a good match from before 4:00."

"Good luck, I'll be here for a while, so if you need help, holler."

"Will do, chief."

Ian collected his notebook, signed out to the crime scene and went out to his car. He drove the length of Lomond Road from North 6th Street to the Ripley Farm. There were three gas stations and two banks where he might find a security camera pointed in the right direction along that route. The most promising was the ATM located in a Credit Union branch near the intersection of Lomond and South Third.

The recording was not the best, a bit grainy, but the little camera did its job. A customer standing at the machine was clearly visible and identifiable, cars passing on the street were not as clear, but coloring, shape and time produced thirty seven vehicles that fit the description, moving north between 8:00 am and 8:00 pm. Unfortunately, not all drivers could be distinguished clearly. In six cases, the view was blocked by a customer using the machine, in another eight cases, the view was blocked by adjacent vehicles moving in the same direction. There was one, time stamped at 10:13:43, that looked very promising. The view of the driver was hampered by the tinting of the window, but the driver was obviously a woman sitting close to the steering wheel.

"A woman," muttered Ian. He thought about Barb Nessman, Sandy Lansing, Lisa Harkins and Audrey Redding. "One of them," he puzzled. "No, I can't see it." He felt relief and hoped the bomber was someone he had not yet met. "A woman?"

*   *   *

"What do we have, Ian?" asked Ned.

"Not near enough to point a hard finger at anyone. These boys were not just disliked, they were hated. Most people believe the four of them were hanging around in town, looking tough, and spotted Darryl as he walked down Garland Avenue on his way home. Now Branch had been embarrassed in front of a cafeteria full of kids a day or two before when he challenged Darryl and a girl made him look bad with her reply. He was the quasi-leader of this group, not the smartest, but the oldest. The assumption is Branch pushed a little harder than he normally would and the others followed suit. They hit Darryl with a piece of wood, poked him with a cattle prod, punched him and kicked him when he was on the ground. They killed him and they walked away, untouched. It was murder, Chief, probably unintential, but murder all the same. Three of them were juveniles at the time, but in most cities, they would all be tried as adults."

"Proof, Ian, we need proof. Do you think Andy withheld evidence back then?"

"From what I can decipher about Detective Ferguson, he's at least guilty of poor judgment. I can't say and I won't say he withheld anything, more likely he turned a blind eye or accepted the word of his girlfriend's kid when he should have been a cop. He should have pushed harder to get the truth out in the open back then. Today, it will be tougher. These four men had nineteen years to imbed their story into their memories. The lies they concocted back then have become truths in their minds. They may really believe they were at the Wharf that night, not downtown and getting them to change their story would have been near impossible."

"Well, then, are you ready to give it up?"

"Hell no, Chief, a crime is a crime and this was the most serious of crimes. Somebody killed that kid and has gotten away with it for the last nineteen years. Now someone has killed the four most probable suspects. Even if they were the bad guys, we can't just allow someone to blow them up. If it was those four that killed Darryl, I want to prove it. If it was not them, then I want to prove that and one way or another, I want to find our barn bomber. The only thing worse than not getting a conviction is getting the wrong conviction."

"So, where was your investigation before the bombing?"

"I interviewed the four victims and was already talking to the other boys, now men, who were at the wharf. Now, I can change my approach and go back at them again. The four musketeers are now dead and can't hurt or be hurt by the other boys at the Wharf. That's on my schedule for tomorrow. I plan to get each one in here and push harder."

* * *

The patient spent hours clearing out personal items no longer needed. All bills were paid and a letter was written to the relative, living in Colorado, letting him know he was named as a beneficiary in one of the patient's two insurance policies. The other insurance policy would cover funeral and burial expenses and anything left would be divided three ways between the high school in Vaneksburg, The University of Virginia and the church the patient had attended as a child. Furniture, clothing, books and collections amassed over the years were sorted, to be sold or donated or passed on to friends. The patient started a list, defining who would get various items.

* * *

The following morning, Ian placed a call to Minnesota. Paul Burger said he now remembered that one of the four, "I think it was Carl," had specifically said they had been at the Wharf since 6:30. "I probably got there after 9:00 and thought it weird he wanted me to know he had been there all evening."

"Are you sure about the time you arrived?"

"Are you kidding? It was twenty years ago. What I remember is that I would have had dinner with my folks and they were pretty regular about dinner time. So there's little chance I got there before 9:00."

"That's interesting. Anything else you remember?"

"Oh yeah, I have thought about the building on Garland. I'm sure there was one time when about ten of us were there. So I'm sure Wilkins and Branch were there too. Wherever we were, they were."

The call to Joe Baines yielded a few items. Joe said he saw Dave and Ron throwing old beer cans around when they arrived. "I'm not sure, but, I think I got there around 5:30 or 6:00 and they came later. Somebody told me it was 6:30, but that didn't sound right because I had been there for a while, like about two hours. And then, there they are dropping beer cans and emptying their pockets."

"What was in their pockets?"

"I don't know, cigarette butts and candy wrappers, you know, trash."

Ian finished his notes and walked into Ned Bowen's office, "Chief, the landscape is changing. The picture of twenty years ago is becoming clearer."

"What'cha got, Ian?"

"What I got is the two remaining boys, now men, are not so sure of the sequence of events for that night nineteen years ago."

"How's that?" asked Bowen.

Ian sat on the edge of the guest chair and continued, "The timeline is not solid. One of them got there around 9:00 or later and couldn't possibly verify what time the four suspects arrived. The other said he arrived around 6:00 or earlier and it seemed like he had been there for two hours, plus or minus, before the four suspects arrived. So the time line would more accurately indicate that the four arrived between 8:00 and 9:00 that night. Also, when the four did arrive they spread trash around the site."

Chief Bowen looked puzzled, "Trash?"

"Yeah, like beer cans and cigarette butts," said Ian.

The chief's eyes widened, "Make it look like they had been there a couple hours when they were actually down on Garland Avenue, hanging out in that building. What else ya got?"

"How about conflicting stories about who had been in that building in the past, before the incident."

"Another nail in their coffin," grunted the Chief.

*   *   *

CHAPTER THIRTY ONE
They did it...

"All evidence indicates that those four boys did in fact cause Darryl's death," said Ian. "The difficulty is proving it beyond a reasonable doubt in a court of law."

Ned leaned back in his chair, "Yeah, now they're all dead, where do we go?"

Ian leaned into Ned's desk and tapped his finger, "Our perp, or unsub, whatever you call him, may well have figured we would not be able to get the job done. These guys continued to get away with killing Darryl and would be walking free as birds on our streets forever. So our perp jumps in and blows them up, seems like a reasonable assumption. A vigilante killing, a revenge bombing. But why now?"

Ned picked up a note on his desk, "Bombing, yeah, the pressure wave from a single stick of dynamite would probably have done the job and it looks like our vigilante used all four sticks."

"Four," quizzed Ian. "Is that the official word from our friends at Quantico?"

"They ran some numbers and talked to Ripley again. Seems he probably had four sticks left and considering the age, probable nitro leakage and the resulting damage, yeah, it looks like all four were used." Ned shook his head and looked at Ian, "Imagine, being all trussed up in cuffs and leg irons, can't get away and you're looking at four red sticks with a detonator, a battery and an alarm clock." He leaned forward and said, "That was not nice. Either this bomber had no idea what effect four sticks would have or he's one very mean, cold son of a bitch. I want him, Ian. I want him in my jail."

Ian saw the look on Ned's face and said, "Chief, the perp doesn't appear to be concerned about getting caught. There is just too much evidence building up. I've already talked to several folks about the restraints and I have a few leads on the perp's car."

Ned scratched his chin as he asked, "You said him, her or them a minute ago, could it be a woman or more than one person?"

"I'm still shaking the tree, but an adult store sold two sets of handcuffs, leg irons and ball gags a few weeks ago to one person. Another store several miles away did the same, to a woman. That makes four sets of each."

"I assume these were all cash purchases, or you would be telling me their names," said Ned.

"Right, in the first store the right sales person was not there when I was in, but should be in today, and in the second store, the guy could hardly see me standing in front of him, but he said the buyer was a woman and he sort of described her."

"What about the shell casings?"

"Somebody, perhaps our perp, used a .9mm, as common as it gets. When I firm up the description of the adult store patron, I may have something to take to a gun shop and see if we have a match."

"What else do you have?"

"The bomber used a stun gun. I'll be asking the local shops about that also."

Ned picked up his glasses and said, "You know, our bomber may have had the .9mm and the stun thing, may have bought them in Maryland or West Virginia."

Ian nodded, "Yeah, or maybe Pennsylvania or California. Might have had them for years, but this smells like a one-time deal. Our bomber used old dynamite that was already in the barn, and used all of it, like he didn't know it was probably too much. He bought new handcuffs and leg restraints, when the victims could have been tied with rope or pull ties." Ian thought for a second and said, "The bombing happened a few minutes after 8:00 pm, when the reunion speeches were being delivered. Remember Chief, the reunion would have been Darryl's 15th. His classmates were gathered at the hotel, celebrating. I think our bomber was at the reunion and timed the blast to coincide with the speeches."

"I think you've already narrowed it down to less than the whole class."

"Yeah, well I don't have enough to point the finger yet, but I have a group of eight people I want to include or exclude as soon as possible."

"Why these eight people?"

Ian stood and picked up his files, "The reunion committee. I have met with them several times and they seem like nice people, real nice people. But the world is a funny place, where really nice people do really nasty things."

*   *   *

It seemed almost too obvious to Ian that the killer was someone who sought revenge for Darryl's killing nearly 20 years ago. Obvious and at the same time, puzzling. Who might have done this? Who would be willing to give up freedom for the satisfaction of a revenge killing? The evidence was piling up and Detective Ian McLarry was getting ever closer to defining the bomber.

As Ian had told Ned Bowen, the most outward of Darryl's advocates were the members of the Reunion Committee. He had befriended them all and did not enjoy the thought of having to arrest any of them. "Not what I want to do, but by the same token, it is what I have to do." His investigation shifted gears into a very deliberate review of each of the committee members. The evidence showed specific things and the committee members were going to be scrutinized.

Ian picked up his files and walked into a conference room. He wrote what he knew on the white board. He talked as he wrote, "The bomber lured these four men into the barn and restrained them. Maybe it was a cooperative effort, two or three people." He wondered, "How could one person have captured all four of these guys? If I assume it was the weakest committee member, Lisa or Audrey, could they physically have managed? If they could do it, then any of them could have." He paced in front of the whiteboard, "A gun, the little equalizer, if Lisa had a gun in her hand, and these guys believed she would use it, she might be able to restrain them." He thought a bit more, "Why was the barn available? How did the bomber get access?" That made him think about the real estate broker again.

He opened his file and started another column of information; "Bomb, dynamite, probably left there by Ripley when he moved out." He browsed the file, "Handcuffs, leg restraints, ball gags, looks like they were bought and used specifically for this event." He flipped a page or two, "Vehicle observed was a silver or grey sedan, looks similar to Chevrolet Cruze." He read more, "Shell casings, .9mm." Ian looked at the whiteboard and then turned another page in the file, "Marks on bodies of victims consistent with stun gun, probably used to control the victims" He paused again, "The autopsy reports indicate the victims all had bagels and water as their last meal, perhaps within 24 hours of the blast." He sat down facing the whiteboard and thought, "24 hours, that would be 8:00 pm on Friday. The guy fed them, so they had been there a while, maybe another eight hours added on, and they would have been there since noon on Friday or longer."

Ian began with Phil Kline. He was Darryl's friend, they did a number of things together and Phil could relate to Darryl's situation. Phil is a veterinarian, with an established practice. He's married and has children. It does not seem likely that he would risk endangering his situation to kill four people.

"Phil is a vet, drives a red Jeep, I wonder if he has access to a silver compact," mused Ian as he leafed through his notes, "Eileen has a silver Honda," he made a note on the board. "Eileen has short dark hair."

"Barb is blond, drives a red van, and she has been very busy coordinating the reunion, Low probability."

"Audrey, long hair, brunette, drives a Cadillac CTS, not a good match. But she is a realtor from Fairfax."

"Jim, drives a blue van, wife drives an Explorer, not good."

"Sandy, brunette, drives a grey Fusion, very vocal, good match."

"Mark, green pick-up truck and a blue Mustang, mechanic, probably has access to any number of vehicles, would probably do anything for Barb."

"Lisa, brunette, drives a silver Toyota, good match."

"Brent, silver Lexus, lives in Leesburg."

Ian continued to leaf through his notes and paused, staring at one word, 'shackled'. He sorted through several tapes from his recorder and played back a conversation. There it was, that one word, 'shackled'. He shook his head, unsettled.

*   *   *

CHAPTER THIRTY TWO
The evidence speaks ...

Ian spent the weekend running various scenarios through his head. Monday morning found Ned in his office poring over paperwork when Ian tapped on Ned's door frame, "Chief, who knew the victims were in cuffs and leg irons?"

Ned took off his glasses and leaned back in his chair, "I don't know, you, me, the Federal boys, the med techs, the hospital staff. I can't think of anyone else. I do know we didn't release that to the press. Where are you heading with this?"

"One of our possible suspects used the word 'shackled' referring to the four victims being restrained. I think someone innocent might have said 'tied up' or 'bound', but not 'shackled'."

"That's thin, Ian, you got anything else?"

"Yeah, a few things."

"You don't look happy, what's the problem?"

"Okay, I have a suspect who almost fits the description."

"Almost?" Ned leaned forward, "Man or woman?"

"Woman."

"One of your friends?"

"Yeah, one of them."

"Are you getting too close to this person? Do we have a little conflict?"

Ian stood, "Chief, I didn't take this job so that I could sit back and only investigate people I don't know or care about. No, I can do what has to be done. If this little lady did it, I will put her in your jail."

Ned watched Ian walk back to his desk and pondered over who had Ian in knots. He watched as Ian picked up a file, looked through it for a minute, then opened a drawer in his desk and took out an envelope. He put a handful of photographs in the file, then dropped the envelope on his desk and headed for the door.

The drive to the adult store on Route 50 took less time than he expected and soon he was walking in the front door with the file in hand. The young man who had helped him before was there and approached Ian.

"Detective?"

"McLarry." responded Ian. "Is Shirley in today?"

"She is," replied the young man. "I'll go get her."

A minute later a well dressed, middle-aged woman came into the showroom, "May I help you, Detective?"

"I hope you can," replied Ian. He opened his file and took out three pictures from the reunion. "I was in a few days ago asking about someone who purchased some restraints in early May. I was wondering if you could look at these photos and tell me if you recognize anyone."

"Well," said Shirley, "That's three weeks ago, let's see what you have."

Ian said, "I believe they bought two sets of handcuffs, leg restraints and gags." He spread the photos out on the counter.

"Oh yes, I do remember her. She teaches a course at NOVA, I think or GMU."

Ian took a deep breath as Shirley looked at the photos. "Hmmm, I'm not sure, this one looks like her," she said pointing at Lisa, "and this one is close, but not her," she said pointing at Sandy. "These other two are not even close," pointing at Barb and Eileen. "And this one is almost right but her hair was shorter."

Ian picked up the picture of Audrey, "Shorter, or could she have had it pinned up somehow?"

"Yes, the more I look at her the more I think it was her. Did she do something wrong?"

Ian put the photos back in his file, "I hope not."

*   *   *

CHAPTER THIRTY THREE
The end approaches ...

The patient visited Dr. Schrader's office on Tuesday afternoon. The pains had increased in frequency and duration and all of the activity at the barn was taking a toll. "Have you been resting, taking it easy?" asked Dr. Schrader.

"Well, I may have pushed a little harder than I should have," replied the patient.

"Overdoing it can cost you time. But then, a little time well spent can be so much better than a long time poorly spent," smiled the doctor. "Did you have fun?"

"I wouldn't call it fun, but it was well worth the time and effort."

Dr. Schrader assumed the patient had done something not up for discussion, something personal and recalled himself saying the patient should do something bad, he didn't pursue the subject, but rather asked, "How was your reunion?"

"It was good, and very interesting. I met a number of people I haven't even thought about in years. It was fun and now I wish I hadn't missed the 10th year event," responded the patient.

They discussed several people the patient had found interesting, including a new detective in Vaneksburg. "He was looking into an old murder case that happened almost twenty years ago and the four most promising suspects were killed in an explosion in a barn."

"I believe I saw something on the news about that," offered the doctor. "Did you know any of the people involved?"

"Actually, doctor, I went to school with the four victims and a number of the people now suspected in that bombing."

"Did you know them, the victims?"

"Not really, they were a few years ahead of the class I was in," responded the patient. "Most of the people I know believe those four were the ones who committed that murder twenty years ago and they got what they deserved."

Dr. Schrader sensed a hard edge to the patient's words. An edge that could mean a number of things, but the doctor didn't want to go there. He brought the conversation back to the patient's condition and the best treatment at this point. The increased level of pain and the reduced effect of the medications, coupled with the patient's increased number of stumbles led the doctor to suggest the patient give up driving. The doctor felt it was time to move into the Palliative Care Center. "I cannot predict what will happen next, and it would be best if you were under constant observation."

"You think it's time for me to move now?" asked the patient.

"Yes," replied Dr. Schrader, "as soon as you can arrange it. The room is ready, all the paperwork is completed and they have your records. I'll go out there this week and meet with the staff to discuss your condition and the treatment plan."

"I only have a few things left to do, doctor. I want to contact the church and the funeral home and make sure all the arrangements are covered. I can be ready by the weekend." The patient's head bowed, "I think I'm as ready as I'll ever be. I did what I set out to do a few weeks ago and everything else has been taken care of, bills are paid, my rent is paid for the next three months and I have written to my cousin in Colorado with a copy of the insurance papers and a list of things to give to the family or donate to charity. Yes, I'm as ready as I'll ever be."

Dr. Schrader looked at his patient, sad to think this young person was fast approaching the end. An unavoidable end, but the quality of that life was important. He smiled, looked at his patient and said, "This is not the end, we still have several avenues to pursue, don't give up. You have done better than expected over these last few weeks and we're still exploring a few possibilities."

Thursday morning, the patient arrived at the Palliative Care Center in a cab with a small bag and a laptop computer. After checking in and being taken to a small, private, assisted living apartment the patient met with a counselor. Living arrangements, dining options, visitor rules and other subjects were discussed. The medical treatments would be determined on a daily basis dependent on the patient's condition and the medical team's recommendations to the patient's primary care physician.

All changes in the patient's condition would be noted and a baseline for that condition would be established over the next two days.

The baseline demonstrated that the patient's ability to walk any appreciable distance was now reduced to several hundred feet and then a rest break was necessary. The prescription pain medications were evaluated and Dr. Schrader made appropriate changes. Dr. Schrader stopped in to see his patient towards the end of the examination.

"Are they treating you nicely?" he asked with a smile.

"Well, I think that the testing is almost over and I have answered more questions than I can remember. They are very thorough."

"Let's hope some of those questions can lead us to some good answers," responded Dr. Schrader. He looked at his patient. The ordeal of checking in, submitting to a battery of tests, answering a long list of questions and trying to settle into a new living arrangement had exhausted his patient. He asked the nurse conducting the test of the moment if they could finish in the morning.

"Yes, of course, doctor." She recognized what a long, tiring day it had been for the patient, "How about a ride back to your room?"

"I would appreciate that," responded the patient.

*   *   *

CHAPTER THIRTY FOUR
Finding a friend ...

Ned was in early on Friday morning. He brewed a fresh pot of coffee and was on his way back to his office when he saw Ian come in. He looked tired and not very happy. "Ian, is everything alright?"

"I have to make a call, Chief, then I'll come over and we can talk."

Ned went into his office and Ian picked up the phone and punched in Audrey's home number. Four rings and the answering machine picked up.

"Audrey, this is Ian McLarry, it's Friday, June 8th about 8:45 am. Please call me as soon as you get this message." He then called her office in Fairfax and spoke to the receptionist. "I'm trying to reach Audrey Redding, is she in today?"

The receptionist looked over her office calendar and replied, "No sir, may I take a message?"

"Can you put me through to her voice mail?"

"Sure, one moment please."

Ian left another message and hung up, He went into Ned's office and sat down. Ned looked at Ian and said, "You don't look happy."

"Well, Chief, I think the person we're looking for may be a very nice young lady, and I don't understand why she would do this."

"Are you sure you have the right person?"

"I'm not sure of anything right now."

"Are you ready to bring her in and interrogate her?"

"I just called her at home and at her office. No answer."

"Maybe she is taking some time off?"

"Yeah, that's possible. I'll give her a few days, try again later this week."

"Is she likely to run?"

"I don't think so, no, she's been very accessible up to now. Maybe I have the wrong person in my sights, I really hope I do."

*　　*　　*

Thursday morning Ian called Audrey's home and office again. She was not home and the receptionist at her office said she was not available and offered to take another message.

Ian was not pleased with the evasive answers and said, "My name is Detective Ian McLarry with the Vaneksburg Police Department. It is important that I speak to Miss Redding, do you have another number where she can be reached?"

"I have her home number and a cell phone number," said the receptionist.

"Okay, I have those numbers. May I speak to her supervisor?"

Within a few seconds a man answered the phone, "This is Dan Merrill, may I help you, Detective?"

"Mr. Merrill, it is important that I speak to Miss Redding. Can you tell me where she is or how I can reach her?"

"Detective, I don't know what to tell you. Audrey was feeling rather ill and decided to take some time off. I thought she would be at home, resting."

"Thank you Mr. Merrill, I'll try her at home again."

Ian tried both Audrey's home and cell numbers and got no answer. She could be staying with a friend or a relative, he had no way of knowing. He decided to take a ride and check out her residence. The drive into Fairfax took less than an hour and he found her address in a newer development of upscale townhouses. He tried the doorbell and waited several minutes for an answer, nothing. A man came out of the home next to Audrey's and Ian approached him, identified himself and asked if he had seen her recently.

"Yeah, the other day she was pulling one of those little suitcases on wheels and got into a cab. She waved, smiled and they took off. Is she in some kind of trouble?"

"No, no trouble. She may have witnessed something and I have a few questions for her. Any idea where she was going?"

"Nope, couple of weeks ago she went away for the weekend and was back on the Monday, maybe she's gone for the same thing again, a weekend trip. She only had one small suitcase and a brief case. Looked like a short trip."

"Do you recall which cab company?"

"No, but it was a maroon colored car, like a Ford, like your car but maroon, with little writing on the door."

Ian noted everything in his notebook, thanked the man and drove back to Vaneksburg.

*   *   *

Monday morning Ian called Audrey's home, cell and office again with no luck. He spoke to her supervisor again, "Mr. Merrill is there any other place she may have gone besides home, perhaps a relative?"

"She mentioned a relative in Colorado, but I really don't know."

"Do you know the relative's name?"

"No, and Redding is a pretty common name. I'll look in her personnel file if you give me a minute."

Ian waited and Dan Merrill came back, "Detective, she has a next of kin listed as George Redding, Colorado Springs, Colorado."

Ian thanked Dan, looked up George Redding in Colorado Springs and dialed his number. The woman who answered the phone said George was at work and would be home around 6:00 pm.

Ian thanked her and asked if she knew anything about Audrey's whereabouts. "No detective, I do know she was very ill and might even be in a hospital." She continued saying her husband was trying to find the time and money to go visit with her.

Ian thanked her again and said he might call back after 6:00. He then looked up hospitals in the Fairfax area and made a list of phone numbers. The fourth one dialed was Inova Fair Oaks Hospital. Ian identified himself and asked if a patient named Redding had been admitted.

"No, detective, but I am looking at our records and we had a Miss Audrey Redding here for some testing several months ago, but I am afraid I am not in a position to discuss her medical condition."

"Could you tell me who her doctor is?"

"We have several doctors who have reviewed her case, but the primary physician is Dr. Albert Schrader."

Ian thanked her and again looked up a number, this time for Dr. Schrader.

*   *   *

CHAPTER THIRTY FIVE
The visit...

Ian left the Police Station in Vaneksburg at 10:00 Friday morning and drove into Fairfax. It took less than an hour to find parking and locate Dr. Schrader's offices. He entered and told the receptionist he had called the previous day and had an appointment with Dr. Schrader at 11:15. "Yes Mr. McLarry, please have a seat and the Doctor will be with you shortly. It appears all of our appointments are running on schedule, so you won't have a long wait."

The clock on the receptionist's wall showed exactly 11:15 when the door next to the receptionist's window opened and Dr. Schrader looked out into the waiting room. Ian was the only man in the waiting room, so Dr. Schrader walked over to him, extended his hand and said, "Detective McLarry, I assume."

Ian stood shook the doctor's hand and followed him through the door. "We'll go to my office at the end of the hall," said the doctor. Ian walked ahead of him, entered the office and the doctor said, "Please sit down." Ian complied, taking a seat in one of the two stuffed leather chairs facing the doctor's desk.

"Doctor, I appreciate you giving me this time," said Ian, "As I stated on the phone yesterday, your patient, Audrey Redding, is a person of interest in a rather serious case in Vaneksburg."

Doctor Schrader looked uneasy, but understood the line of questioning. "Can you tell me which case you are referring to, Detective?"

"I would rather not disclose too much, as it may turn out she had no involvement in this incident."

"Detective, I read the papers, watch the news and have a radio in my car. The media has been full of news about an investigation into a bombing in a barn in Vaneksburg. I assume there has not been that many serious crimes in your neck of the woods and anything less important would not bring you here to my office. Are you referring to the barn bombing?"

"Touche´," grinned Ian. "Now it's my turn. Miss Redding is a person of interest in this investigation and in other ways to me. I consider her a friend and would enjoy finding something that proves she is not involved. Everything I have found thus far has left her high on the list. She is not alone there, but she is definitely on the suspect list."

"So what do you want from me, detective?"

"Right now, just a few answers."

"Okay, let's hear the questions."

"First, is she alright? I mean she has disappeared and I haven't found her yet and as a friend, I am concerned."

"That's a rather difficult question, detective. Audrey is ill, very ill. She has been admitted to a Palliative Care Center in Fairfax and we are trying to keep her comfortable. This incident in Vaneksburg, is she involved in some part of this thing?"

"Right now I am trying to reduce my suspect list and I'd really like to remove her. On that note, doctor, let me ask you, considering her physical condition, is she capable of moving bales of hay around a barn and could she move a full grown man onto one of those bales?"

"I don't understand, move a full grown man?"

"The four victims were men, not the biggest guys off the street, but certainly not the smallest, so let's say they were all between 175 and 200 pounds. Could Audrey Redding, in her current condition, maneuver four men to sitting positions on bales of hay?"

"The incident you are referring to happened in May, almost three weeks ago. At that time, my response would have been, no, detective. No, at least not picking them up and putting them down on the bales. I might say yes if it were just moving them from a slouch to an upright sitting position. You should understand that any exertion on her part would have exhausted her. She could walk around a shopping center, through a park, even do the five mile hike around Burke Lake, but she would probably want to sit down several times and catch her breath. Now, if she bought several items at the shopping center or had a dog on a leash in the park or had a backpack with lunch at Burke Lake Park, I would say no, that would be pushing it. This week, when she was admitted to the center, her condition was much worse. Today she can't even stand on her own. Her great adventure each day is walking about one hundred feet, and then sitting in a wheelchair and being pushed around the hospital campus. Twenty minutes of fresh air, a little sunshine and she is exhausted again. No, Detective, if your bomber had to lift and move those men, I would say no, she could not have done that."

"Thanks, Doctor. You have been very helpful and now I would like to stop at this Care Center and see her, if that is alright?"

"Sure, she could use a friendly visitor. Can I assume you are not thinking of arresting her or pummeling her with questions? That would not be good."

"I won't pester her with questions, promise. This will be a friendly visit."

*   *   *

The Fairfax Care Center is located near the intersection of Route 50 and the Fairfax County Parkway. Ian covered the distance in less than 10 minutes and was at the door to Audrey's room in five more.

"She's awake," said the nurse just about to leave her room. "Probably day dreaming about some tall, handsome gentleman coming to visit her." The nurse turned toward Audrey and touched her shoulder and said quietly, "Audrey, you have a visitor."

Audrey's eyes opened, focused on Ian and a smile grew across her face. "Ian, or should I call you Detective?"

"I like the way you say Ian. I also like the way you smiled when you saw me."

"Are you here to arrest me?"

"Well, if I was, you would have to call me Detective. I was going to interrogate you, but I left my rubber hose and brass knuckles in my office. How about I take you for a little walk in the sunshine instead?"

Audrey smiled and said, "That would be very nice, a slow walk would be best."

"I'll get the nurse to bring a wheelchair in." Ian went out to the nurse's station, "Can I get a wheelchair and take her for a little walk?"

The nurse smiled at Ian, "If you hold her, she can walk a short distance. I think she would like that and I will be right behind you with the wheelchair."

Ian went back to the room and Audrey was sitting on the edge of the bed. The nurse came in with the wheelchair and gently scolded

Audrey for trying to get up herself. "Honey, that's why God made these big strong men, to take us for walks now and again." She took Audrey's robe from the door and helped her put it on. "Now you two go ahead and I'll be right behind you when you get tired."

Audrey smiled and said, "Thanks, Jess." She curled her arm around Ian's, and began to walk very slowly out to the hall toward the elevators. The walk was very short, once outside, Audrey made it less than 100 feet and started to sag.

Jess brought the chair close and helped her sit down. "Now, I have other patients, so you two try to stay out of trouble," she joked as she turned and went back inside the building.

Ian took the wheelchair handles and said, "What's your pleasure, young lady, should we go straight, left or right?"

Audrey pointed to a small garden with benches and said, "That looks nice."

Ian pushed the wheelchair across the open square and helped Audrey to a bench. He sat next to her on the bench for almost an hour with Audrey leaning on his shoulder. They talked about sunshine, birds and squirrels. Ian never mentioned the barn, the bomb or even his visit to Dr. Schrader. Audrey squeezed Ian's arm and he felt a little shudder. He looked down at her and saw a tear in her eye. "Are you alright?"

"No, damn it," she whispered, "I hate that I am so weak. I don't want to die." They sat there until her tears stopped and a cloud covered the sun. "We should go back," she said, "I'm very tired."

He helped her back into the chair and slowly wheeled her toward the building. A raindrop fell first on Ian's face and then on Audrey's. Ian started to walk faster until Audrey said, "I like the rain." Ian slowed and Audrey smiled again.

As Ian was leaving the hospital, Jess caught up to him. "Hey tall, man, what's your name?"

"Ian, Ian McLarry."

"Well, Ian McLarry, you gave our little friend a wonderful afternoon. I hope you come again, soon. She is asleep now and still smiling."

* * *

CHAPTER THIRTY SIX
Passing away...

A week passed and Ian made the trip into Fairfax every day, taking Audrey for shorter and shorter walks and very light conversation. Friday morning a gentle rain began and a light breeze moved the leaves in the trees. Clouds still cluttered the sky and promised to continue with more rain through the rest of the day. Ian received a call from Dr. Schrader's assistant at 9:25 Friday morning and he told Cindy he might be gone for the remainder of the day. The drive to The Fairfax Center took about half an hour and he arrived at the hospital a few minutes after 10:00.

Dr. Schrader met Ian at the nurse's station and told him that Audrey's condition had deteriorated and the end was very close. "She has been in and out, conscious only for a minute or two at a time," said Dr. Schrader, "I know you still have questions for her, but the drugs that we have pumped into her to ease the pain make any statement from her absolutely worthless."

"I understand," replied Ian, "But I'm not here to question a suspect, I'm here to see a friend." He walked into the room where Audrey was sleeping. Jess had just adjusted the monitors and the IV drip.

"Well, good morning, Ian McLarry," said the nurse with a smile.

"Good morning, Jess, how is she doing?" he asked as he walked over to the bed and touched her hand.

"She had a rough night, but we gave her some more happy juice and her pain has subsided," said Jess. "Give her a few minutes and she will wake up again."

Ian stood staring at the small woman lying in the bed. He wondered what he would have done if she had not been ill. He wondered if he would have treated her as roughly as others he had questioned or arrested in the past. Did he feel something beyond a friendship for this quiet, shy little woman? His mind was reaching out in all directions trying to grasp what he felt and what he was doing.

"You should sit here," said Jess, moving a chair next to the bed, "Sit down and wait, she'll be awake soon."

"Thanks Jess, I'm not in a hurry, I'll be here for a while."

Jess walked out of the room and her smile faded. She had other patients who needed her attention and she had done all she could for this one. She took a deep breath, let out a sigh and moved on to her next patient.

* * *

At 10:47, Audrey moved slightly and opened her eyes. She saw Ian sitting at her side and tried to speak, but her voice was raspy and the words did not form. Ian lifted his head, "Hey, good morning, sleepyhead."

She tried to speak again and couldn't. Ian lifted a water glass with a straw to her lips, "Shush, drink and relax, I'm not going anywhere."

She sipped a little water, coughed and a little drool flowed from her mouth. Ian took a napkin and wiped it away. She was embarrassed and her eyes showed it. Ian smiled and said, "Did I ever tell you that you have beautiful eyes?"

She looked at him, relaxed, smiled and said in a gravelly voice, "I wish you had." She wanted to touch him, but her hand would not respond and she started to cry. "Ian, I don't want to die. I know it's coming and I'm scared." She coughed again and started to say something that came out all wrong. Her eyes closed and she was asleep.

An hour later, she woke again and Ian was still there. He gave her water and she cleared her throat and said, "I lied to you, I'm sorry, I shouldn't have lied."

"I know, and I know what actually happened, but I am not here to talk about that. I'm here because a friend of mine is in a tough spot and I want to help her any way I can."

"But what I did, Ian. You know what I did."

"Let's make a deal, you get better and I will arrest you and charge you with something, until then, you are my friend and I came to visit you because I…," Ian paused, not sure what to say next, so he looked in her eyes. She smiled and fell asleep.

Ian looked at her and thought about what he had almost said, "Because I what?" Thoughts ran rampant through his head. "I wanted to say because I care, because I like you, because you are." His head dropped, "I don't know what I want to say."

Dr. Schrader entered the room and looked at the monitors, read the chart and put his hand on Ian's shoulder. "Right now, Detective, you are her best medicine. She may be out for a while."

Ian held her hand even though she couldn't feel his and said, "I'm not going anywhere Doc."

Dr. Schrader nodded, patted Ian on his shoulder and walked out of the room. As he approached the nurse's station, Jess looked at him with a question in her eyes. He looked at her and said quietly, "She may not wake up again."

*   *   *

CHAPTER THIRTY SEVEN
The Wake...

Audrey's wake was held in Vaneksburg at the Taylor & Bennett Funeral Home. People from Fairfax who had known Audrey in the Real Estate business came, said a prayer, offered condolences and went back to their lives. Local representation was primarily from the class of 1997 and a few others who had known the shy and quiet little girl. A few of her old neighbors who remembered her mother came and went. On the second day of the wake, a man came in, walked directly to the open casket and stood silently for a few minutes looking at Audrey. Finally he turned away, walked over to a man dressed in a dark suit, standing alone next to the door. "Excuse me, but could you tell me who is in charge here?"

The man replied, "My name is Franklin Bennett, I am the funeral director here, how can I help you?"

"Could we step out of the room, I have a few questions for you."

"Certainly sir, we could go into my office, if you would prefer."

Twenty minutes later the two emerged from Bennett's office and the man was led over to Barb Nessman.

"Ms. Nessman, my name is George Redding. Audrey was my cousin. I live in Colorado and couldn't get a flight in any sooner. I landed at 12:35, got to Audrey's apartment, picked up the car and drove straight here."

"The car, you are driving Audrey's car?"

"Yeah, she gave it to me. Sent me the spare key and the title a week or so ago, I certainly did not expect to be picking it up so soon," he said bowing his head. "I wish I could have come sooner."

"You're here now, and that's what matters," said Barb.

"Please, Ms. Nessman, I really didn't know her. The thing is, she knew who I was and wrote me a letter a few months ago. She said that since I was her closest relative, she wanted me to handle her estate after she passed. It took me by surprise, but family is family and as soon as I received the letter, I called her. She told me she had some condition that was incurable and her time left was limited. We reminisced about the last 30 years. I live in Colorado and I wished I could come and visit, but I just couldn't hop on a plane, we have three kids and my wife was laid off a year ago. So we called back and forth every few days until about a week ago. She said her time was short, but I thought perhaps a few months or a year, not a week. I didn't know it was that bad. When I couldn't get hold of her, at first I figured she was out doing things and we would hook up later, after a few days, well, I guess now is later. I should have come right away and at least seen her."

Barb touched George's arm, "Audrey was my friend. I think that we all feel she was a good person and taking care of her was our privilege. She was so special in a number of ways." They both stepped over to the casket and gazed down on her.

"She looks so small, like a little girl. She should be raising her own family now, Ms. Nessman."

"Please call me Barb."

George straightened up, took a deep breath and said, "I guess I am the extent of the family that is going to be here. I want to thank you for all you have done for Audrey, arranging all of this, the flowers, the church. I have spoken to the funeral director here and we have agreed on the final payments for their services. I will cover any expenses you may have incurred in this process also."

"Thanks Mr. Redding, as I said, Audrey was my friend, and it has been my privilege to see to this for her."

George looked about the room noticing the number of people, "The last time I saw her was about ten years ago. She was on her way back to college and we said hello, then she was gone." He continued to scan the crowd, "I had business in Philadelphia back then and took an extra few days to stop over here in Northern Virginia and visit my dad's sister-in-law, Beth, Audrey's mom. She passed away a year after that when my wife was in the hospital delivering our third child so I didn't make it to her funeral and I always felt bad about that."

Barb took George's arm and began to lead him across the room, "Let's go meet some of Audrey's friends."

George continued, "We're not a big family by any means, our next of kin is somewhere in California or Texas. Folks I have never met. Anyway, Audrey wrote to me a few months ago and we began to talk. She never said how little time she had left, just that it was incurable and she was getting ready."

Phil Kline and Eileen were talking to Sandy and Barb led George to their group, gesturing to each "Phil, Eileen and Sandy, this is George, Audrey's cousin. He lives in Colorado and just arrived."

Phil shook Georges hand and said, "My pleasure to meet you, George. Audrey was a beautiful person. One of those people that couldn't buy an enemy."

"Thanks, Phil. As I was telling Barb, I'm sorry I didn't come sooner. If I had any idea how little time she had, I would have."

Eileen stepped forward and shook George's hand, "I'm Eileen, Phil's wife. I was just getting to know her."

Sandy said a quiet hello and added, "I've known her since we were little, she has always been such an angel."

Barb led George around the room introducing him to everybody she could, all with similar reactions, Audrey was a wonderful person and the world was diminished by her passing.

They were talking to several new arrivals and Barb noticed George looking toward the casket. "Barb, excuse me for a minute," he said and he walked over to Audrey, bowed his head and looked at her for a few minutes, then turned and went back to Barb.

"Well, Barb, Audrey never said there was someone special in her life, but I had the feeling there must be. Do you know who that might be?"

Barb smiled, "No, not for sure, but I guess it's probably Ian. He's a detective with our police force and we all met because of an old cold case he was working on. I noticed that Audrey seemed a little happier when he came to our reunion meetings and at the reunion, well, they made such a nice couple."

"Ian McLarry, he's the detective that called me a few weeks ago asking about Audrey. Were they close? Has he been here?"

"Yes, he just came in, I see him over there," said Barb, pointing across the room to a tall man in a dark suit. "You should meet him," she said as she led George across the room.

Ian was talking to Phil and Eileen Kline as Barb and George approached. Phil looked at Barb and Ian turned to see her coming directly at him.

"Ian, this is George Redding, he is Audrey's cousin."

"George, I'm pleased to meet you."

George looked uneasy as he shook Ian's hand. "I feel like a complete outsider and I may be her only family here. We hardly ever met, but over the last few weeks, we started to get to know each other. Ian, she mentioned your name a number of times, did you know her very well?"

Ian bowed his head slightly and replied, "Not nearly as well as I had hoped. She was very quiet and liked to take her time. We had a number of conversations about a case I was working on and, well, time flies by so quickly, all of a sudden she was in a palliative care center and then, then she was gone."

"A case you were working on," said George, "was she involved in something?"

Ian straightened up and replied, "No, that case involved a boy she had known in high school. His name was Darryl and the two of them were apparently very much alike. They were bright kids, both rather quiet and shy and got along. He liked her and respected her and her funny ways. Then someone killed him." Ian cleared his throat, "The killer or killers were never found and I was looking into it when we met. I liked her from Day One."

*   *   *

The funeral was held at the same church Audrey had attended when she lived in Vaneksburg and she was buried in the local cemetery next to her mother. Barb arranged a gathering at the Tavern after the services and everyone was welcome. George found Barb talking with Mark and Ian and asked if they could discuss a few of Audrey's wishes privately.

"Sure, George," said Barb, "There's a room over here that may be free," as she touched Jim and asked if they could use the small dining room.

Mark excused himself and Barb, Ian and George went into the small room. They sat at the large round table the committee had used and George began, "Audrey planned ahead. She paid all her bills and left an insurance policy naming me as the beneficiary. She asked me to be sure the expense of her funeral was covered with these funds and the rest was to go towards helping my kids pay for college. I have to file some papers with the insurance company later this week and it will take a few weeks to go through the system, but when it does, I want to honor her wishes and cover the cost of all this. So please, send me a listing of anything, including this lunch, in the way of expenses and as soon as the money comes in, I will reimburse you."

"George, that is very nice," said Barb.

George smiled, "As I said, she planned ahead, and she knew it would be a sizable chunk of money. I would not be surprised if the total bill was nearly twenty thousand dollars. That's what insurance is for, these kinds of expenses."

Barb's eyes opened wide, "Twenty thousand."

George continued, "My wife's brother lost his wife a year ago and the cost of the casket alone was several thousand, then there are the cemetery costs, the funeral home fees, the church, the headstone."

Ian looked at Barb and said, "I know the cost of a full funeral can be a lot, but I never had to add it up before." He looked at George, "Do you think it will be that much, twenty thousand?"

"I hope not, but as I said, Audrey planned for this and as soon as the money comes in, I'll pay it out. I have an appointment with an attorney on Monday here in town to cover a few legal items and I have already asked the funeral home to send me the bill for their services. As soon as the meeting with the attorney is over, I plan on starting the drive back to Colorado."

"You're driving back, I thought you flew in?" asked Ian.

"Audrey left me her car, and we can really use it," replied George.

Ian smiled, "That's a nice car, a Cadillac CTS as I remember."

George grinned, "Yeah, I wish. That was her company car, she left me her personal car."

Ian bowed his head, smiled and said, "A silver Focus?"

"Yes," replied George, "you've seen it?"

"No," said Ian, "Just a wild guess."

Barb looked at Ian, "I didn't know she had another car."

Ian smiled, "Neither did I, Barb. When I asked her if there was a second car, she said there wasn't and I didn't check the DMV records. my mistake."

"So, she lied?" said Barb.

"Did she?" said Ian. "She had already sent the title to George, so it could be looked at either way."

George looked confused, "Does this mean something?"

Ian looked at the ground pensively, continued to smile and said, "No," as he glanced at Barb, "As we all know, she was very quiet and there are lots of things about her we will never know." Then Ian asked George if they could have a private conversation. Barb excused herself and left the two to talk.

Ian began, "George, I don't know what will come out eventually about this, but, I felt it best that you hear it from me."

George hesitated, "Was Audrey in some kind of trouble?"

"No, not exactly," said Ian. "First, no charges have been filed, no arrest was ever made and I don't know if we have enough to try and convict her of anything." He looked around the room and saw nobody else about, and continued, "There was an incident and she is the only one thus far who stands out as a viable suspect."

George held up his hand, "You're referring to the barn bombing in May."

"Yes," said Ian. "Those four men in the barn were the main suspects in an investigation I was conducting. It was a cold case, almost twenty years old and this high school reunion was an excellent opportunity to meet the people surrounding the victim. He would have been one of their classmates if he had not been killed in '93."

"But, Audrey," said George, "She was such a nice person. Was there a dark side I never saw?"

"I struggled with the idea that she was involved too," said Ian, "But when I saw her in the Palliative Center, she all but confirmed it. We never talked specifics, but I know she did it and she knew I knew."

George was staring at the floor, "So she murdered them?"

"I won't go that far," said Ian. "I think her condition probably played havoc with her reasoning and she stumbled into this bombing of the barn with them in it. She may have meant to scare them or hurt them short of killing them. Again, we'll never know."

"So, how solid is your case?"

Ian thought for a moment and replied, "There are holes, but, depending on the specific charges and if the DA pushed hard, they might have been able to get a favorable verdict."

"Might? Favorable?" quizzed George.

"Yeah," said Ian. "Depending on the specific charges, the verdict could vary."

"So will there be charges filed?" asked George.

"No," returned Ian. "Audrey is gone, and there are no other suspects and the case against the four victims of the bombing was very convincing but not enough to prosecute."

"What if there was new information to be considered?" said George.

"Like what?" asked Ian.

"A smoking gun, for instance."

Ian sighed, "What do you mean?"

George hesitated, "I have something you should see."

Ian looked confused, "What should I see?"

"In cleaning up Audrey's apartment in Fairfax, I found a hand gun, ammunition and a taser."

"A hand gun, there is no record of her owning a handgun."

"It was her father's. She kept it locked up in her apartment and didn't use it. Took it out a few weeks ago and found a shooting range around here somewhere and started learning to shoot."

"The bullets and handgun may be traceable back to the crime scene. The taser could be additional corroboration. But when the suspect is dead, there are typically no charges filed, unless she had an accomplice. The case gets closed.

*   *   *

EPILOGUE

Ian was sitting at his desk when Jim Schuster came into the station and asked to see him. "Sure, Monica, send him back." Ian stood and turned toward the door as Jim walked in. He raised his hand and said, "Jim, over here."

"Hey, Ian, how are you doing?"

"Things are quiet; I guess that's a good thing."

Jim sat at the guest chair next to Ian's desk, "Ian, there are a number of little groups here in town. Some of us get together to play golf or softball. Some of us go down to the river and try to catch some fish. There's a bowling league. Does any of that appeal to you?"

"Well, I've killed a bunch of golf balls trying to play that game, I'm probably better at softball and bowling."

"Great, we have an informal gathering at the Tavern on Friday, different guys set up different things to do. You should stop by."

Ian smiled, "Do you have a dart league?"

"As a matter of fact, yes," said Jim. "Hey, have you closed out the bombing thing yet?"

"Well, I have cleared a number of people, there are a few loose ends to seal off, but I think we are real close to putting this one away. Just one or two little details and we'll hold a press conference."

"Great, remember, Friday night, any time after 7:00."

"I'll be there," said Ian.

*   *   *

Ian walked over to Chief Bowen's office. He was reviewing a file and noticed Ian approaching. Ned leaned back in his chair, "Come on in, sit and talk to me for a minute."

Ian sat in one of the two chairs in front of Ned's desk. "I've been invited to join a group of guys at the Tavern."

"Friday night," confirmed Ned, as he laid the file down on his desk.

"Yeah, they talk about stuff to do."

Ned grinned, "Well, it's about time they called you. Every Friday night around 7:00, several guys gather to see what might be fun or interesting over the next week or two. It's as loose a group as you will find. I come once in a while, just to see what's going on. Sometimes I end up with a golf game or a ride into the District to see the Capitals play. They go to most of the home games for the Potomac Nationals and make the trip into Nats Park once a week during the season."

Ian grinned, "Sounds like fun."

"Ian, you didn't come in here to tell me you're going to a baseball game."

"No, I'm kinda' wrestling with this barn bombing."

"The Feds will want closure, we can't just sweep it under the rug," said Ned.

"Yeah, I know. So do I, we all do," said Ian.

Ned scratched his chin, looked at Ian and said, "So, how do you want to close this one out?"

Ian replied as he sat up straight, "Darryl's family is gone, but he had a lot of friends and the result may be significant to them."

"So, what do you want to do?" Ned reiterated.

Ian leaned forward, "Well, by the time I had it narrowed down to Audrey, and I had enough to make an arrest, she was in a Palliative Care Center with very little time left to live. I, or we, know damn well she put that bomb in that barn. We know how the bomb was triggered. We know why she did it, but I still don't know how that tiny little lady got all four of those characters all trussed up in the barn." Ian shifted in his chair, "She never confessed. I guess if I had pushed her she might have, but I didn't and she didn't."

"You still haven't answered my question, Ian. What do you want to do?"

"It's not what I want to do, Chief, it's what I have to do. All we had then and all we have now is circumstantial. I don't know if she was a master criminal or if she bungled her way through it with luck. I'm sure she acted alone. I can show she bought restraints at a few stores, she picked up a stun gun at another store and the bullets we have recovered are the same caliber as her gun. A good lawyer could make all that seem innocent. If we had arrested and charged her, she could have gotten off. We'll never know."

Ned leaned forward in his chair, "Yeah, Ian, but you know she did it. So once again, what do you want to do?"

Ian looked at Ned, "The easy thing would be to say we'll never know for sure who did it. Just like the Zamanski case, it could have been someone just passing through town."

Ned leaned back in his chair, "You think that's the easy way out of this?" He watched Ian consider his options, "We're going to get questions from the press until we make a statement."

Ian stood and as he was turning toward the door, looked back at Ned, "Yeah, easy and I don't think anybody would protest. But as much as I would like to protect her memory, I have to write it up as it really went down, Capital Murder, four counts. Prime suspect, Audrey Redding, deceased, never arrested, never charged. All evidence collected thus far, circumstantial. No witnesses, no other suspects under consideration. Case closed." He turned toward the door again and said, "That's what I'll say at the press conference."

Ned watched Ian walk back to his cubicle. He picked up the file again, grinned and mumbled to himself, "Got me a real cop, a bulldog."

END

*   *   *

ACKNOWLEDGMENTS

How many people have I talked to about some minor facet of my writing? From a casual conversation in a parking lot about hand guns to a discussion about state police procedures with a friend, there have been so many people who have contributed to my writing of this and other books. I cannot thank them all individually; it would fill several pages, so please allow me to mention with special note my friends at the Northern Virginia Chapter of the Virginia Writers Club. Every meeting has been a continuation of my education and every event a lesson in the fine art of marketing our works. To my wife, who has read each version of this book and offered critical assistance, and to my editor, Gail Lord, who has read and edited the last few passes through this manuscript. Finally, to Katie G. Jones who designed the cover as she has for my first two novels. Any lingering errors remaining are my fault and mine alone.

Thank you all.

ABOUT THE AUTHOR

John B. Wren worked as a consulting engineer for over 40 years. He began writing in 2009 as a hobby and upon retiring in 2012, turned most of his efforts to writing. He has published three novels as of the summer of 2014 and has two more in the works. Wren lives with his family in Northern Virginia.

He was born in Pittsburgh, Pennsylvania, grew up in western New York State, went to college and lived in Northeast Ohio for 25 years and now resides in Northern Virginia.

*   *   *

ALSO BY JOHN B. WREN

To Probe A Beating Heart

In the Autumn of 1991, a young girl disappears from a Cleveland Heights, Ohio neighborhood. She was last seen talking to a man as the clouds opened and a rain began. The only witness is an elderly woman whose description of the possible kidnapper could fit any number of people.

As police, friends and family search the immediate area for Annette, she is taken farther away and becomes one of the predator's first victims. The police narrow their search over several years, but cannot find enough evidence to identify or arrest Averell. Annette's family, part of an Irish Clann, becomes involved in the pursuit and eventually, ask the questions, get the answers and find their own version of justice.

Killing His Fear

The films of the forties and early fifties depended on lighting and sounds to convey terror. They didn't have the advantage of color and computer graphics nor did they delve into the same level of gore and violence that we see today. Such was the world of Brandon, a young impressionable boy, who watches a Frankenstein movie on television one night and begins a trek through life in an ever deepening spiral of FEAR of the grey men and shadowy characters of these early films.

Losing his father to a hit and run driver and his mother to her own mental hell, Brandon leaves his home in suburban Detroit, seeking sanity in Florida. He arrives in Washington, DC and decides to earn a little money as a dishwasher before continuing his journey to Florida. He stays and eventually begins to see hope in his dark tunnel as a few life changing events begin to lift his spirits.

Brandon may be on a track to come out of his hellish spiral, or he may be boring deeper into oblivion.

* * *

COMING SOON

An Trodai: Scolai

From a time before history, Eirinn was an island nation of many tribes, kingdoms and sub-kingdoms. Disputes between these groups pitted countrymen against countrymen in battle after battle. The invasions by raiders from northern countries dating from 795 AD to the end of the first millennium aided in maintaining a near constant state of warfare somewhere on the island.

In 894 a Viking raider takes a young girl during a raid and leaves her raped, beaten and bloodied. Ceara dies nine months later in giving birth to a boy, Scolai who grows up in this world of constant battle and becomes a warrior in the army of Cennetig mac Lorcain.